MW00944469

B.L. BERRY

Copyright © 2014 by B.L. Berry
Editing by Jennifer Roberts-Hall
Cover Design by Najla Qamber Designs
Formatting and interior design by JT Formatting

Printed in the United States of America
First Edition: September 2014
Library of Congress Cataloging-in-Publication Data

Berry, B.L.
Love Nouveau – 1st ed
ISBN-13: 978-1501086304
ISBN-10: 1501086308

For my husband,

who has taught me more about

selflessness and sacrifice

than I ever could have imagined.

My love for you is incalculable.

And for my children,

When you find yourself standing on the precipice

of something truly terrifying,

May you find the courage to jump,

take flight

and find greatness.

My dear,

Find what you love and let it kill you.

Let it drain you of your all.

Let it cling onto your back

and weigh you down

into eventual nothingness.

Let it kill you and let it devour your remains.

For all things will kill you,

both slowly and fastly,

but it's much better to be killed by a lover.

~ Falsely yours

Anonymous

Four Months Earlier

I'M BLINDSIDED WHEN THE MUSTY throw pillow from the loveseat smacks me in the face. Popping the buds out from my ears, I give my flatmate Robyn a cross look.

"What?"

"Your phone. It's been ringing nonstop. Answer the damn thing already."

Oh.

I snatch it off my nightstand and look at the screen, cringing when I see three missed calls from home flashing across the window. It's just after one in the morning and I'm in the zone writing a term paper on the influence of ancient Greek Architecture in modern America, a requirement for my Art History track. When the call comes through a fourth time, I click the accept button, mildly annoyed at the lack of consideration for the seven hour time difference since technically I should be in bed.

With any luck, someone is dead.

"Ivy! He proposed! I'm getting married!" a voice shrieks into the phone before I can even extend a greeting.

"Who is that?" Robyn asks curtly as I pull the phone away from my ear.

"My sister," I whisper back.

"You have a sister?"

I roll my eyes and return my focus to Genevieve on the other end of the line. Yes, I have a sister. No, I don't talk about her, let alone *to* her ... or anyone else in my family on a regular basis for that matter.

"CJ proposed tonight! I am so excited! I'm getting married!" she squeals again before pausing. "Hello? Ivy? Are you there?"

"Sorry. Yes, I'm here. Congratulations, Gen," I reply with a heavy sigh and try to hide the annoyance in my voice. "That's really great. I'm happy for you." There are no sincere words I can offer her. The purpose of her call wasn't really to tell me that she's engaged. She and I both know that this call is to remind me of how superficially amazing and perfect life can be when you fall into line in the Cotter household. Something that I'm simply *not* willing to do.

"Oh my God! I cannot wait for you to meet him, Ivy! He is absolutely amazing. And last night was so romantic. He took me on a horse-drawn carriage ride through downtown and he slipped the ring into my glass of champagne. It had just started snowing and we were all bundled up under fleece blankets and it was just so, so beautiful! I wish you could have seen it since it will *never* happen to you ..."

I tune her out. I'm not sure when clichés became romantic, but this guy sounds like a winner. My eyes return back to my computer screen and I continue to edit my paper as I toss in an obligatory overzealous "yay" and "mm-hmm" to appease the princess while she motors on with mundane details.

How she can be this far along with wedding plans baffles me. The poor sap *just* proposed. Oh, who am I kidding? She's had her wedding planned since she was six years old.

"Anyway, Daddy said we could have the wedding anywhere we wanted, but there is, like, a wait list everywhere for at least two years. Then it turned out that The Drake had a cancellation for this June, so we snatched it up and we're getting married in six months. Six months! Can you believe it? There is so much to do! You'll need to find a seamstress in Italy to take your measurements so I can have your maid of honor gown designed, and when you get back you'll have to plan a bachelorette party for me, but don't worry, I'll tell you exactly what I want and can even make a few calls for you, and—"

Wait. What?

"What do you mean maid of honor?" I ask, cutting her off.

"You, silly! You're my sister, and I can't possibly have one of my girlfriends outshining me. You'll be my maid of honor and then some other girls from my sorority will be standing with you. I was thinking a deep red, but I don't know how well that'll work with your skin tone. We can't have you sticking out in photos."

She can't be serious. This five-minute conversation is the most we've said to each other in nearly four years.

"Listen, Gen. Surely there is someone else you'd rather have as your maid of honor. I really don't think I could do the job justice and help you out like you'd need me to. I'm halfway around the globe."

"Oh shush. You're my only sister. You're standing up there with me. Non-negotiable," she barks back.

Suddenly, I find myself overjoyed with the fact that I'm halfway across the world, divided by the expanse of the Atlantic Ocean. But something tells me I could be living on a different planet and Genevieve would still find a way to bridge the gap and torment me.

I've spent my senior year in Europe studying art history. Partly because it's my major, but more importantly I'm here as a means to get away from my family. I fed my parents some bullshit about how it was necessary to immerse myself in antiquity and art and embrace ancient cultures to truly make myself marketable after graduation. In reality, I needed to disconnect from them, but more importantly, disconnect from myself and who I had allowed myself to become. As much as I love the University of Wisconsin, the one hundred and fifty miles between campus and my home in Chicago were just too close for comfort.

And at this moment, being a continent away still doesn't feel far enough. Hell, I didn't even return home for Christmas break. Instead, I flew to Prague for a few days with a stopover in Budapest. Exploring a foreign country by myself is one of the most liberating and terrifying things I've ever done. I learned to eat by myself in public, smoked some damn fine weed with two tourists from Australia in a youth hostel, and experienced my first Thai massage. Unlike romance novels, but not unlike my life, there was no happy ending.

"Fine, Gen, I'll wear whatever you want. Listen, I need to get going. As much as I'd love to rack up Mom and Dad's phone bill with this call, it's late and my roommate is trying to sleep. I guess just email me with the details and we'll chat more when I'm home for graduation, okay?"

"Sure, okay."

"Bye," I chirp before I realize that Genevieve has already hung up the line. Fitting, after all this time she still thinks she has the right to the last word.

Robyn pulls herself out from the novel she has been reading and gives me a pointed look, mouth agape. I run my fingers over the threadbare quilt I bought from a thrift store on the square, avoiding her stare. The teal and gray details have faded over time, but the weathered weaves are soft and comforting. Italy feels more like home than anywhere else.

"I don't want to talk about it. Okay?"

"Whatever you say, girl."

And with that, she snaps her book shut and clicks off her lamp, leaving me alone in the glow from my laptop.

Mid-May

I LEAN MY HEAD AGAINST the window and look out beyond the wing to the twinkling city lights below. As we descend toward U.S. soil, I can't help but think about how things have changed over the past nine months. And when I say 'things' I'm really talking about myself. Who knew that it would take an escape to realize that I am not my mother's daughter and that who I've slept with is certainly not a reflection of my true self.

When I left for Italy, I wanted to get away from all of the drama with my family and with my now *ex*-boyfriend, Matt. I had become the girl who would excessively drink to avoid actually having to feel something, and I'd slept with countless guys who most definitely were *not* my boyfriend. I desperately wanted to disconnect from the world around me.

So I ran.

I ran halfway around the globe to a place where I knew not one soul and where the Cotter family name would have no consequences. And just to be sure, I took up my grandmother's last name—Phillips.

It was a glorious nine months abroad. I learned more about myself than I'd ever imagined possible. The old Ivy feared parental reaction from each tiny act of defiance. But the new Ivy says, "Fuck 'em all!" a sentiment that Rachel will surely appreciate. My new motto? Be who you are and own that shit—because only with true self-acceptance comes peace and joy.

No more self-loathing.

No more hiding behind the guises of liquor and meaningless one-night stands.

No more fearing living life *my* way.

No more aiming to please my parents, especially when they don't see the value in me.

I, Ivy Cotter, am returning to the states a completely different woman … Ivy Phillips.

It took all of three bags to pack up my belongings. Last August I brought one trunk of clothes, some toiletries and a few supplies for classes. The only memories I packed were a few photos, mostly of me and my best friend Rachel. She was really the only one I'd actually missed. We'll be reunited in a matter of hours, and in a few short days we'll walk together in the University of Wisconsin commencement ceremonies, entering the proverbial real world. I've never understood why they call it the real world. The past twenty-something years of my life sure as hell have felt real, absolutely painful. And there's nothing like pain to prove you're really alive.

The captain announces preparations for the plane's final descent and I realize just how anxious I am to get back to Madison. Only within the past few weeks have I really started to crave the familiarity of home. A few weeks ago I even sought out the American sports bar La Botticella so I could watch the Chicago Cubs on opening day. They lost, which was more comforting than surprising. It's good to know that some things will never change.

I can hardly contain my excitement when it comes to Rachel. It feels like we've been separated for a decade. I've missed everything about her, especially her energy and her ability to make me forget about my bat shit crazy family. But the best thing about our friendship is the fact it is so effortless. The moment we see each other, I know it will be as if no time has passed at all.

Our time together is numbered, though. Rachel is returning to Chicago, presumably to live off of her trust fund for a while as she figures out what she wants to do next with her life. Not that I blame her. While majoring in Political Science, she still has no idea what she wants to be when she grows up.

I, on the other hand, have known what I've wanted to do ever since a junior high field trip to the Art Institute of Chicago for the traveling Monet exhibit. I wandered off on my own, and as all of my classmates were waiting for me on the bus, Mr. Moyer, my Art Appreciation teacher, found me sitting in front of the *Water Lilies* painting, lost in thought. Rather than turning angry because I'd separated from the group, he'd sat down next to me and talked about Impressionism—not so much about the art itself, but how it made each of us feel. I have Mr. Moyer to thank for opening my eyes to countless other movements like Surrealism, Constructivism, Cubism, Pop Art and more. And when he showed me how I could have a career in art without actually being an artist, I knew I had found my calling.

Majoring in Art History has been one of the most ful-filling things I've ever done for myself, much to my family's chagrin. And while I don't have anything lined up after graduation, I'm hopeful that I can find work. I'd give anything to work in an artist's studio or even an art gallery. Then again, Kate Middleton majored in Art History and that seemed to work out well for her, though my life is anything but a fairytale with a crown prince waiting for me in the wings.

When the wheels finally touch the ground, a strange combination of relief and anxiety wash over me. I inhale deeply and swallow down the sensation. *A fresh start.*

I can do this.

MY EYES SCAN THE EMPTY apartment. It's strange to be here without Rachel's boisterous personality filling the space. When I told Rachel about my plans to go abroad senior year, I insisted on helping her find a suitable roommate in my absence, one who could handle her quirks and habitual study partners (her code for hook ups) every weekend without fail. But she refused, saying no one would ever take my place. Really, we both knew she was looking forward to having some space and freedom to walk around the apartment in nothing but her unmentionables. Not that my presence ever stopped her before.

Walking into my old room, I see traces of my life before Italy scattered everywhere. This is the room of a completely different girl. Photos of a questionably happy Matt and I smile down at me from the corkboard above the desk. Movie stubs, concert posters and old Badger football tickets from Saturdays at Camp Randall Stadium litter the walls.

The only thing that has changed is the fine layer of dust collected upon my former life. Walking to the bathroom, I trace my finger along the bookcase, leaving a trail of cleanliness in its wake.

I take my time and unpack enough to get me through the next few days. No sense in unloading all of my belongings for my brief graduation layover here in Madison. Looking around the apartment, I can't believe how much I've missed this place. Wisconsin was always more of a home to me than Chicago ever was.

Snagging a soda from the fridge, I settle into the overstuffed love seat that is too large for our modest living room. Frankly, the yellow and blue paisley pattern is hideous but adds character to an otherwise drab space.

When we found it the summer before our sophomore year, Rachel demanded that it be the focal point of the room, deeming that it would make us sit closer to the guys we brought home. In reality, the most action it saw was the pair of us huddled together under a blanket gossiping. The one time Rachel tried to get lucky on it, she put too much weight against the backside and the whole thing flipped over in the throes of passion. I stormed out in a sleepy daze, convinced we were being robbed, and beat the hell out of the nameless naked jackass with a golf club. Since then, we've agreed to relegate all promiscuity to our respective bedrooms.

I open my laptop and instantly connect to the wireless network. It's true what they say—home is where your Wi-Fi connects automatically. I load my email page and key in my password. Six new messages flash the top of my inbox. After deleting a plea from a Nigerian prince and several solicitations for black market penis enhancers, I click on an email from my favorite professor with a smile.

Professor Whitman is an elderly stout gentleman with a refined penchant for Renaissance and Baroque art. And when I say gentleman, I mean it. He's a true southern beau at heart and vigilant proponent of random acts of chivalry. I never did learn how he ended up in Wisconsin for the long haul, but if I had to guess, I'd venture to say it was a hopeless act of romance that kept him here.

I had taken nearly all of my Art History cornerstone classes with him and he'd become fond of me when I practically begged him to take me on as a teaching assistant for the entry-level Art History lecture. He saw it as enthusiasm. I saw it as a paycheck to bring myself one step closer to living independently from my parents. Most of all, I liked Professor Whitman because he was simply a nice guy. He knew how to make learning fun and, as Associate Dean of the Fine Arts program, he made it his business to know who's who among the student body. Over the past four years, he'd evolved into the dad I had always wanted but never had. Don't get me wrong. I have a father in the sense of an overbearing, controlling, ATM machine. But he isn't a *dad*.

As I open his email, it's impossible not to imagine Professor Whitman reciting it aloud with a cigar in one hand, whiskey neat in the other, his over exaggerated gestures sloshing the amber liquid through the air.

> *Ivy,*
>
> *Welcome back! I trust that your European adventure has served you well and that this message finds you in the comforts of*

home. Teaching Art History 101 to a lecture hall of freshman thinking they were in a blow off course was not nearly as satisfying without you joining me as my T.A. again. I always appreciated your snark and ability to break through to them. But I digress.

James Horejsi, a friend and former colleague, contacted me last week about a new endeavor. Last year he opened Gallery 545 in New York and now has an opportunity for an Associate Curator. James asked me if I knew of anyone who would, theoretically, be worthy and knowledgeable enough to take on such a prestigious position. I replied that, theoretically, if I did have someone in mind, I would need to talk with him or her prior to handing him his or her personal information.

Naturally, with your passion for art, you were the first student to come to mind.

So, Ivy, if you are—in theory— interested, just say the words and I will put him in touch with you. James has worked at countless art museums around the world including The Louvre and Prado Museum, and within the last decade has begun opening art galleries across the globe. Opportunities from him are rare and tend to be available for a fraction of a millisecond. He's good people and you would get along swimmingly, of this I am sure.

Feel free to stop by during my office hours so we can chat a bit more. I would love

to hear all about Italy and learn if you are in-
terested in scheduling an interview with
James. Theoretically, of course.
    Sincerely,
    Dr. Elias Whitman

Flattered, I shoot him a quick message back and make a mental note to head to campus and visit him tomorrow. My insides fall through my feet when I click open the next email. Her inevitable acrimonious tone floods my head as I start to read.

Ivy Elaine,
    I am writing to let you know that your
father and I will be unable to attend your
graduation ceremonies this weekend. Gene-
vieve and Cortland have their tasting for the
wedding, along with a few other important
appointments that simply cannot be missed.
As maid of honor, you need to reconsider
your stopover in Madison and join us to fulfill
your sisterly obligation.
    I do not understand why you have cho-
sen to fly directly to Madison upon arrival in
the States. We will see you when you return to
Chicago. I will plan to send our driver up to
collect your belongings and take you home
this weekend.
    — Mother

Seriously? Reconsider staying in Madison. Miss graduation? This woman is ridiculous. Puckering my lips and releasing a drawn out exhale, I click reply.

> *Don't worry about it, Mom. I'll have Rachel bring me home after graduation. And Italy was amazing. Thanks for asking.*

That woman is impossible. She clearly still hasn't forgiven me for "bringing shame to the family name" as she so eloquently called it during my rebellious phase in high school. She called it shame, but I called it, "showing the world not everyone in the Cotter family is a stuck up asshat."

I'm sure her face is still void of emotion, pulled skin-tight from the copious amount of Botox she injects, trying to make herself look younger and become the perfect trophy wife on my father's arm. My mother never wastes an opportunity to remind me that she wanted Genevieve to be an only child. I was the accident—the accident that ruined her life. My mother resents me for it. She doesn't need to say it aloud, though; her actions tell me everything I need to know. But I stopped taking offense a long ago and realized that my value goes far beyond my mother's opinion of me.

I snap my laptop shut and head back to my room so I can decompress in the shower. I don't want to think about my parents or Chicago, and I certainly don't want to think about Matt, who is looking at me smugly from the confines of a picture frame. As I walk by, I rip down any photographic evidence of him, tossing the shreds into the wastebasket in the corner.

I don't want to think about what the future has in store for me. I just want to enjoy my last few days of freedom in Madison with Rachel and not have to worry about any impending responsibility.

Retreating to the bathroom, I crank the water to scalding and slip inside, washing the grime and my worries away.

I SCREAM AS I'M STARTLED to my senses when the bathroom door flies open. Popping my head out from behind the shower curtain, I see Rachel bouncing around frantically. She never was one for social protocol. If only her energy could be bottled, we would surely have the world's most effective antidepressant.

"I haven't seen you in ages, Ivy Cotter ... Phillips ... whatever the hell you are calling yourself these days! Get your cute little ass out of the shower and hug me. Now!" Rachel commands in an enthusiastic fashion that only she can pull off. I manage to finish rinsing the conditioner out of my hair and turn the water off just before she tosses a towel over the curtain. She drags me out, near naked and envelopes me in a bear hug worthy of grizzlies. We are just one towel drop away from a ridiculous lesbian love scene— moments like these are what teenage boy fantasies are made of.

The steam from my shower has fogged over the mirror, where Rachel has written 'Welcome Home!' surrounded by stars. When I pry myself from her grasp, I wrap my bathrobe around me as Rachel jumps up on the counter and proceeds to tell me about everything I've missed over the past nine months.

God, how I've missed her incessant babbling.

When she finally comes up for air, the fog on the

glass has dissipated and the air between us has chilled. My eyes meet Rachel's in the mirror and she pauses with a deep breath and a look of worry in her eyes.

"So I guess I should tell you … Matt called me the other day. He wanted to know when you were getting back into town."

Her words ricochet right off me and I continue to brush through my hair, unaffected. "That's nice, I guess. I hope you told him I had no plans of returning." And as far as he's concerned, that's the truth. I have no intention of seeing him again. Ever.

"Ivy…" She touches my arm, and I stop brushing my hair to look her in the eye. "Our friends back home have told me that ever since you left last year, he's really changed. I know you don't talk about what went down with you guys, but maybe you should consider hearing him out. Give him a chance."

"Don't you dare go defending him. And for the record, I've changed too. Like my tolerance for his bullshit? It's nonexistent now. So what did you tell him?" I start brushing my hair again, each stroke getting increasingly more aggressive. I do not want to be discussing this with her right now. Talking about Matt will only sour my mood and spoil our reunion.

"You know I can't lie."

"Rachel!" I whine as I rip a knot out from my scalp, yelping in pain.

"He knows you got back in today. But don't worry. Matt has a life of his own set up back home in Chicago, working for some big fancy ad agency downtown, so I don't think he'll be making the three hour trek up here just to surprise you, especially since we're headed back to Chicago this weekend."

"Good."

I'm honestly not sure if I'd run away from him or run right into his bed, so it's best for everyone if he keeps a safe distance from me.

I know why I started dating Matt, but I never really understood why I let it go on as long as it did. I was emotionally checked out after a month of dating and Matt seemed to like the *idea* of me far more than he actually liked being with me as an individual. I always had the sneaky suspicion that it was because of my parent's money. Early on I'd learned not to complain and that it was good to keep him around for three reasons:

One, he was great in bed. And by great I mean he gave me the ability to completely disconnect from all of life's bullshit and see stars for days.

Two, my parents adored him and as long as they believed that I was with him, they tended to stay off my back—a major plus for me, and if we're being honest a necessity to my survival.

And *three*, he was insanely easy to cheat on.

By the time I'd finally ended it, I was repulsed by everything little he did, so I decided to cut my losses and fled to Italy. Don't get me wrong, I miss the sex; I just don't miss the person on the other end of the dick.

At all.

"So when do your folks roll into town for the main event?"

I can't help but laugh. "They don't."

She looks at me slack-jawed. I fight the urge to reach out and close Rachel's mouth. Really, this move shouldn't surprise her.

"My mom emailed me earlier to let me know they aren't coming up for graduation. Apparently Gen and her fiancé have some wedding crap they've roped the whole family into attending. Then she laid it on thick about me choosing to be here, at my graduation, and not back in Chicago with them. All of this in an email when I haven't heard their voices in nearly nine months. She may as well have sent me a telegraph by way of pigeon."

"That's bullshit."

"No … that's my family," I say with a sigh. It's sad but true. I have always played second fiddle to Genevieve. I'm just ready to be done with it all and get myself as far away from them as possible. Italy was a welcomed taste of independence, and I'm dreading being back under their roof for even a short amount of time while I figure out the job situation.

It's unfair that I've had to deal with this nonsense for so long. You would think they'd be proud to have a daughter who actually has a spine and a fuck it all attitude, but instead I get to spend the rest of my life being cast away as the black sheep for refusing to fall into line. I come from a family with serious control issues. My parents try to control everything in sight, and I refuse to be controlled. It's a nightmare for everyone.

"You know what I say, girl? When all else fails, eat your feelings. I'll be right back," Rachel says with an infectious smile that touches her eyes.

Right. It's all fun and games until your pants don't fit anymore.

Rachel disappears down the hall and I quickly toss on a pair of cozy sweatpants and my favorite Chicago Cubs T-shirt. When I sit down on the bed, I realize just how tired I am. All this traveling is starting to catch up. Rachel returns moments later with two spoons and a pint of Ben and Jerry—my two favorite men. Her grin is electric and I realize just how much I've missed her since August.

"I suppose it's not all bad news though."

"What do you mean?" she asks, offering me a spoon.

"Well, for starters, my parents won't be here to dictate how I curl my hair for graduation," I smirk. "Anyway, I really don't want to think about them right now. Besides, I have something to tell you."

"Lay it on me."

"There's a job interview in—"

"An interview!"

I nod and fight my grin, trying not to come off as overeager. Rachel hasn't had any luck finding an internship for after graduation. She smacks my arm with the back of her hand.

"Ivy! That's incredible! Tell me about it," she begs, eyes wide as she takes an unhealthy-sized scoop of ice cream. It baffles me that she can eat such crap and still look like she just stepped off the runway.

"Well, I don't *officially* have the interview yet. But Professor Whitman is recommending me to a friend of his for an Associate Curator position. In New York City." Rachel screams and tackles me in another bear hug, overcome with excitement.

"Whoa, whoa, whoa. Settle down, Rachel. I don't even have the interview scheduled."

"But you will, and you'll absolutely get it. I mean, have you met you?"

I laugh at her energy. Some things never change with Rachel and me. I am the Daria to her Quinn. She is the

Prozac to my Valium. We are the perfect balance of sweetness and cynicism.

"This calls for a celebration!" She jumps up and drags me into her bedroom. "Screw jetlag, we're going out to-night," she announces prolifically.

"Oh, we are? And where exactly are we going?"

If I'm being entirely honest, I really wouldn't mind crashing early tonight, but it would be nice to party with folks who actually speak the same language. Plus it's graduation weekend, so it will be the last chance I have to see a lot of my old classmates.

"There's a party at some house down by Lake Mendota. No idea who's throwing it, but Cassie told me the whole gang will be there. Should be a good time."

"Really? A house party?" I whine. I can't believe she thinks this is a good way to kick off graduation festivities. We haven't stepped foot inside a house party since spring semester freshman year when we scored our fake IDs.

"It should be fun," she reassured. "Let's stop by for a little bit and if we aren't having fun, I promise we can leave and hit up The Great Dane."

She knows just how to placate me. I love that pub and had spent most of my free time there two years ago. "Fine. But I'm holding you to that."

Rachel leaves me with Ben and Jerry, shooting me a flirtatious wink before sashaying into her bathroom to get ready.

MY FAVORITE RED PEEP TOE heels hit the pavement with a dull click, and a splash of water coats my toes as I step into a puddle, the aftermath of an early evening storm.

The house is quaint and perched upon a slight hill, staking prominence over its neighbors. The striking cobalt door and country white trim read contemporary, which is odd for a lake house. It's a crisp late spring night, the scent of alcohol and possibility lingering in the air. Above us, the moon is painted in the sky, casting a soft glow across the front yard and lighting our way to the door. Rachel and I lock elbows and surrender to the pull of the house party, the bass line vibrating and electrifying the air, luring us inside.

Tonight, I feel good. Invincible, even. I don't have to think about my family or stress out about what I'm doing after graduation. Tonight I am just going with the flow. And if I'm lucky, I won't be going home alone. Now that I'm back in my element, my inner bad girl is just dying to come out and play.

It's just before eleven; late enough for our entrance to go unnoticed, but early enough to avoid being the only sober ones on site. There are easily sixty people crammed inside, mostly huddling in the kitchen with the kegs and makeshift bar. Through the window, dozens more litter the backyard, and I can see people all the way down to the lake. Admittedly, I'm a bit surprised the cops have yet to break up the party.

A blond-haired god obstructs my view as he squeezes in front of me, heading toward the alcohol. He looks as if he walked right off the page of a menswear catalog and into my life. Muscular, sophisticated and mysterious, he is easily one of the most attractive men I have ever seen.

"Hellooo there," I muse under my breath in a sing-song whisper. He casts a confident smile over his shoulder and his green eyes pierce right through me. This man is officially locked in my crosshairs and doesn't stand a chance for survival. "I wouldn't mind tasting him later this evening," I quip at Rachel.

Him. I could easily turn into the girl I used to be for one night with him.

"You are so bad, Ivy. You haven't even been home for twenty-four hours and you're already on the verge of pouncing on some unsuspecting guy." Apparently subtle gawking still isn't my strong suit.

"Guys like him are anything but unsuspecting," I correct Rachel. "He's practically eye-fucking anything with two legs and breasts in this place."

I crave nothing more than one night of unattached company. It's been too long. And Rachel can see it in my eyes. My instincts kick into overdrive and every guy in the place becomes an opportunity. A challenge. A missing name on my roster of conquests.

For the past year, I have been angelic. They should

have a patron saint named after my celibate efforts. After all this time, you can't fault a girl for wanting a good, rough roll in the hay.

Rachel playfully rolls her eyes at me and bumps my hip with hers. "Let's go, Ivy. I need a drink."

Never one for waiting, Rachel bypasses the snaking line and walks right up to the keg, grabbing two beers from the fraternity guy manning the tap. She whispers something in his ear and his face flushes crimson before she pecks a kiss on his cheek and turns back to me.

Looks like I'm not the only one fishing for company this evening.

We make several rounds through the house and find our way outside, reconnecting with classmates I haven't seen in ages. I'm in the middle of recounting the tale of getting locked in the restroom of the Galleria dell'Accademia at closing time when Rachel's eyes go wide.

Strong arms wrap around my waist in a vice from behind as a wolfish voice husks in my ear, "I heard you were back in town." I freeze, stunned at the intimate touch and hot breath against my neck. I recognize the voice instantly and it sends a warning chill down my spine.

"Jesus, Matt. Get off me," I reply, weaseling my way out of his grasp, then turning around to face him.

"Come on, Ivy. I've missed you so much this past year." He eyes me with a certainty reserved for a lion on the cusp of tasting its prey.

"You mean you've missed having a Cotter girl on your arm."

"Well, yeah. I mean ... dating you certainly came with its ... privileges," he smirks.

Privileges. *Right*. That's just another way of saying he

enjoyed being so close to my parent's money. And while I wasn't exactly the portrait of fidelity, he practically had a love affair with my parents every time I brought him home.

Matt pulls me away from the crowd to talk on the side of the house. It's a little quieter here so I can hear myself think over the thrumming bass line of the music.

"When did you get back?" He seems genuinely interested, but if he thinks I'm going home with him tonight he's sorely mistaken. I look over his shoulder, trying to find someone, *anyone*, who can rescue me from this conversation. He flashes that mischievous smile capable of dropping panties from miles away.

"I know that you harassed Rachel about my travel plans and that you were well aware I got back this afternoon, so don't even try to play this off like a coincidence." I defensively fold my arms. "Shouldn't you be back in Chicago?"

"Why do you have to go and be like that?" He crosses his arms defensively.

"Like what?"

Matt looks to the ground in thought and sighs. "Never mind."

I cannot even believe that we are having this conversation. Just yesterday I was saying goodbye to Italy, and after only a few hours in Wisconsin I already have pieces of my old life trying to suck me back up in its drama. I should have never come home.

"Let me take you out."

"We *are* out, Matt," I state obviously.

"That's not what I meant. Come on, Ivy. You know we're great together. Our parents loved us together."

My gaze is vacant at his statement and I want to hole up into myself, disappearing completely. "Right. Because we should be doing everything our parents expect us to do?"

Matt opens his mouth to say something and snaps it shut quickly, looking away.

"We broke up for a reason," I remind him curtly.

"And I've spent the last nine months trying to figure that reason out. I was willing to overlook you sneaking around behind my back just so I could be with you."

My stern exterior cracks a little at his admission. But mostly, I just feel really sorry for him knowing that he only stayed with me because of my last name. It's impossible to respect someone who knew they were being cheated on and never did a damn thing about it like a little bitch. *Grow some balls, man.*

But it's true. I never did tell him how unhappy I was and that I never really gave a damn about our "relationship." His very existence grated on my every nerve. It got to the point where watching him chew his food made me want to strike him with the back of my hand. How the mere sound of his voice would make my insides coil with nausea.

In spite of this, Matt was always reliable for one thing, allowing me to close my eyes and lose myself at the touch of his skilled hands. I could spend days between the sheets of his bed, forgetting about the expectations of my parents, the expectations of myself ... hell, even forgetting my own name. You could say I used him and I would be the first to openly admit that.

Ultimately though, I didn't end things because of him. I ended things because I hated who I had become when I was with him. Our relationship, if you can even call it that, was all for appearances. I had become unapologetically slutty, and frankly, I didn't care.

At the end of the day, I played along for so long because my parents adored Matt, which meant they stayed out of my hair as a result. The less involved they were in my life, the better. Matt adored having an elusive Cotter girl on his arm, and I simply adored the cover he provided for my outrageous collegiate shenanigans.

Matt's remorseful eyes capture mine and I'm reminded of the unspoken words that passed between us when we first met. We started dating spring semester of my freshman year at UW. I bumped into Matt at the student union, literally. I stopped by the cafeteria in between classes to grab a soda, rounded a corner too quickly, and turned his white henley into a piece of Orange Crush modern art. As I stood there horrified, he gave me the comforting look as if to say, "Everything will be all right but you are *so* going to make this up to me." Matt never technically asked me out, but we were pretty much inseparable from that day forward, and things progressed to the physical realm rather quickly.

I used to think we had instant chemistry. But I now know that if you think something often enough, it becomes reality.

"Please?"

I'm not sure exactly what he's asking, but he is obviously hurting. Frankly, I don't have time for his charade. Matt is part of my past and that's exactly where I need to leave him.

"Come with me." He pulls on my hand. "Let's go grab a drink together, catch up." Quickly, I draw my arm back to my body, grinding my teeth.

"Matt ... just go. Okay?" He needs to leave me alone before my open fist meets his face. I really don't want our exchange to cause a scene, but I'm not above it.

"One drink. That's all I'm asking."

"No."

His face contorts as if he's swallowed something bitter and we stand there in a Mexican standoff, each waiting for the other to make a move. He can't seem to get it through his thick skull that we are never happening again. *Ever.*

I turn to move back to the party and Matt panics, knowing that I'm on the verge of slipping through his fingers. He's desperate and gives me that piercing look that made my insides tingle once upon a time.

"Pleeeeeease?" he pleads.

Jesus, stop begging. This boy is pathetically relentless.

A heavy sigh escapes my lips as I calculate my next move. "Fine."

"Really?" Matt's eyes light up with surprise. I purse my lips together and nod, pausing to make sure no one is watching.

I think to myself, *bottoms up, asshole,* and throw the remaining contents of my beer in Matt's face. Shock registers and he mutters a string of indecipherable obscenities under his breath. I turn on my heel and make my way back into the party to find Rachel.

I catch a glimpse of Matt storming toward the front yard in haste. If only he had stormed away that day in the cafeteria, I wouldn't be in this position right now. Hopefully, he's gone. *Indefinitely.*

22

Empowered and invincible. That's how I feel in this moment. Adrenaline pulsates through my veins and the natural high makes me untouchable.

Rejoining Rachel, I'm pleased to see that Cassie and a few other folks I recognize have finally made it. Cassie squeals and pulls me into a tight hug, spilling her beer on the ground. It feels good to be among my closest friends again.

"Now," I breathe, "where were we?" I shake off my exchange with Matt and twirl a few loose hairs around my finger, tucking the locks behind my ear.

"Oh no … what'd you do, Ivy?" Rachel deadpans. Out of everyone on this Earth, Rachel can read me like an open book. I really need to work on my poker face.

"It's nothing, really."

"No," she says pointedly, "you're doing that thing. With your hair." Damn it. *My tell.* "What'd he do this time?" she asks with a sigh.

"He insisted on getting a drink with me. I insisted he leave me alone. And so he left me with no other choice than to give him *my* drink," I spat quickly. "If you'd like to catch up with him, just look for the pissed off soaked shirt in the front yard."

"You didn't," Cassie gasps.

"I did." I can barely contain the smirk on my lips.

"You think he'd take a hint by now," Rachel comments.

Unfortunately for me, he has never been that smart. To him, I was the answer to all of his problems. To me, he was a mindless escape from all of the drama and troubles I left behind in Chicago. Eventually, he found himself twisted into my life and went so far as to make a home for himself with my family. It's completely my fault for ever allowing it to get that far.

When I elected to take my senior year abroad to get away from him and everyone else in my life, Matt was less than thrilled. I broke his heart, and from what mutual friends had told me, he'd found solace in the bed of a few dozen girls. Even through his haste, Matt continued to claim that I was the one for him and constantly pleaded his case to be together. He wrote me nearly every week while I was in Italy, even though it fell on deaf ears. Then, he went as far as finding a job at a major ad agency in downtown Chicago with the intent of winning me back together after I graduated. While most girls would be thrilled at the thought of an old flame pining away and turning their life upside down waiting for their return, I was turned off.

"Well, let's go get you another drink. You know, in case Matt decides to come back," Cassie chimes, pulling us back inside the house. Her blonde ringlets fit her personality—bouncy and out of control.

It isn't until this very moment I realize just how much I'd missed my friends while I was away. My heart aches a little for the time lost.

ON OUR WAY BACK INTO the house, Cassie gets lost in the crowd and I can only assume she has made her way onto the makeshift dance floor in the backyard. The attractive guy in Greek letters is lingering by the keg and gives Rachel a sly smile. She wraps one arm around his waist and he leans over, kissing her hair.

Clearly I've missed something as they obviously already know each other. He tucks his hand in Rachel's back pocket and runs his finger tenderly down the edge of her nose, and I can't help but feel like a Peeping Tom as the pair flirt shamelessly. *Get a room, already.* It's clear she wants to spend some time with this guy but her eyes read guilty for leaving me to fend for myself.

I kiss Rachel on the cheek and shoo her and the hottie away with a flick of my wrist. I'm a big girl and perfectly capable of entertaining myself at a party.

The crowd inside the house has finally thinned out, and almost everyone is in the backyard grinding on each other to the beat of the music. Alone in my thoughts, I fight the annoyance of Matt's surprise visit. Why the hell did he bother showing up? He lives in Chicago and needs to stay there. I haven't even been home for twenty-four hours and I'm already itching to put space between me and the drama of my former life.

I snatch the tap from the keg, furiously pouring myself another beer, not caring about the two inches of foam on top. On the counter is a colorful rainbow of Jell-O shots, so I quickly grab one and throw my head back, swallowing the citrusy libation whole. Then another.

And another.

I wasn't planning on going on a bender tonight, but after my run-in with Matt it seems as though the universe has other plans for me.

I spy Rachel and her 'beau du jour' in the crowd of people below the porch, their lips locked tightly together as they move to the music. I mentally calm myself with each passing sip of beer and fresh air. The crowd in the backyard is thickening, booming speakers beckoning everyone to dance as a sea of limbs pulsates with the music below me.

"Well, *that* was an entertaining performance," a deep voice says next to me.

I look to my right and the lickable, green-eyed man from earlier is standing there smiling in all of his golden-haired glory. It should seriously be illegal for anyone to be this good looking. "You know, you should be more careful. I'd hate for a girl like you to get a bad rap," he says, eyeing me slowly before nudging my shoulder.

"Girl like me?"

"Yeah." He pauses thoughtfully. "Beautiful. Mysterious. Confident. And pissed off."

Ah, he must have seen me with Matt. I give him a sly, flirtatious smile. "Don't worry. He deserved it," I reply sweetly, my voice void of tension. He seems a little older than the typical college crowd. A grad student, perhaps? Too old to be in classes, but too young to be staying in on a weeknight.

"Are you graduating?"

"Nah, I'm just in town from Chicago for a long weekend. This is my younger brother's place. He's only twenty and lost his fake ID when he got pulled over with a DUI last month. Since he has no way to hit up the bars without it, he went the old fashioned route with a house party." He gestures grandly with his hand. "Hence, the soiree, and you existing in my very presence. You're welcome." He playfully smirks as his eyes zero in on an athletic, olive-skinned, black-haired sorority girl grinding on one of her girlfriends. His gaze is so intense he's practically devouring her in his mind. Cocky much?

An athletic, dark-haired guy walks up and stands on the other side of the blond, interrupting our conversation and my chances of hooking up. His white polo shirt is just tight enough to showcase his muscles, and the faded navy Bermuda shorts look soft, and accentuate his perfect ass. His dark locks hit the ideal length, just before it needs a haircut—long enough to grab in the throes of passion, but not so long it hangs in his eyes. He's effortlessly attractive in a not so obvious way.

"Hey, Sully," the newcomer says, gesturing my neighbor. I take note of his name. It's unique and I can't help but assume that it's a nickname.

"Nix," he responds with a tight mouth and subtle nod.

Our conversation comes to a screeching halt, and the three of us continue to look out over the party. A dirty rap song fills the awkward silence between us.

"Welp, my work here is done. I'm out." Sully lazily toasts his glass my direction, his tone instantly bored. "Have fun, kids."

The friend glances over his shoulder and slides over to me, filling the space Sully just vacated. A small laugh escapes my breath and I shake my head in disbelief.

"What?" He eyes me curiously.

"Wingman?" I question, glancing over my shoulder to look back at Sully, trying to mask my disappointment.

He gives me a toothy grin worthy of a dozen Boy Scout merit badges. "Something like that." He reluctantly extends his hand to shake mine. "I'm Phoenix. But everyone calls me Nix."

Phoenix. I like that.

"Ivy," I respond, shaking his hand firmly. Phoenix's hand lingers just a beat too long on mine. His fingers are calloused, but his palms are soft.

"Ivy? Like the plant?"

"Something like that," I repeat his words, mirroring

his intonation. Silence lingers in the space between us and I can't fight the urge to fill it. More information than necessary spills from my mouth. "My dad named me. He's a huge Chicago Cubs fan and apparently wanted a year-round reminder of Wrigley Field."

Phoenix's eyes grow wide. "Well, that's strike one. I'm a Cardinals fan," he ribs proudly, a smile lighting his eyes. "When was the last time your team won the World Series?"

"Hey! It was 1908 and any team can have a bad century," I tease defensively. Growing up a Cubs fan gave me thick skin and an affinity for disappointment, perfect for moments like these. I look out over the crowd and see Sully dancing quite inappropriately with the black-haired girl, then look at plan B standing next to me.

Phoenix is certainly attractive. Not necessarily the kind of guy I would typically go for, but I'm more than willing to make an exception.

"At any rate, my mom only agreed to the name because she felt it gave me the aspirational essence of being out of everyone's league." I flit my hand in the air at the thought.

He laughs through his nose and takes another sip from his red cup.

"And are you, Miss Ivy League?"

"Only to assholes," I affirm, repressing a smile, thinking of Matt storming away earlier. I certainly don't want to go into my thoroughbred upbringing with this guy. It always comes with unnecessary judgment.

"Well then…" he pauses, leaning over the railing. "I'm in luck."

"Why's that?"

"Because I'm not an asshole."

The sincerity in his eyes tells me he truly believes that of himself, and at this moment, I am given no reason to think otherwise. His boyish charm shines right through and it starts to bubble my insides.

With an inviting tilt of my head, I lead him to the old-fashioned porch swing on the side of the wrap around deck. It reminds me of something you'd see in the south—little old biddies sitting together, sipping their mint juleps and gossiping about the latest town scandal. It's a little quieter over here away from the main speakers and we can at least attempt to have a decent conversation without screaming over some top forty dance remix.

Phoenix and I talk until the red moon crosses the night sky. He tells me about life as a freelance landscape architect in St. Louis and I'm surprised to learn that even though he's lived there most of his life, he's never been down to the Gateway Arch. It's one of my favorite places in his city. When you stand underneath the arch, it's impossible not to feel like you've shrunk in size. It's a little like magic.

I gather that Phoenix loves his field of work, but he doesn't love the uncertainty of freelancing. He's hoping to find a permanent gig by the time summer comes to a close and is open to relocating. The market hasn't been strong since he graduated two years ago, so I mentally place him at twenty-four, maybe twenty-five years old. Phoenix seems especially interested in my European travels this past year, eagerly asking questions about visiting world-renowned museums and exploring ancient ruins in Rome and Greece.

I learn that he and a bunch of his guy friends are

spending the weekend in Madison for a bachelor party. Wisconsin is a far cry from the stereotypical Vegas bachelor extravaganza, but who am I to judge? Had they gone to Las Vegas, I wouldn't be sitting here in this moment, so I'm certainly not complaining.

Never before has a conversation with the opposite sex come this naturally. It could be the three rounds of beer we've thrown back together, but Phoenix makes it easy to be honest, to be myself. I can forget about who I was before I ever left for Italy because, let's be truthful, I kind of became a horrible person. Instead, he makes me feel good about who I truly am, who I want to be. Suddenly, life doesn't seem so bad after all. His hazel eyes are inviting and I find myself wanting to reach out and grab hold of his hand. At one point, I nearly do but get nervous and lean over to scratch my leg instead. Bold Ivy is long gone, replaced by a timid girl bubbling over with giddiness inside, trying to keep her cool over this boy.

Talking with him has a calming effect on me. I don't find my mind wandering to my family or graduation, or even what I'm doing next week. It's refreshing. I'm right here in this moment with Phoenix, and everything is seemingly in its right place. At times, it's as if his shyness matches my own which explains the need for a wingman … something has rattled his confidence.

As we gently swing together, I take a long draw from my beer and discern that Phoenix is right. He definitely isn't an asshole. He's the kind of guy you'd want to bring home to Mom and Dad. Well, not *my* mom and dad, but rather nice, normal parents. But the best part is that he can hold my attention, a welcomed change from the roster of guys I've hooked up with and tossed away with the light of day.

"Hey … nice phone case," he says as I fish my phone from my back pocket. "I had a poster of Edvard Munch's *The Scream* in my dorm room freshman year."

I smile at his admission and find myself impressed that he recognized not only the painting, but the artist as well. But I don't tell him that I hung the same poster in my flat in Italy.

I check the time on my phone and notice it's nearly two thirty in the morning, much to my surprise. This party is still going strong and Phoenix and I have been talking with the greatest of ease for hours. It's impossible not to notice the subtle frown on his face when I glance up from my phone. I want to reach out and caress his face, letting him know that I'm not looking for an escape route, but for some reason, I can't muster the courage to make a pass at him. Under normal circumstances, the alcohol would have pushed me to make my move hours ago.

But these aren't normal circumstances.

Phoenix intently looks at the bottom of his empty cup. "Can I get you anything?"

"I kind of want to eat some waffles," I say, playfully nudging him with my shoulder. While he may take that as a request to have breakfast with him in a few hours, I really do legitimately want some kind of breakfast food.

Phoenix throws his head back in laughter. "I'm fresh out of waffles. And I think you're a little tipsy," he says, reaching out to gently touch my cheek with his fingers. His hand is warm and my face instantly melts at his touch. The look in his eyes is so endearing … God, I want to kiss the shit out of him right now.

Yep, I'm tipsy. Maybe even more than tipsy. There's

no sense in trying to deny it.

"And you're cute," I slur. "But seriously, eating breakfast food could solve all of the world's problems right now." It could help me sober up, for starters. I may need to call for a cab sometime soon if my nerves keep getting in the way of this thing with Phoenix. It appears that Rachel left hours ago, and Cassie is probably lost in a sea of drunkenness, and who knows where things with Phoenix will end up.

"All right. Let's go get me a refill and see if there's anything to snack on for you." He extends his elbow my direction as we stand and escorts me into the kitchen. By some divine force, I'm able to walk upright without tripping over my own feet.

Entering the kitchen, I spot Sully sitting on the countertop with the tan, black-haired girl now perched between his legs like a poodle begging for a treat. His treat. *Good grief, desperate much*? For one fleeting moment, I realize that is likely how I've looked time and time again. God, how pathetic. I will *never* be that girl again.

We scan the kitchen and there is no food in sight. The hell with it … I grab another Jell-O shot, chasing it with the last of my beer. Jell-O is technically a food, right? And more liquid courage is just what I need to get my nerves in check and make this night a little more interesting, moving from conversation to some action. At this point, I'd just settle for a good old-fashioned make out session. His lips look absolutely delicious and I want them plastered to mine.

Making my way closer to the keg, I catch Sully giving Phoenix a questionable glare, eyes serious. Nix subtly shakes his head no as Sully's eyes hide a sinister laugh.

The silent exchange brings unease, but rather than focus on it, I let my head drift into the fizziness of the last shot. I feel it in my bones that Phoenix is a good guy and there is a shortage of good guys in my world these days.

I turn to look at him and he's already staring. The feeling that takes over is indescribable. Suppressing a flirtatious smile, he simply says, "Let's dance."

"Put on your red shoes and dance the blues," I sing back, quoting my all-time favorite David Bowie song.

His face lights up with childlike delight as he takes my hand and places it over my heart. "Did you really just say that? I think I may have just fallen in love," he muses with a twinkle in his eye. "I grew up listening to Bowie."

It's as if the powers that be have plucked this guy out from the sky and put him in my presence.

Anxiously, I let him lead me out under the night sky. Oak trees in the backyard are strung with Christmas lights, like twinkling stars winking fatefully down upon us. In my intoxicated haze, they cast an ethereal glow. Phoenix and I move in sync with the bass line of some ridiculous nineties R&B song, our hands exploring each other's bodies. He smells sexy, like damp earth and musk, and it's easily the manliest scent I've encountered.

The contours of his arms are magnetizing; I couldn't pry my fingers away if I tried. Beads of sweat snake their way from my hairline, between my shoulders, and pool in the small of my back. It's difficult to tell if the salt I taste is from the alcohol or my skin melting into itself. I grip my hands around his neck and gently twist his hair between my fingertips. Phoenix rests his forehead against mine, eyes cutting right through to my soul, and I hear a soft groan escape the back of his throat.

I trace my tongue over my lips in anticipation and take slow, deep breaths, committing myself not to screw this up. More than anything I want to know what he tastes like.

Everything about his presence feels right. We fit together is like two pieces of a puzzle. We read each other's body like we've done this before. Phoenix licks his lips and I can taste a sweet blend of alcohol and sweat in the space between us. Heat rises from deep within me and I close my eyes, willing him to make a move.

Kiss me already, damn it!

We get lost like this for a few songs—me, a siren, working to bring him into my possession. I sense him leisurely eyeing my body, inhaling my hair, soaking me in as much as he can. And when his soft lips delicately press against my temple, relief washes through me. He wants this too.

Our gravitational pull is undeniable.

Phoenix traces his tongue teasingly to my jawline before nibbling on my earlobe. I can't help but moan as the sensation resonates deep inside my body. My pulse quickens and I'm breathless. I need his kiss to fill my lungs with air. I need his touch to make me believe that good guys like him *do* exist. I need him to …

I need him to get out of here.

My head snaps back involuntarily and my eyes shoot open in surprise. I'm drunk.

So very, very drunk.

And I'm overwhelmingly desperate to get away from this party. The earth shifts on its axis and my sense of security goes askew. I scan my eyes through the crowd, desperately searching for Rachel … Cassie … any familiar face. I have to get out of here. Go home. Sleep the alcohol off.

Now.

"Ivy?"

I hear him call out to me. But his voice is muffled. I'm underwater. Phoenix's nails dig into the flesh of my arms ... my head fills with stars ... my legs are lead, but I find myself floating weightlessly, dancing in slow motion.

Try as I might, words fail me. I attempt to respond to him, but each thought is trapped inside my mouth, clinging to the back of my teeth like an insect struggling to free itself from tar.

My body shakes in Phoenix's arms.

Darkness begins in the corners of my eyes and seeps through, taking over my line of sight. A blank page bleeding ink. The crisp music turns murky.

My brain ... slurs.

My knees ... buckle.

Give ...

Out ...

Heaviness ...

Darkness.

THE FIRST THING I NOTICE is my pulse.

Behind my eyelids is a furious pushing and pulling of angry seawaters beating against a rocky shoreline with each beat of my heart. The morning sun melts through the blinds, cascading stripes against the far wall, and the aura makes my insides heave as I choke back the rising bile in my throat. Slowly, I sit up and fist my hair.

What the fuck happened last night?

This is easily the worst hangover in the history of hangovers. I know my limits, but more often than not I just simply ignore them. Case and point? This very moment. With the way I'm feeling, I clearly drank half the party.

That's it. I'm never drinking again.

This time I think I might actually mean it.

I spy my phone on the nightstand, next to a large glass of water. That's…*thoughtful?* I chug the full glass in three gulps.

I grab my phone to check the time and notice a text message.

Rachel: *Hey, girl! Call me when you wake up*

and I'll come get you. Hope you had fun with
that lickable blond hottie! XO

I don't think Rachel could be more awesome if she tried. As for the blond … well, that didn't go as planned. I quickly fire off a reply.

Ivy: *Rescue me. Stat.*

Moments later she texts back to let me know she's on her way. Which gives me roughly ten to fifteen minutes to get my shit together and out of this place.

I examine myself. Clothes, while disheveled, are still on. I look around the room and observe my surroundings and then it hits me—I have no idea where I am. I catch a glimpse of my reflection in the mirror. Raccoon eyes, bird's nest hair, sallow cheeks … whatever happened once the shots took over must have been fun because I look, and feel, like hell.

I sit up to gather my belongings and find a bathroom. As soon as I'm vertical, sea legs hit and I'm woozy. My thighs throb and my entire body aches, clear indication that a good time was had, although I don't recall dancing all that much.

When I emerge from the bedroom, the pieces begin to fall into place. Clearly, I crashed at the party, which is rather adventitious of me. I chalk it up to blacking out.

The hallways are quiet and I am certain there's no one else awake … that is if there is even anyone else in this house.

I open a door, praying it's the bathroom and not a bedroom holding half naked, passed out strangers on the other side, but all I find are rolls of towels twisted like cinnamon buns with extra bed linens and blankets stuffed along the top. I reach for a washcloth and try the handle on the opposite of the closet with success. Quietly, I slip in and close the door, locking it behind me.

My stomach grumbles, but thankfully it isn't lurching in the aftermath of a long night of drinking. I ransack the medicine cabinet, searching for something, anything, to help relieve the pounding inside my skull.

When I spy the bottle of generic aspirin, I can't get the lid off fast enough. I toss three little white pills in my mouth and stick my face under the running faucet. Next, I splash cold water across my cheeks, wiping the mascara streaks from underneath my bloodshot eyes and make plans to beeline it out of this house as quickly as possible.

Creeping back into the hallway, I tip toe my way to the living room so I can sneak out the front door. My efforts are foiled with each passing step as the floor creaks beneath me, and a pair of warm hazel eyes meets mine as I walk through the doorway into the living room.

"Well, well, well, look who decided to join the land of the living. It's Ivy, of the Wrigley Field variety!"

Shit.

It's him.

Beautiful, perfect, quirky him. And, of course, he's sitting there looking like a shiny new penny while I unequivocally look like hell. I should have searched for mouthwash in the bathroom. I would give anything for a breath mint right now, or better yet, a brown bag to put over my head.

It's clear that I wasn't wearing beer goggles last night because Phoenix in the light of the morning sun is infinitely sexier than Phoenix after a keg of Wisconsin's finest cheap beer. I didn't notice the slight copper tint to his hair last night, or the playful dimple on his right cheek. He's wearing a vintage Led Zeppelin shirt from when they played Knebworth Festival back in '79, and it takes all of my willpower not to throw myself at him right here and now.

"Come on over here, Cubby Bear," Phoenix teases, patting the spot next to him on the couch.

"Oh God," I groan. "Please don't call me that." Rolling my eyes, the motion sears deep inside my head.

"Not feeling so hot?" The dimple on his cheek mocks me as he smirks. How the hell he doesn't feel the same way I do is baffling. I give him my best 'don't fuck with me' stink eye as I collapse next to him on the faded leather couch. Surprisingly, there is little evidence of last night's party, save for a few garbage bags full of red cups in the corner.

"So … um … what happened to you last night? You seem like the kind of girl who can hold her liquor, but one minute we're having fun, and the next I'm carrying a passed out chick." The look in his eyes tells me that was not how he had hoped our evening would end. God, even in disappointment this guy is hot as shit.

"I was about to ask you the same thing."

A tiny worry crease flashes in between his eyebrows.

"We didn't …" I don't know how to put this politely, so I give him a questioning look. "You know … did we …" Not that I would have minded, especially with him, but if I'm going to have a romp between the sheets, I would at least like to have the decency to remember the occasion.

"No, no, no. We didn't do anything. In fact, I was a perfect gentleman." His smile melts my insides and he marks the letter X over his heart. "After you passed out, while dancing no less, I carried you into the spare bedroom, took off your shoes, and tucked you in. I even slept on the couch after everyone left. It wasn't exactly the most comfortable arrangement," he says, rolling his neck around. I notice the heap of a blanket on the floor with a spare pillow and suddenly find myself appreciative of the gesture.

"And they say chivalry is dead." I beam back at him, the smile hurting my eyes.

Phoenix adjusts himself on the couch so he's turned, facing me. I refrain from reaching through the space between us and brushing his dark shaggy hair away from his eyes. Fresh bed head is a striking look for him.

The stench of stale alcohol has aired out and the mouthwatering aroma of coffee wafts through the air. Phoenix sits up from the couch and walks into the kitchen to pour a cup.

"Want some?" He lifts the fresh pot into the air as I nod.

"Oh God, yes." The words slip out in a seductive groan and the sexual intonation is not lost on either of us, but caffeine is exactly what I need to start to jump start my body today.

"Sugar?"

"No, just black, please." I never understood the point of diluting coffee with sugar, creamers and flavored syrupy shit. Coffee should always be bitter and unapologetic, much like me.

Phoenix presents me with my morning brew in an

oversized mug reading "World's Greatest Teacher," then sits back down next to me. We sit in comfortable silence as I blow over the coffee, a feeble attempt to cool it off. He chews on the inside of his cheek and looks up toward the ceiling, seeming to debate something internally.

"I'm gonna take you out tomorrow night," Phoenix says matter-of-factly.

"Oh, you are?" I challenge.

"Yes. Just dinner."

"Just dinner." I do my best to mask my disappointment. What would be so wrong with more than dinner?

"Well, we could do drinks, but I would guess you're swearing off alcohol until you're forty-two."

"Forty-three actually," I reply with a light laugh. The movement rattles my skull.

I look at Phoenix intently for a moment. He has hints of laugh lines tracing his eyes which I find endearing. It is such an attractive, subtle feature, making him seem wise beyond his years as if he's endured far more than any twenty-something should have.

I certainly wouldn't mind spending more time with him, although what's the point for anything other than a fling if we're both leaving town? The smile playing at my lips suddenly turns down at the corners when I remember that Rachel and I made plans to leave tomorrow after graduation.

"When you're done thinking, say yes," he tells me.

"I wish I could, but my best friend and I are leaving to go home to Chicago tomorrow."

"So? Push your departure back. I'm not leaving until Sunday night." The hopefulness in his stare is irresistibly endearing.

He makes it seem so easy. And maybe it is? Seeing as how we're both only in town through the weekend, making myself available is the least I could do. Still, it feels a bit silly to rearrange schedules and commit myself to a date when we're never going to see each other again.

"Don't you have bachelor party things to be doing?"

"Meh." He shrugs nonchalantly. "I'll catch up with the guys after we eat."

I catch my bottom lip in my teeth, thinking of what Rachel's reaction will be if I ask her to stick around longer just so I can meet up with this guy. Surely she won't mind. I've moved mountains for her over far more petty things.

"Okay."

"Okay?"

I nod my head, fighting a cheesy grin.

"It's a date!" he exclaims, clapping his hands together once. Phoenix seems like the traditional type, so I don't have the heart to tell him I don't date. *At least not anymore.*

"No, it's not a date. It's *just* dinner." I give him my best teasing smile. I'm certain Rachel won't care if we extend our stay. She technically can't even get into her new apartment in Chicago until the middle of the week.

He pulls a bulky black chunk of metal from his back pocket and flips it open. "What's your number?"

"What is that thing?" I ask, stifling a laugh.

"Uh, it's a cell phone?" His response comes out as more of a question and less of a statement.

"Um, no. That's an artifact. That relic belongs in a museum," I proclaim in disbelief. I haven't seen a phone like this in well over a decade. It's a miracle he doesn't have it firmly attached to his hip on a belt clip. "What is this? 2001? You don't have a smartphone?"

"Nope, I don't need one of those fancy things," he says, looking at me with a ferocious intensity. "I think people spend too much time staring at meaningless screens, updating statuses, and fooling themselves into thinking they're being social when in reality they need to spend more time actually talking to the person directly in front of them. How can you really connect if you're too focused on one-way communication?"

Seriously, who is this guy? Is he for real? Everything about him surprises me. Simply being in his presence improves my whole mood, in spite of this wicked hangover from hell.

I take the fossil of a phone from his hands and dial my number, feeling it vibrate from my back pocket. I allow it to ring twice before ending the call.

"There. Now I have your number too." As I pass his phone back to him, our hands touch, and in that sober brush, electricity passes between us. His eyes widen in surprise and I can tell that he feels it too.

I sit back on my side of the couch and take a large sip of my coffee, looking at him over the rim of my mug and trying to figure him out. His beautiful maple eyes meet mine and pierce right through me, incinerating me to my core.

Suddenly, my phone vibrates from my backside, startling me and breaking me from his gaze. I quickly pull it out to find a text message.

Rachel: *Outside!*

"That's my cue." I quickly finish my coffee and make

my way to meet Rachel in the driveway. Phoenix stands up and walks me to the door.

I'm a little eager to get out of this confined space we've been sharing the past few minutes. Not because I'm uncomfortable, but rather because the way he makes me feel is unfamiliar and a little unnerving.

"See you tomorrow night." He looks at me with longing in his eyes.

I unsuccessfully try to hide my smile and give him a tight nod. "Tomorrow night. I'll text you the address."

I'm halfway out the door when I feel him pull on my hand, tugging me back inside. His eyes burn through to my soul and my knees weaken. Ever so slowly, he lifts my hand to his lips and places a delicate kiss on my palm before curling my fingers in a fist.

"Hold onto this until tomorrow," he whispers.

Warmth radiates from my palm to my arm and throughout my chest. I can't help but smile.

Promise lingers in the air between us as I float down the driveway.

"Shit, girl. You look like you had a great time last night." Rachel gapes as I slide into the front seat next to her.

"That's a thoughtful way of telling me I look like hell." The world is so bright it's screaming at me, so I reach between the seats and put on her spare pair of sunglasses. "But yes, I had a great time."

"So what happened?"

I wince as Rachel drives away from the curb with such force that I slam my head against the back of the seat. "No idea. I can't remember half the party," I confide, bringing my hands to my forehead and slowly massaging my temples.

"So you blacked out again?"

I knew Rachel would call me out on that. Before I left for Italy, I had a habit of drinking myself into oblivion. Within our circle of friends, I was the one who always had the crazy stories of waking up in bizarre locations … the stacks of Memorial Library on campus, in the Chancellor's garden, and then there was the epic moment when I woke up on the fifty-yard line on the "W" signifying Wisconsin in the middle of Camp Randall Stadium. It's not something I'm particularly proud of, but it always made for a great story. But last night … last night something was different.

"I guess. After you left to go hook up with that frat guy, I kind of went overboard."

"Ivy!" she scolds. I can't help but blanch at her volume. My insides curdle and I'm torn between needing to vomit and wanting to cry.

"I know. I was just pissed at Matt. Who the hell does he think he is showing up unannounced and expecting me to fall back into his arms? I am so over his shit."

"Yeah, well some guys will never change. Hopefully, he took the hint. So how'd it go with blondie?"

"It didn't."

"But you never just crash at someone's house," she says in disbelief.

"I know," I admonish myself. "Sully, the blond, only started talking to me to introduce me to his friend Phoenix."

Rachel throws her head back against the headrest and releases a deep belly laugh. "Guys are such idiots. Grow some balls and drop the wingman act already. Sorry it didn't work out."

"I don't know if I'd say that..." I linger, deep in thought and suppressing a smile. "Phoenix was ... he was different."

"Different?"

I nod in response. Unlike most guys, he seemed genuinely interested in what I had to say, unafraid to tease me, and didn't have a main objective to get me into bed. Ironic since that's usually *my* M.O.

"He was just an all-around good guy. Apparently, after I passed out, he tucked me in one of the spare bedrooms and slept on the couch."

Rachel gives me a cautious, side-eye glance. "Really? And you actually believe that he tucked you in and slept on the couch?" she parrots in distrust.

"Yeah. I do, actually." If he tried something I'd know, right? And if he had done something, he certainly wouldn't have asked to see me again. I look down at the palm of my hand, feeling the heat from the touch of his lips.

We ride in silence, turning onto State Street in the direction of the capital. State Street is the quintessential downtown stretch found in every college town—local retailers, affordable restaurants, used record shops, all with a kitschy vibe. But there's something extra special about the strip here in Madison.

"Hey, can we stop somewhere and get some grease with a side of breakfast?" With coffee and aspirin already in my system, grease is the last key ingredient to ridding myself of this hangover.

Rachel smiles at my request. "I thought you'd never ask."

We find our way to our favorite greasy spoon. It's just a few blocks off of State Street and usually frequented by locals instead of the standard college crowd. We discovered this dive our freshman year and would grab breakfast here at least once every weekend as it was our surefire hangover cure. Although, the last time I was here I was surrounded by friends right before I went abroad. It was also the morning that I dumped Matt.

When we arrive, Jody squeals from behind the counter and comes around to meet me. She still has the same beautiful round face with friendly wrinkles highlighting her smile. Over the past four years, nothing about this place has changed, not even the wait staff.

"Oh, Ivy. It has been far too long, honey! Welcome home."

In this moment I realize that Madison really is my home. I would give anything to stay here after graduation, but Wisconsin isn't exactly the art capital of the northern hemisphere.

"Hi Jody. I've missed you!"

"Oh, honey. You haven't missed me. You've just missed Bert's famous pancakes. I, on the other hand, have missed your tips." She teases with a wink. "Can I get you your usual?" After all this time, Jody still remembers my favorite.

"Of course."

Rachel and I are both halfway through a pile of blueberry buttermilk pancakes with sausage links when my headache finally subsides. Grease really does work wonders. Now is as good a time as any, so I decide to ask the question, hesitant to let her know the motives behind the request. She would certainly never let me hear the end of it.

"How would you feel about sticking around for one more night before heading back to Chicago?"

Rachel's fork hangs in the air as syrup drips down off of her pancake. She eyes me curiously, processing the request.

"Why?" she asks slowly.

I shrug. I should just tell her I'm not ready to see my family again just yet, but I've never lied to Rachel before and I'm not about to start lying to her now.

"This wouldn't have anything to do with that guy Phoenix, would it?"

I feel my face blush scarlet as I think of *that guy* and mindlessly twist a piece of my hair between my fingers. "Phoenix is only in town for a few more days. He wants to go grab dinner tomorrow night," I say casually.

The clanking of Rachel's fork dropping against her plate startles me. "You want to see him again?" I realize how uncharacteristic this request must be to her. I could never stay faithful to Matt, and even then I never saw the same guy more than once.

"Yeah, I do. I feel kind of bad for passing out on him like that."

Rachel mulls over my request for a moment and shrugs her shoulders.

"That's fine. Plus it'll give me one more night with Eric before he moves back home to Seattle next week."

Ah, the mystery man has a name.

Rachel springs into a long-winded story about how she met Eric at a Halloween party when they both showed up as Princess Leia in the iconic gold bikini. Eric was drawn to her body and bold costume choice for a chilly

Madison night, and Rachel was drawn to Eric's ridiculous sense of humor. Apparently he even shaved his chest and legs for the part. They have been hooking up nearly every weekend since. It's obvious to me that she likes him way more than she wants to let on, but I understand her reservation for commitment with him moving halfway across the country.

As I lay down my debit card to pay for our meal, I notice the time and realize I have a little over an hour to get myself together and meet up with Professor Whitman before he closes his office door for the summer.

Within the past twenty-four hours, my future has gone from uncertainty and some dread to a future full of promise and exciting unknowns.

GRADUATION COMES AND GOES WITH the usual
pomp and circumstance. Donning our caps and gowns,
Rachel and I take photos throughout campus together,
committing the best years of our lives to memory.

Walking down Linden and knowing I am leaving this
weekend for good inevitably makes me sad. Madison has
become my home, the place where I really established who
I am and who I want to become completely untainted by
my family.

I was okay not having my parents in town to witness
the momentous occasion. I thought for sure I'd be upset at
some point, but a long time ago I realized that just because
someone is of the same blood, it doesn't make them family; and really, Rachel and her parents and stepdad are more
like my family than anyone else in my life.

Packing the apartment was bittersweet. Rachel re-
called, in grotesque detail, the various encounters she'd
had while I was away. She had a penchant for stealing
something small from each of her hookups—a shot glass
from a guy with jet black hair whose name she couldn't
remember, a hockey jersey from Roen, an avid San Jose

Sharks fan, and an entire drawer of T-shirts she nabbed from Eric. I thought she'd eventually outgrow it, but as the adage says, old habits die hard.

I will miss her ridiculous stories and klepto tendencies when we leave this place, but it's not like I'll never see her again. At least we'll be in the same city, if only for a little while. *Unlike Phoenix.* He seems really sweet, which makes me feel like I'm not good enough for him, and with us both going our separate ways tomorrow, I can't help but wonder if it's even worth it. I'm only setting myself up for inevitable disappointment.

I swallow that feeling down, and try to convince myself that I'm a brand new person and worthy of good things.

I am.

Really.

My mind drifts off to thoughts of him and suddenly I can't help but wonder what he's doing this very moment. If he's thinking of me like I'm thinking of him. If I make him nervous like he makes me.

Rachel snaps me from my drifting thoughts. "Stop looking at me like that."

"Like what?"

"You're all doe-eyed and just … not here."

I roll my eyes and shake her off as I finish packing the contents of a bookshelf into a box. If I give her any indication that I'm thinking about a guy, it is going to open up the dam and I will never be able to shut her up. So instead, I do what I do best with her. I divert.

"So … this job in New York City sounds promising."

Rachel stops packing up the dishes and looks at me from across the room. The emotion on her face is a cross between pride and heartache. Me officially leaving will inevitably be hard for her to swallow. We've been friends since elementary school and never lived more than ten minutes apart except for this past year.

The light in her eyes and her slow, timid smile tells me pride is winning over heartache.

"Tell me what happened."

Catching up with Professor Whitman went as expected. I made it to his office hours about thirty minutes before he closed up for the summer, and we talked for close to three hours. He even missed his afternoon doctor appointment to catch up with me.

"Well, by the end of our conversation he'd called this James guy who owns the gallery to introduce me personally over the phone. And you know how Whitman gets. I barely did any talking, and he made me sound like I was God's gift to the industry."

"So you got it?" Rachel asks, bubbling over with excitement.

"Well, no. I still have to meet him in New York in a few weeks. Assuming he likes me and finds me competent, it sounds like it's a done deal."

I try to play it off casually but I know securing a job of this caliber right out of college is a huge deal. Actually, securing any job in this field without having to use my parent's contacts is a huge deal. Surely my parents will see it that way, right? Regardless, I need this job to prove them wrong. Show them that Art History is a worthwhile path that can help me make a living and a name for myself professionally.

"Do you know what the best part of all this is?" Rachel asks. I arch my eyebrow, curious to see where she's going with this one. "*When* you get the job," she emphasizes, "I will never have to pay for another overpriced hotel in New York City ever again!" And with that she quickly changes the subject.

I'm really going to miss her mindless chatter. After all of our years of friendship, I've learned that Rachel doesn't do farewells. She's more of a "see you later" kind of gal. And as the closest thing she has ever had to a real sister, I know me leaving is going to take its toll on her.

No matter how much she masks it.

I'M LOOKING IN THE MIRROR trying to decide if I'm overdressed when I hear a knock on our door. Rachel runs to answer and I give myself a final once over.

Since most of my clothes are still packed up from Italy, Rachel dressed me in one of her jean skirts and a cabernet-colored eyelet blouse. Admittedly, I look cute, even if it makes me come across a little more innocent than I'd like. She forced me into a pair of her wedge heels, but I'm feeling a bit more down to earth tonight, so I kick those off and slip into my favorite pair of black Chuck Taylors.

The light that hits Phoenix's eyes when I walk into our living room instantly brings butterflies to my insides. The nerves take over again and I feel the heat in my palm from when he kissed it yesterday morning. But that look … I would be content spending our entire date here in this living room staring at each other if he wanted to keep looking at me like *that,* like I'm the only female in existence.

It makes me feel like … well, no. It just makes me *feel.*

"Hey," he says softly with a smile.

"Hi," I respond in a shy whisper.

I run my fingers nervously through my hair, tucking a piece behind my ear, but the strand falls loose. Magnetized, he quickly closes the gap between us and takes the strand of hair within his fingers. He smiles and tucks it behind my ear again.

I inhale slowly, willing my heart to slow down. He still smells of musk and damp earth, that familiar scent after a spring rain shower, such a heady combination.

And for a beat, I am certain he is going to kiss me.

After saying only one word to me.

And in front of my best friend.

That's not awkward or anything.

From the corner of my eye, I see Rachel look from him to me, then back to him again. Then she clears her throat. I abruptly take a step back to put some space between us, feeling embarrassed.

"Before we go, there's just something I need to do," Phoenix says. He reaches for my purse, raising an eyebrow. "May I?" I give an approving, but curious nod, and watch him open it up, and fish around for something. Grabbing my iPhone, he holds it up triumphantly. "Found it!"

I watch him place it on the coffee table and give him a questioning stare. Just what are his motives?

"You won't be needing this tonight." He smiles smugly. I open my mouth to protest, but he beats me to the punch. "I know what you're thinking. What if I need an exit strategy?" He grins boldly. "I can promise you Ivy whose last name I don't know, you won't need an escape. And if you're having a truly horrible time with me, you can borrow my phone to call your roommate to come and save you."

It's impossible to not smile ... and not be slightly annoyed. I'm an independent gal and having something like this out of my control makes me a little uneasy. Plus, this bolder side of Phoenix is a little surprising.

"Phillips. My last name is Phillips," I say, slowly forcing the words from my mind to my tongue to my lips.

"Well, Ivy Phillips, like I said before, I hate it when people spend more time on their phone than with the person they're with. It's my biggest pet peeve."

Phoenix walks to the center of the room, tears off a piece of packing paper and writes something down. As he leans over the table, I can't help but admire how striking he looks in his loose fitted jeans and well loved, faded cranberry T-shirt. When I notice he's wearing black Chucks, I suppress a laugh. We match.

"There," he says, handing the slip of paper to Rachel. "In case of an emergency, you've got my number. But unless someone's dead, please don't call."

Well, then!

He turns back toward me and winks. He actually winks! Where did the shy guy who couldn't approach me without the help of his friend go? That guy had my insides tied up and twisted. This Phoenix has me hot and bothered. Not that I'm complaining because I certainly like his more confident side.

He extends his elbow and I slip my arm through it. As we walk out the door, I look over my shoulder and see Rachel standing there bug-eyed. She mouths, "Oh...My... God..." and I blow her a kiss, trying to contain my excitement.

I'm guided out of the apartment and he opens the car door for me. Charming. That's the word that comes to mind. He's charming and so old school. But I keep my guard up ever so slightly. I learned long ago that the charming guys are usually the most dangerous.

Besides, we're just out for one night of fun, nothing more. Tomorrow we will both go to our respective corners of the country and carry on with our lives. So really, what's the point of letting my guard down and allowing myself to enjoy this evening for more than it's worth? Or better yet, why shouldn't I let my guard down for one night knowing this isn't going to go anywhere after this date?

"So where are we eating?" I ask once we're both settled into the car.

Phoenix smiles as he reaches over to turn down the stereo. The Airborne Toxic Event softly serenades us with an acoustic rendition of *Sometime Around Midnight*.

Focusing his eyes back on the road, my question goes unanswered.

"You told me we were having dinner."

He nods. "Just dinner."

"Just dinner." I affirm.

"And maybe more," he throws in casually, "but that'll depend on you."

If this is this his way of coming onto me, he seriously needs some new material.

Phoenix looks across the front seat and smiles at me again. He is very tight lipped about this evening's plans, and the anticipation he's building has a strange effect on me. I feel like I'm thirteen years old again and crushing on the popular boy who is a few grades ahead of me.

I can handle a little mystery, can't I?

The drive doesn't take us long as he pulls onto campus and parks in a staff parking lot behind one of the science buildings. He holds up a single finger, indicating he wants me to stay put. I'm confused as to why we're on campus, but I decide to go with it rather than say something and ruin whatever plan he's concocted.

Phoenix runs around to the back of the car and pulls something out of the trunk before coming to the passenger side and opening the door for me, his boyish grin melting my heart. As he pulls me to my feet, I notice a picnic basket.

"I thought you might like to do something different for dinner."

He reaches out and grabs my hand like it's the most natural thing in the world. I can't help but believe that it belongs there, my hand molds perfectly inside of his, and I suddenly find myself self-conscious of sweaty palms.

It becomes obvious that Phoenix isn't sure exactly where he is going when we walk by the same building a third time.

"There's a grassy area on the other side of Agricultural Hall where we could eat," I suggest, trying not to make him feel bad. I really have no idea what he's looking for and he is tight-lipped on our destination.

"Which one is Agricultural Hall? We're going somewhere close to there."

I point to prominent building down the way and lead him to the lawn on the backside. Phoenix pauses for a moment and evaluates the domed building in the distance. Tugging on my hand, he pulls me toward Washburn Observatory, one of the oldest buildings on campus.

"Have you been here before?" he asks as we approach.

I shake my head. I passed by this building nearly every day my freshman year but never stepped foot inside. Rachel and I learned about this place on our campus tour during orientation. It's one hundred plus years old and, at the time, housed one of the largest telescopes in the world.

It's a Saturday night and I know for a fact that the building is closed. Only on an occasional Wednesday is it open to the public. Otherwise, it's restricted access—astronomy students and staff only.

We approach the main entrance and Phoenix smiles at me knowingly, before knocking on the entrance. A short guy with dirty blond hair and thick-rimmed glasses opens the door and lets us inside.

The ground level is dimly lit and it takes my eyes a moment to adjust. A century of must fills the air even after multiple renovations. The scent reminds me of old books and mildew.

"How...?" I eye him cautiously as the door pulls shut behind me.

Spending the night in a holding cell for breaking and entering, no matter how innocent it may be is not how I want to spend my first night as a college graduate.

"I know someone," he says proudly. "Okay, that's a lie. I actually know someone who knows someone."

My feet are firmly planted and I can't seem to make myself walk further. He senses my hesitation.

"Seriously, Ivy, it's okay. One of the guys I'm with this weekend is an astronomy grad student. He helped coordinate everything for us. Just don't break anything."

He doesn't have to worry about that. I won't touch, or

even breathe near anything inside this place for fear of destroying it. What have I done to be worthy of orchestrating such a huge favor? And what are his expectations after this little adventure? But one word gets caught in my chest. *Us.*

Instantly I feel guilty for these thoughts.

Phoenix reaches for my hand again and I follow him toward a narrow stairwell in the corner. He gestures for me to walk up first.

As we climb to the second floor, a wave of fresh air hits me. The dome is pulled back, revealing an exquisite technicolor sky over Lake Mendota. I have never seen anything like this before and it is absolutely breathtaking. From our vantage point, you can't see the sun, but it's evident that it's on the cusp of disappearing for the evening.

"Have a seat," he tells me as gestures to a blanket that's laid on the ground.

This really is over the top. And thoughtful. And something that only happens in the movies or romance novels—never to me.

We are only thirty minutes into our evening and already I'm certain that any date I go on for the rest of my life will have a hard time outdoing this one. Seriously, what twenty-something does this kind of romantic gesture? What's his game?

As I settle onto the ground, he sits down next to me and opens the picnic basket.

"I hope you don't mind, but I was working with limited resources," he says as he hands me a peanut butter and marshmallow fluff sandwich with the crust cut off. "If it's not up to your caliber, we can blow this place off and find a restaurant. But I'll warn you, reservations are tough to come by since it's graduation weekend."

I look at the sandwich in my hands and can't believe how absolutely perfect this moment is. I haven't tasted a fluffanutter sandwich since I was a little girl. The sentiment he evokes from me is indescribable.

"Don't be ridiculous. You can't get a dinner like this anywhere downtown," I reply with a coquettish grin.

He pops open two sodas and pulls out a bag of pretzels, some cheese, and a pair of gourmet cupcakes from my favorite local bakery. My stomach relaxes at the realization that he left the alcohol at home.

We eat our sandwiches in comfortable silence. I find myself subconsciously mirroring his movements. Taking a bite when he does. Following his lead as he drinks his soda. It's hard to believe that I just met him the other night. Having him here next to me feels as natural as breathing. The way my body is in sync with his makes me feel like I've known him for years, as if our souls are connected.

As I savor the last of the sandwich he made, my mind drifts off to thoughts of Thursday night. What if we didn't go to that house party? What if I had blown him off, or worse, thrown myself at Sully?

Sitting here in his presence makes me want to be a better person. It's easy to let the past be done and focus on what is right in front of me this very moment.

Twilight is upon us and the air is starting to chill as the sky fades from blue to purple to pink and red then orange before settling on black spotted with flecks of glitter. The stars twinkle, making their presence known on this cloudless night.

We make small talk as we finish our food and a slight shiver runs down my spine. I realize that there is nothing sexier than a good conversation. His words alone are enough to disarm me. After putting the remainder of the cheese back in the picnic basket, Phoenix takes the blanket and wraps it around me, letting his hand linger around my back.

I pick at my cupcake, amazed that of the dozens of flavors he managed to buy my favorite one—chocolate sea-salted caramel. Our eyes meet and he reaches over, picking a small piece off the side of my lips.

"Lucky crumb," Phoenix says, putting it in his mouth. He looks up into the sky, his eyes full of wonder. "That's some serious moonlight."

I smile and turn my gaze toward the sky. His David Bowie reference is not lost on me.

"If you could go back to any age, how old would you want to be?"

What a peculiar question to be asked. Most of the time my parents treat me as if I'm a ten year old in a twenty-something's wardrobe. Not because I'm immature, but I think because I was far more impressionable and easily put into line.

"I think I'd want to be fourteen again. Fourteen was a very good year. Things were much simpler and the toughest choices I had to make were what to wear to school any given day. My folks weren't such assholes back then, and there were no exes or complicated adult relationships to navigate. No games, either. If you had a crush on someone, it was easy. You'd just pass a note in math class asking 'Do you like me? Check yes, no, or maybe'. If they checked yes, or even maybe, then you were automatically a couple."

He chuckles, presumably recalling his own prepubescent memory.

"What about you?"

"I think I'd be eight. I wanted to be a superhero when I grew up. Fly in and save the damsel in distress. Be someone's knight in shining armor. Life was a lot less …dramatic back then. Sometimes being naïve is a blessing."

The way he says it is almost heartbreaking, and I want to ask him what happened, but he stands and walks toward the telescope on the other end of the dome, effectively ending this portion of our conversation. When he looks back, he catches me checking out his ass, and I flush crimson, feeling the urge to quickly change the subject.

"So you're missing the last night of your bachelor weekend extravaganza?" I ask, pushing myself up to my feet to stand next to him.

"Nah, I'll catch up with the guys later. They're probably so drunk they don't even realize I'm gone." He runs his hand down the length of the telescope with an intense look in his eye. "I'll let you in on a little secret," he says, lifting his eyebrows. "I'm totally using you right now."

"Is that so?" He nods once, not breaking my gaze. "You're not a very good user apparently. I still have my clothes on and you've tipped me off on your plans. Rookie mistake," I tease.

Casually, he runs his hand through his hair and confesses, "Actually, I'm using you as an excuse. The whole bachelor party thing? Not my scene at all. I'm not big on drinking until I puke. And if you've seen one stripper, you've seen them all."

I'm not sure if I should be charmed by his honesty or offended that he claimed me as his excuse to ditch the guys.

"Besides, not to be all negative, but I don't think it'll last. Sully has never been a one gal kind of guy. Don't get me wrong, he's a good kid and has always been a loyal friend when I needed him the most, he's just not what I'd call monogamous material."

I snort involuntarily. What he said isn't funny in the slightest, but I can't say it surprises me. Men, as a collective whole, tend to have a problem keeping their dicks to themselves. With my previous affinity for whoring myself out, sometimes I wonder if I should have been born a guy.

"Apparently he got lucky at the party on Thursday night. We had to listen to him boast about it all day yesterday," he says in disbelief before giving me a curious glance. "You wouldn't know anything about that, would you?" he questions me, wiggling his eyebrows in jest.

"Oh God! No!" I say, trying not to sound defensive. "I most definitely did not hook up with him." My cheeks flush scarlet at the thought of initially wanting to take Sully ten ways to Sunday, and my mind wanders back to the black-haired girl with tanned skin. I wonder if she had any clue that he was engaged. If she did, would that have changed the fate of her night?

I nudge Phoenix over a little and bring my face to the eyepiece on the telescope. Turning a knob on the side, I watch the blurriness subside and focus on the brilliant stars light years away. It's truly breathtaking. When I feel his hand on the small of my back, my heart skips a beat, and I step back from the lens and nod for him to take a peek with a small smile on my lips.

As he looks through the telescope, Phoenix goes on to tell me all about how Sully never had a girlfriend he was completely faithful to, but in spite of his tendency to sleep around he is a fiercely loyal friend and has been there for him his whole life. Sully actually starts to sound like a decent guy, if it weren't for cheating on his fiancée time and time again. I chew on that thought for a few moments, feeling bad for his unassuming blushing bride.

In turn, I tell Phoenix more about my adventures in Italy. How I took the time away from home to really focus on myself and making me a better person. Phoenix senses my hesitation that comes with talking about my past, but is genuinely interested in listening to me talk about learning Greek and Roman architecture firsthand.

We're standing fairly close together, taking turns getting lost in the stars and telling each other stories. If ever there were a moment to kiss me, this would be it. I know Phoenix can sense it too. He becomes increasingly more nervous and is the first to look away.

We linger in this moment a touch too long, evident that neither of us is bold enough to make a move. It takes all of my energy to suppress the urge to plaster my lips on his, wrap my legs around his waist and take him right here and now.

But I am *not* that girl anymore. I will not shamelessly take what I want whenever I want it. I force myself to step back and allow him to make the first move, relinquishing control and allowing him to take the lead.

"Come on," I say, tugging on his hand. "Let's go for a walk."

We make our way down through the observatory. Phoenix gives a nod to the young man who let us in. I didn't realize he was still on site waiting for us.

I lead him down Observatory Drive, cutting down a side path taking us to Lake Mendota's waterfront walkway. This place is the epitome of peace in a vibrant college town. Darkness consumes the world in front of us and city lights strike the sky off in the distance.

We cross a wrought iron bench with a small memorial plaque affixed to the back of the seat and pause together to read the words etched for eternity.

For my dearest Delilah who loved this bench
nearly as much as she loved her family.
One day, we'll enjoy this perfect view together again.

"Fancy a seat? See what Delilah thought the fuss was all about?" Phoenix gestures to the bench, then sits down beside me.

I lean over and rest my elbows on my knees, gazing upon the lake. I can't help the wistful feeling taking over, knowing just how much I'm going to miss this place when I return home to Chicago.

What a perfect way to spend my last night in Madison. We haven't spent a dime and yet we've managed to experience the beauty of this city. Phoenix has opened my eyes to a side of this place I've never even appreciated.

He mirrors my position, leaning over his knees. I can't read him as well as I can read other people, but I *think* he's into me. I get the feeling that he is just as cautious and weary of starting anything because we both go our separate ways tomorrow and it seems silly to explore this connection we share. From what I can tell, Phoenix could take me right here on this bench just as easily as he could give me a hearty handshake with a "thanks for the company" before turning and walking away.

"What are you thinking about?" he questions.

"You."

"What about me?"

I take a deep breath and allow myself a collective moment to summon my bravery, thinking back to our earlier conversation about Sully. "Are you monogamous material?" I blurt out without considering that I might not want to know the answer to the question. My attempts at being coy are pathetic at best, but I'm feeling bold and discretion was never my best quality.

"Well, I have certainly never cheated on anyone like Sully has, if that's what you mean. But I've never met anyone who struck me to the point of wanting to be in a serious, long-term relationship. I dated this one girl for a year or so, but she wasn't the right one for me. I honestly don't buy into the whole notion of marriage."

His proclamation does not surprise me at all. I'm not sure I've ever known any guy to be into marriage without external pressures from their significant other, family, or society.

He takes a deep breath before continuing the thought. "When I was little, I walked in on my dad and another woman. It was devastating and practically tore my family apart. I was only nine years old at the time, but it completely wrecked my sense of security." I suddenly understand his earlier comment about wanting to go back to being eight years old. It was a time where his family was still whole and his father was undoubtedly his hero.

"After Mom and I left him, I had to step up. Work granted her unpaid temporary leave, but most days she could barely function and I'd have to remind her to eat. She loved my dad so ferociously, but it was obvious her love was unmatched. I think the intensity and depth in which you love someone is directly proportional to the amount of hurt they are capable of bringing. It's why I don't judge Sully for sleeping around. It's why I don't buy into the theory of marriage, though I'm not opposed to it entirely for other people. It's why I'm not sure one guy can just stay happy with one woman for all of eternity. How can something so sacred be fragile enough to shatter with one weak moment of stupidity?"

Phoenix bites his thumbnail and looks down at the ground, and I give him the silence he seems to need. My heart aches for nine-year-old Phoenix. But his last comment is what burns me. It's *exactly* the reason why I've avoided truly opening myself up to anyone. Even with Matt there were always walls built, never letting him in entirely because I'm absolutely petrified of love and the pain it can bring. I gathered from my mom a long time ago that the person who loves the least is in control of the relationship. They are also the least likely to get hurt. And I hurt enough without love complicating things further, thank you very much.

"My dad spent the next thirteen years trying to prove his worth to her," Phoenix continues. "He forced his way back into our lives. I'm not sure how much of that was because of me, because of guilt, or because of genuine love for my mom. God only knows how much therapy he went through, both by himself and with my mom. I don't know how, but eventually she trusted him enough to let him in once more. I mean *really* let him in. Over time, they fell in love all over again and he re-proposed to her on the anniversary of the day they first met back in college. In spite of it all, all of his mistakes, I'm not sure they ever really stopped loving each other."

I try to hide a smile and raise my eyebrows in delight. For some reason, his parents' sweet story tugs on my heartstrings.

"I know, right? I've had a lot of friends whose parents divorced and remarried someone else, or filled the void with drinking, but I've never heard of anyone remarrying the same person they split from. My mom wanted something simple, just the three of us at the Justice of Peace. My dad insisted that he give her the wedding they never had twenty years earlier—the friends, the dress, the huge party. None of that mattered to my mom, but she wanted him to be happy, and allowing him to make her happy was part of their healing process."

Phoenix takes a thoughtful pause as if he's making a decision and cracks his knuckles.

"The week before their wedding date, my mom was on her way home from her shift at the hospital," he looks from me to the ground and then back to my eyes again, like he's willing me to fill in the blanks so he doesn't have to say what happened next.

He swallows hard. "She was hit head on by drunk driver. First responders pronounced her dead at the scene," he says, voice cracking.

I exhale a breath I didn't realize I was holding. There are no words that I can offer up to ease the pain that he is still obviously feeling. Instead, I trail my fingertips along the back of his hand, a comforting, silent touch.

I watch Phoenix bite his lower lip as he collects his thoughts, and his face turns from hurt to seemingly angry in one quick moment. "Do you want to know the worst part about it all? The worst was everyone, even my dad, telling me that she was in a better place." He laughs inwardly. "She's dead, Ivy. My mom is in the dark, cold ground, not on a fucking beach in Tahiti. She's not in a better place. There isn't anywhere else she would have rather been than with her son and best friend."

We're both swallowing back the tears. I want to tell him that it's okay for him to break down, but I know firsthand how awful it is for other people to tell you how you should feel.

"I ... I'm so sorry, Phoenix."

I know he doesn't want my apology, but it's all I can offer. His pain is still raw. Why does horrible shit happen to good people? Why doesn't it happen to someone who deserves it?

Phoenix shrugs his shoulders. "I've come to terms with it, or at least I convinced myself I have. And while it's clear mom forgave my dad, I'm not there just yet. I'm not sure I'll ever be." He gives me a quick sideways glance. "I haven't seen or spoken to him since her funeral."

Holy shit. I suddenly find myself heartbroken, not just for Phoenix, but for his father too. Not only did he lose the love of his life that day, but he also lost his only child.

I tuck a loose strand of hair behind my ear and look out over Lake Mendota. It's not awkward. It's not uncomfortable. It just is.

"So to answer your original question, monogamous material? Probably. Marriage material? The jury is still out. I don't want to end up like him. I don't have it in me to cheat, but I'm not confident in the institution of marriage."

I understand him on levels he doesn't even realize. Honestly, I'm not sure I buy into the idea of marriage either. Or perhaps I'm not sure I buy into my own personal ability to stay faithful to one person for the rest of my life. Then again, maybe I haven't met a person worth staying faithful for?

"What about you? What's your story?" he asks softly.

"Well, as you know I'm Chicago born and bred. Up until last year I—"

"No. I know all that already," he cuts me off. "I want to know *you*. Not the you that everyone else sees." His eyes pierce right through me, daring me to tell him a secret. Something I would never willingly offer up.

I exhale slowly and ponder his request. At this moment, after Phoenix's admittance, I'm feeling especially vulnerable and honest.

When you first meet a stranger, you have a choice. You can redefine yourself to be anyone you want to be, or you can be completely and totally honest. Radical honesty, to me, always felt perfect in the presence of complete strangers. And for some reason, I feel compelled to be radically honest with Phoenix, just as he has with me.

And technically, we all start as strangers. And aren't strangers simply friends we haven't made yet? All strangers have the capacity to become best friends, enemies, the other woman, husbands and wives.

"My family hates me." The words spill from my mouth in an abrupt exhale. "I slept with my sister's boyfriend after graduation my senior year of high school and I never lived it down. Well, more like *they've* never let me live it down. Glen — that was his name — was visiting over the summer break from Cape Cod. I was drunk. He was hot. And everyone and everything in my world was really pissing me off. I made a pass at him, not thinking he'd bite. In the end, he bit off more than he could chew."

I glance sideways at him and he's studying me intently. This is the first time I've ever even mentioned Glen to someone other than Rachel. I want to come clean and tell him that Glen wasn't the only one. That I also slept with two other boyfriends of Genevieve's that she never found out about. And then there is Matt and the laundry list of trysts that transpired over the past three years.

Damn, when I put it all together like that, I really do sound like the village tricycle where everyone gets a ride.

Silence fills the void between us and I can tell he's judging me by the way he clenches his jaw. God, I hate being judged. I want to tell him how I've changed, but really if he's not willing to find out for himself, he isn't worth my time. I'm not normally in the business of defending my past indiscretions to anyone.

I refrain from telling him about all my promiscuity over the years. At an age I'm embarrassed to admit, curiosity killed my virginity. It wasn't amazing or anything. It was just fine, I suppose. It was awkward and messy, nothing like the movies. So much for life imitating art.

But I wouldn't say that sleeping around makes me a bad person. Just like going to church doesn't make you a good person. My parents go to church every Sunday and they most certainly are not good people.

It's obvious that he's reevaluating my "other woman" status. He seems really uneasy about it. I feel a sudden urge to try and explain myself. "I usually would blame being young and stupid, but—"

"Hey, don't waste your breath explaining yourself to me. Just allow yourself to let me in. I can decide for myself."

I like that my reputation doesn't precede me with this guy. "Thanks," I say genuinely and touch my hand to him arm. "When I look back, I think I wanted nothing more than to make a statement."

"A statement?" he asks with slight amusement in his eyes.

"I'm not exactly proud of it, but it was more of a 'fuck you' to my entire family. I needed to ruin their expectations of me. For years, they've tried to prime me to live up to their standards. To marry rich, join the country club, become successful ... a lawyer ... a doctor ... whatever would make the most money, whatever would help stamp continued success upon the family. When I told them I wanted to major in Art History and work in an art gallery or museum you would have thought I was confessing to murdering puppies in my free time."

I will never forget the arguments that ensued after telling them my plans. They threatened to stop paying for my education, and I received daily emails from my mom detailing how deeply I had shamed them and how following this minimalist dream of mine was a waste of such intelligence.

Frightening as it was, I never wavered. Even without their support and approval, I knew I would find a way to get through school and follow my passion, no matter how strongly they disapproved. I made a promise to myself a long time ago that I would not be made to feel guilty for being who I am, and that I would stop pretending to be their perfect little daughter.

"Sounds like you've got quite the family," Phoenix says as I try to gauge his reaction.

While no one was married, I certainly played the role

of home wrecker back in the day. And knowing what he went through with his dad's infidelities, I highly doubt he has any tolerance for anyone who openly admits they slept with someone who was spoken for.

"I've just made it clear from very early on that I could not be controlled. My sister lived to make them happy and everyone saw me as a thorn in their side. They never once cared about what made me happy, but rather that the Norman Rockwell illusion of family and perfection remained in place. But I am anything but Rockwell. I'm more of a Seurat."

Phoenix nods as if he understands what I'm saying. "From afar, it looks like you have it all together, but when you examine it up close … it's nothing but a blur of colorful dots and beautiful chaos."

He must read the surprise on my face. "What?" he asks, masking his smile. "I know what Pointillism is. Art History was a requirement for my degree."

He gets me.

He *actually* gets me.

He may be the only guy in existence who does.

Anxiously, I bite my lip. I desperately want to lean over and kiss him, but the moment isn't right. Since when do I care about waiting for the right moment?

I look out to some boat lights floating in the distance along the horizon.

"Just so you know, I'm not judging you for who you were or what you did."

I press my lips in a tight, appreciative smile. He may be one of the few people in this world who doesn't judge me for that. "So yeah, when I get home tomorrow I am re-entering my own personal hell. My sister is getting married, so naturally everyone is going to be keeping close tabs on me, making sure I don't sleep with the groom." I can't help but roll my eyes. "How taboo would that be? The maid of honor screwing the groom. My family would have a field day burning me at the stake."

Phoenix mouths the word "wow" and looks out to the water, shaking his head in disbelief. "Why do you even bother? You could have just said no to your sister."

Oh, if only it were that easy. Turning her down would only make things infinitely worse for me in the long haul. As much as I don't want to be tied to my family, I need to rely on them just until I can get up and running on my own two feet. If I don't comply, there are consequences, and those consequences could ruin everything I have going for me.

"I can't. The only reason I have any kind of relationship with my sister is because I'm guilted into it. It's why I'm her maid of honor. Not because we're close, or because we're friends, but because she's my sister. It's out of obligation."

He nods, seeming to understand my predicament.

"But from what I've gathered, this guy seems like an ass." And I kind of hope he is. Maybe then Genevieve will finally get what's coming to her for making my life hell the past few years.

"Seems? Wait a minute … you've never actually met him?"

"Nope," I say, popping the p for dramatic effect. I can only assume I was never introduced for fear of what I would do to ruin their relationship.

"That seems a bit judgmental, even for you, Little Miss I Don't Give A Fuck."

"Usually I don't judge, but from what I've pieced together he's a piece of work. He's been mercurial for years with this on again off again relationship. My sister has suspected him of cheating multiple times, but she doesn't have the balls to leave him. She fears having a failed relationship. Gen would rather be married and miserable than single and happy. Plus, I'm fairly certain he just wants to marry into my family for the money."

I divert my eyes and bite my tongue. I've said too much. I certainly don't want him to think I have money. My parents may be loaded, but I'd love for nothing more than to disassociate myself from their wealth. While I was in Italy, I came to the realization that you aren't rich until you have something that money can't buy.

"Well, that's a good thing I suppose."

"What? That he wants in on the inheritance?" I'm taken aback by his forthright comment.

"No." He cracks a grin. "That she doesn't have balls."

I laugh under my breath and try to shake the thoughts of my family. I don't want Genevieve to be a part of our evening any longer.

Silence passes between us and he nudges my elbow with his. Reaching out for my hand again, he delicately traces the inside of my palm where he kissed it yesterday with his fingertip. Goosebumps rise and my body hums with anticipation. I turn to look him in the eye again and he has a charming, yet shy, look on his face.

For the love of all that is holy...lean over and kiss me, already!

"You know … if you're wondering whether or not I want to," he pauses for a quick breath and stares at my lips before continuing. "I want to. Or rather, I want *you* to."

I can hardly control myself and double over in laughter.

"What?" Phoenix asks, his eyebrows knit together.

"I cannot believe you just said that! You just turned one of my most favorite songs into a cheesy pickup line!"

He chuckles softly and tries to pull me back toward him. "Yeah, you got me. At least now I have confirmation that you have good taste in music."

Pfft. As if there were ever any doubt. I'm becoming increasingly more aware of how he works. Clearly he has issues making the first move, but once the door is open, the shy guy dissolves.

We stare at each other in silence ... staring *through* each other ... his hazel eyes pleading for what we both want to say ... for what we both want to do.

For something that has been so easy to do so many times before, I'm surprised by my nervousness.

Then, as if on cue, the world starts moving in slow motion. I watch Phoenix close his eyes and lean toward me, and I swear ... I *swear* I see his lips quiver.

"Ivy..." he whispers. My name tastes of chocolate and caramel from the cupcakes we shared and my heart sighs at the sound of my name rolling off of his tongue.

I lean forward and close the gap between us, running my fingertips down his face and committing his stubble to memory as I slowly part his lips with mine.

I fall into this kiss...

Fall into him...

Fall for him.

This kiss. *God*, this kiss is deliciously slow like honey. Instantly I can feel it everywhere in my body, blazing in my palm ... my chest ... my toes. He takes his time, his hands outlining my neck to my shoulders and down to my arms.

I kiss him like I'm starving and I only now realize that I have been hungry for the past twenty-two years, savoring every last bite, committing it to memory for both the present and the afterlife. I take my time memorizing his mouth with my tongue.

The fresh taste of his lips …

The way his arms envelop me, delicate but firm …

The tender moan that rises from the back of his throat…

I've come undone.

Pulling back, I watch him bring his fingertips to his lips in wonder. When his lips struck mine, tiny sparks jumped. Heat flashed. Instant combustion.

With that one kiss, an ember hidden deep inside my soul awakened a sleeping shadow. A kindling in my hollows started a slow burn. The ember becomes light, a twin flame illuminating my heart.

It's strange to think that something as innocent as pressing one's lips to another's can so drastically alter the course of your entire life. But with that single kiss, I know that he is important.

That single kiss has changed everything.

Everything.

This single kiss has ruined all future kisses for me.

We look at each other deeply and a smile hints at my lips as he wraps his strong arms around me. "Delilah was right," he whispers.

I give him a knowing nod with a shy smile. This place is absolutely perfect.

He leans in and kisses me again for a few minutes,

maybe a few hours. Who knows, really? I am only aware of being completely lost in his lips and arms. It's a foreign feeling and it excites and scares the hell out of me.

I wish more than anything that we could stay here kissing all night long, but when I hear his cell phone ring, I'm abruptly reminded that he has places to be.

"Sorry," he mutters, taking his cellphone from his pocket and silencing it instantly. "I'll call them back in a bit."

"It's okay. I know we're on borrowed time right now." I stand and he follows suit, adjusting his pants before reaching for my hand. I stifle a giggle knowing the effect that I have on him.

I find myself thankful for the little time we have shared, though my head is telling me to guard my emotions. As we head back to his car, my head and my heart wage war against each other. I so badly want to wrap myself in this … whatever *this* is, but it's pointless. He's headed to St. Louis, I'm hopefully headed to New York City, and that's just too great a distance to overcome for having just met.

On the drive back to my apartment, I convince myself that it's a good thing we live hundreds of miles apart because he makes it exceptionally easy to see myself falling for him, and this would only end with one, or both, of us getting hurt.

When we pull up to my apartment, I want to beg him to blow the guys off the rest of the night. I want to invite him in and show him just where that amazing kiss can go. Perhaps one night is all I'd need to get him out of my system. And as difficult as it would be to say goodbye in the morning, I'm confident he'd oblige.

Phoenix reaches out and wraps his pinky around mine, walking me to the door. It's a gesture so sweet and so innocent, taking me back to the days of schoolgirl crushes and making my heart flutter at the speed of a million hummingbird wings.

When we reach the threshold, I bite back thoughts of inviting him inside. I know I need to cut him loose.

Right here.

Right now.

Before I'm in too deep.

He turns to face me and takes both of my hands in his, running circles in my palms with his thumbs. Silence wraps its warm embrace around the pair of us and he looks intently in my eyes as if he's reading a novel.

And in a way, he is.

"I'm not going to say goodbye to you," he whispers.

My heart clenches. I don't want to say good-bye to him either, but I don't know if I can turn around and watch him walk down the hallway and out of my life because when he does, I know he's taking a piece of my heart with him.

Instead, he leans in and feathers a tender kiss upon my lips, the kind so impossibly delicate it wouldn't stir a sleeping baby. It's passionate, but not feverish. Controlled, but feral. I reel in my hormones or else this evening could have an entirely different outcome. Pulling back, his eyes burn to my core. He feels it too.

"I'll see you soon, Cubby Bear." He gives my hands a tight squeeze.

This is not good. There is no way in hell I'm going to be capable of cutting him loose. This man is going to wreck me.

Turning on his heel, he walks down the hall leaving me speechless, breathless. Before making the final turn to walk out of my life, he looks over his shoulder and winks, lifting his hand in a faint wave.

I let myself into the apartment and press my back against the inside of the door, eyes shut tight.

Shit.

THE MOVE BACK TO CHICAGO was uneventful. Rachel and I drove mostly in silence, save for the top forty radio station blasting between us. I wish she'd turn this crap off and allow me to give her an education in alternative rock.

When I finally tune out the whining vocals of the latest pop hit, I replay last night over and over and over in my mind. I can still feel Phoenix's soft lips against mine and the chivalrous touch of his hand pressed against the small of my back.

It's a shame that he lives so far away. There could have been something great between us.

I try not to dwell on the disappointment and instead, focus my mind toward my interview in New York. When I get back to Chicago, I have calls to make and travel arrangements to coordinate.

Just past Rockford, Rachel turns the radio off and gives me a stern look.

"Spill it, Ivy."

I've managed to evade her inquisition all morning. And now that we're trapped in a confined space for a few hours, she's going to badger it out of me.

"What?" I feign ignorance.

"You're hopeless, you know that?"

There is so much truth in that statement, I can hardly count the ways.

I smile to myself and look out the passenger window at the fields of northern Illinois, wondering if Phoenix is looking out the window of his airplane and seeing the same thing I am.

"Oh my God, has the unthinkable finally happened?" Rachel gives me a wide-eyed smile. "You actually like this one! You *do* have feelings inside that icy heart of yours."

I unsuccessfully fight a smile. She's right. I do. I like this one a lot.

As we barrel down the highway, I recount the evening for her—the picnic, the stars, the walk … *the kiss*. The palm of my hand is still burning at the memory of his touch. Describing everything to her in detail makes me feel like I'm sitting on a bench in a museum, gazing upon my night inside of a picture frame. I can see the details and the brush strokes, but it's what I feel when I look at it that breathes life into the canvas. It's that indescribable feeling that moves me, that makes me want to throw away everything I've worked for and take a dare on my instincts.

"You have to go for it, Ivy. I mean, this could be the guy to turn your life upside down in all the best ways possible."

"You seem to be overlooking the obvious problem," I say.

"Screw the distance. You never turned your back on a challenge before. The risk could totally be worth the reward with him."

I can't help but think that for once, Rachel might be right.

After she helps me unload the last of my belongings, Rachel makes me promise to get together a few times over the next few weeks. She gives me an overenthusiastic hug before I begrudgingly turn and head into my parent's house.

It's strange being back in Chicago under this roof. I can't remember the last time it actually felt like home. The houses on Astor Street are a symbol of old money in this city. Its residents include some of the most renowned surgeons in the Midwest, successful litigation lawyers, and Fortune 500 executive officers. My dad falls in that last category as Chief Operating Officer for the largest financial firm in the Loop.

I know I should feel fortunate enough to have grown up so privileged, but honestly, it was hell. My parents like to constantly remind me that they own everything within its walls, including myself. Being back here as an adult feels all wrong. In fact, I didn't really miss this place at all.

That's the thing about my parents. I only miss them when I'm *with* them. Their presence reminds me of the fact they never really were parents at all. A commanding hand, a means to a financial end, and a roof over my head—that's about it.

Now that I'm a grown woman, I can't help but think I am better off without them. It's a wonder I was able to co-exist with them as long as I did. I'm eager to break free of them and be truly independent.

Standing in my childhood bedroom, I realize that I am looking at a ten-year-old Ivy frozen in time. Autographed photographs of professional ballerinas are still framed on the wall, and the faded pink paisley comforter is tucked neatly in place under a mountain of pillows. I haven't liked the color pink since I was five years old, and I haven't danced ballet in over a decade. Madame Alexander dolls line the shelves of a glass curio cabinet, never to be played with, just admired from afar. This room is a reminder of the "me" my parents wanted me to be.

The me they tried to mold but never succeeded.

The me I worked so hard to avoid.

Small acts of defiance throughout my teenage years were the tiny victories I relished in. The fake ID I secured. Successfully sneaking out of the house to go skinny-dipping in Lake Michigan with some hot upperclassmen at my prep school. But sleeping with Glen behind my sister's back was the final dagger that sealed my fate with my family.

That was the moment they seemed to give up hope. I like to think that I never did care, but the truth is that hurt.

A brusque knock at the door pulls me from my mental revelry.

"Ivy. You're home." My mother observes as steps into my room, arms folded. She doesn't come near. She doesn't hug me or tell me how much I was missed while abroad. She just stands there, coldness emanating from her expression. She is quite the welcome wagon.

I take a deep breath and remind myself that this is only temporary. Her eyes do a once over and I can read disapproval in her pursed lips.

"Yeah, Rachel dropped me off a little while ago," I say, matching her stare.

She responds with a silent nod. "Dinner will be at six. Please shower and make yourself presentable before then."

It's comforting to see that some things will never change. The ice queen that is my mother remains frozen in spite of the looming summer heat. It's amazing just how lonely I feel when I'm around my family. Surely Genevieve has never felt this way. After all, she is the golden child.

DINNER CAME AND WENT WITHOUT fanfare. As expected, Genevieve gushed over mundane wedding details with my mother. Does anybody really give a shit if the napkins are folded in a French Pleat instead of an Opera Fan? As the pair drone on, my father flashes a tight, sad smile as we both eat in silence.

In another place and time I think my dad would not be all that bad. If you could just peel back the designer suits and mutual funds and my mother latched to his hip, I really think he'd be a decent, humble man. He seems to understand my pariah status in this family, even if he doesn't actively do anything about it.

Sometimes just understanding isn't enough. I might actually like him if he weren't under my mother's influence.

I didn't bother making plans tonight as things have been so exhausting the past week. I'm still not entirely over the jetlag and I want nothing more than to retreat to my bedroom and watch reruns of sitcoms I missed while abroad. I pass through the library to grab a glass of water before retiring to my room for the night.

"You look different, Ivy," my dad observes with a lightness in his voice. "Italy must have treated you rather well."

I smile and my heart swells ever so slightly. "Thanks, Dad. The experience was more than I ever dreamed it could be. I'm really glad I made the decision to go abroad."

"Did you meet a boy there? I haven't seen you look this way since you brought Matt home the first time."

Ugh. I cringe at the sound of his name. It will take a miracle to erase him from my family's grasp. I settle on a half-truth. "No, I didn't meet anyone in Italy, Dad." My lips form a tight smile. I really don't want to be talking about this with him.

"Oh, okay then."

I walk toward the kitchen, but he calls back to me. "Don't think you're off the hook with me just yet, young lady. When you're ready I want to hear about all Italy and whatever is taking up space in that pretty little head of yours," he teases.

My cheeks turn scarlet as I think back to the past few days. Even after all the time away from my dad, I still can't fool him.

AS I LIE IN BED, I find myself wanting to turn back the clocks and unkiss Phoenix just so I can experience the magic of that first kiss all over again. His tender lips, assertive grasp, his amazingly delicious scent, his sweet taste. It was an assault of all my senses.

I drift off to sleep, dreaming of hazel eyes and telescopes and wrought iron benches along the lake.

THE NEXT DAY I WAKE in the early afternoon. After nearly a week of trying to adjust, the hours of jetlag have finally caught up to me. I stare wide-eyed at the textures in the ceiling, finding shapes and scenes like I used to as a child. I have no idea how I am going to get through staying here. Only another week or so and I'll be in New York City, hopefully securing my future.

"Why aren't you ready to go?"

Startled, I sit up and give Genevieve the side eye I perfected after decades of being under this roof.

"I told you last night at dinner that I needed you to come with me today. The florist? We're meeting CJ there, remember?"

"I … I'm sorry. I must've been so exhausted that I didn't hear you."

At least I'll finally get to meet the infamous Cortland James. There is a special place in heaven for anyone willingly enlisting themselves for a lifetime of my sister's bullshit, even if they're enlisting for all the wrong reasons.

"Well, we're leaving in ten minutes. I'll see you downstairs." She turns, leaving my bedroom door wide open. I can hear her heavy footsteps as she makes her way to the main foyer in a huff.

I shower in record time and twist my dark hair into a loose, wet bun at the nape of my neck before tearing my favorite vintage sapphire sundress from my closet. Dabbing on some gloss and mascara, I pin my grandmother's pearl studs in my ears and slip on my strappy sandals.

Racing down the stairs, I find Genevieve waiting for me with a bored expression. "Ready?" she asks with a hint of annoyance.

I grab my purse from the console table and open the

door, escaping from her nonsense. "Let's go," I call out over my shoulder.

When we get to the town car, I can't hide my elation when I see Harold standing there, waiting to open the door. Officially, Harold is our driver and has been a permanent fixture in our family as long as I can remember, but to me, he's the grandfather I never knew. He is incredibly kind to my family, especially since my parents don't deserve his respect the vast majority of the time.

Harold greets me with his megawatt smile and I can't fight the overwhelming urge to run and hug him. "It's good to have you home, Miss Ivy." He pulls back and gives me a once over proudly. "Italy looks good on you."

"Thanks, Harold." I reach up on my tiptoes and give him a soft kiss on his cheek, smiling as he blushes. "I've missed you too."

Behind me, Genevieve haughtily clears her throat and waits for Harold to open the door. I step out of her way and give Harold an overdramatic eye roll as I climb in after her. Now, more than ever, I am thankful for his years of service to our family and to the old friend he has been to me.

As we pull onto Lake Shore Drive, Genevieve's phone shrills to the tune of church bells. "Hi, baby," she coos into the receiver.

I turn to look out the window and give her as much privacy as the backseat of a town car can afford. Outside, the path along Lake Michigan is filled with runners and cyclists soaking in the beautiful weather. What I would give to escape the insanity of my family and join them in their free afternoon.

"What do you mean you can't make it?" Genevieve

exasperates. "Damn it, CJ! You have to be here today. We're finalizing the centerpieces. I can't do this without you."

I want to tell her that she is fully capable of making these kinds of decisions without him, that he likely doesn't give a shit about these kind of things, but I hold my tongue. It's not my problem.

"You've got to be kidding me. Tell him that there are plenty of other fish in the sea. Tell him … tell him that life is tough and to wear a helmet." She shuts up momentarily, finally listening to what he has to say. "Fine," she growls. "You owe me."

Genevieve dramatically throws her phone into her clutch. No good-bye, no I love you, no nothing. For the first time ever, I look at my sister and feel an overwhelming sense of pity. If she is going to handle her marriage like that, like our parents did, she is in for a lifetime of disappointment. Assuming they even make it that long.

She releases a weighted sigh and turns to face me. "I'm so sorry, Ivy," she croons sweetly at me. "Apparently, CJ is unable to join us this afternoon. It appears that one of his groomsmen is having girlfriend troubles and started drinking with breakfast. My darling feels it's necessary to interfere and do damage control before things with him get worse. Rain check on meeting the love of my life?" The plastic smile on her pretty little face is a perfect match for her plastic life.

It's revolting.

"Yeah, that's fine," I reply.

"It'll probably be a few weeks before you get to meet him now. He is heading out of town on business," she tells me, swearing under her breath.

I can't help but think she has a thing or two to learn about love. My thoughts are interrupted by her detailing a recent rift she had with the florist about her tropical flowers. It seems as if this florist reassured her that tropical flowers flown in from Hawaii would be more sustainable than the tropical flowers she demanded from Tahiti.

First world problems.

If she put half as much effort into her relationships as she did with this wedding, she would be set for life.

As we drive through the city, I can't help but wonder what Phoenix is doing today. I grab my phone and fire off a quick message his way.

> **Ivy:** *Thanks again for Saturday night. I hope you're having a good day! Catch up soon?*

I toss my phone back into my purse and brace myself for what will inevitably be the world's longest afternoon.

By the time we finally get home I'm exhausted. Not only did we spend three hours at the florist, but we also dropped off the name cards at the calligrapher's studio, stopped by the seamstress to make sure that my monstrosity of a dress fit, then ran to a local bakery to design a groom's cake as a surprise. To top off our day, we had dinner at my favorite pizza joint in the entire city where Genevieve proceeded to order a salad—a criminal offense in the presence of deep-dish lovers, but I really shouldn't be surprised. She probably hasn't touched a carb in eight years.

I checked my phone obsessively throughout the day, but there was still no response from Phoenix. I feel slightly wounded, though I try to brush it off. Maybe he's not into me nearly as much as I am with him. I mean, it's not like I'm dating the guy or anything. Instead of dwelling in disappointment, I power up my laptop to check my email.

At the very top of my inbox, there is a message from James Horesji's personal assistant with a few flight options for my upcoming interview. It's surreal how fast everything is happening. I email her back and ask her to book my flight for Tuesday, the first available option next week. Anything to get me out of Chicago sooner rather than later. I go through and start deleting junk mail and nearly trash a message from P. Wolfe. It's the subject line that grabs my attention.

"The stars shine brighter when I'm with you."

My insides swell ever so slightly and I open the email, hoping that it's from who I think it's from.

> *At risk of sounding resoundingly pathetic, I miss you. I miss you so much that I want to write "I miss you" on a rock and throw it at your face so you know just how much it hurts to miss you. But then, if I were that close I would have every reason in the world to kiss you and make you feel better.*
>
> *If missing you this much is wrong, I don't want to be right. Please tell me you want to throw rocks at my face too?*
> *Phoenix*

He misses me!

I breathe a sigh of relief and thank the maker I'm not the only sap still dreaming of two nights ago. I read his email over and over, my smile growing bigger each time.

Laughing under my breath, I open up a blank email and craft an equally smart-ass response.

> Rock throwing aside, I really miss you, too...but probably not as much as you miss me. After all, I am pretty awesome. ;)
> Ivy
>
> P.S. How'd you get my email?

Feeling fifty pounds lighter, I float off my bed and traipse into the bathroom. I'm in the middle of brushing my teeth when I hear my phone ringing from the other room.

"Huwwo?" I muffle into the phone over the sound of my faucet.

"Uh, Ivy?" a male voice asks hesitantly. "It's Phoenix."

Oh, shit. I quickly spit the toothpaste from my mouth and shut the water off in what is arguably my classiest move to date.

"Hey! Sorry, I thought you were Rachel." I try to control my emotions so I don't come off as overeager. It's a good thing he can only hear me and not see the ridiculous grin on my face.

"I'm so sorry," he croons into the phone, "but my phone battery died earlier, so I didn't get your text messages until a little bit ago. I rarely use this thing. I'll try and do a better job of keeping it juiced up. Is this a bad time?"

"No, I was just getting ready for bed. How was your day?"

"Long. I spent most of the day working on some blueprints from home and dealing with an overdramatic Sully on the side. Yours?"

I know firsthand how draining it can be dealing with other people. Dealing with Genevieve was a full-time job growing up. Hell, we're not even close anymore and it's still a full-time job.

"Sounds better than mine. Bridezilla towed me all around Chicago obsessing over mundane details." I yawn and lie back into the cloud of pillows on my bed. "Did you know that you can have monograms hand painted on rose petals in gold leaf? Or that you can have a cake built into three-dimensional shapes?" The absurdity of Genevieve's wedding decisions knows no bounds.

Phoenix chuckles softly in my ear. "All in a day's work, maid of honor."

He's such a good sport letting me unload. Normally I hate talking on the phone, but there's an ease with Phoenix on the other end of the line. My guard is down and I will-ingly offer up all more information than what is socially acceptable.

"Seriously, though. How'd you get my email?"

"Well ... I tried Googling you." He sounds a little embarrassed by his confession.

Admittedly, I'm a bit flattered that he has taken to cyber-stalking me. "And what did you find?" I bite my lip flirtatiously, even though he can't see me.

"Nothing, actually. It's like you don't even exist online. And believe me, I tried just about everything."

And that makes perfect sense considering Ivy Phillips does not exist outside of the boundaries that I put in place. Had he been Googling Ivy Cotter he would find pages of high school swim meet results, newspaper articles from my time on the Junior League board, and all of my tomfoolery plastered on my Facebook page. There is no reason he needs to see old pictures of me with Matt. Or me dancing on bars. Or me on one knee taking a beer bong like a champ. Though that was one of my crowning collegiate moments.

I make a mental note to go through and clean up my Facebook pictures … just in case.

But the truth is, I like being incognito with him. I can be *me* without my family's notoriety getting in the way. He gets to be my little secret. And I, his.

"Anyway … the morning after the bachelor party one of Sully's brother's roommates said that you were his Art History TA. So when I couldn't find you online, I reached out to him to get it. It only put me back a case of beer."

"For being so anti-technology, you sure know how to use it to your advantage."

"I never said I was anti-technology. I only said that I much prefer the company of an engaging person rather than the backside of their cellphone."

When I look at the clock, I'm shocked to see it's nearing one in the morning and we've been talking for more than three hours. It feels like we've been on the phone for thirty minutes. I hear him stifle a yawn on the other end of the line.

"I better let you go, sleepyhead. You've got work to take care of in the morning."

Phoenix hums softly into the phone, a sign of contentment. "Promise to text me tomorrow?"

"I'll see your text, and raise you a phone call."

"Then I will have hit the jackpot." The smile in his

voice warms me. "Good night, Ivy."

"Night, Phoenix."

As I fall asleep, I succumb to the overwhelming urge to take a gamble on this man, this distance, and this undeniable connection threading us together.

WITHOUT EVEN KNOCKING, RACHEL BARRELS through my bedroom door and stands at the edge of my bed, arms crossed. She looks livid. But that's probably because she is. The last time I saw her this angry, Garrett Gregory had ditched her at senior prom and went back to his ex-girlfriend.

I have no idea what time it is, but I'm exhausted and just want to go to finish texting with Phoenix and just go to bed. That seems to be all I do these days, not that I'm complaining.

When I'm not talking with Phoenix on the phone, we're texting. When we're not texting, I'm thinking about him, daydreaming of all the wonderful things we would do together if our current circumstances were different. Envisioning all of the scandalous things I want to do to him … the sounds he'd make … the way he'd taste … he was consuming my every thought in the most amazing ways possible.

Nearly every night this week, I have stayed up late texting and talking with him on the phone. Last night, or rather this morning, we even saw the clock hit four in the morning. He's just so easy to talk to. Being on the phone with him is like slipping into my favorite pair of yoga pants—comfortable and inviting. We talk about everything and nothing all at the same time. And I learn something new and endearing with each call. Phoenix has quickly become my favorite reason to lose sleep.

Much to Rachel's chagrin, I've blown her off—twice—so I really shouldn't be surprised to see her standing in my doorway with a pissed off look on her face.

"What the hell, Ivy?"

"What? I'm tired. Leave me be." I bury my head under a pillow.

"No. You're texting. With him. And you were supposed to be at my apartment an hour ago. This is so unlike you."

I rollover and glance at the clock, then groan. It's only eight forty-five. I could have sworn it was after midnight. I sit up and look at Rachel.

"You look cute," I say with a smile, hoping the compliment will take down her edge. Only Rachel can pull off bright red skinny jeans, a backless black top and studded heels. Her blonde bombshell status certainly doesn't hurt her appeal either.

"I know. And it's because we were supposed to get cute together and go dancing. Now get your tiny ass up. You're not ditching me again. Who knows how many more nights out we'll have together."

She's right, even though I honestly have no recollection of making plans with her.

Just last week, Rachel was pushing me to go for it, to be with him any way I possibly can. And now that I'm putting myself out there for this long-distance … well, whatever *this* is, she chastises me. I sigh and remind my-self that even in the midst of relationships, we always make time for each other.

I drag myself out from the comforts of my bed and slip into the bathroom. This past week I have mastered the art of the five-minute shower and I'm ready to go in record time.

"You can't wear that."

"What's wrong with my outfit?" I look down at my favorite pair of black jeans and plaid, capped-sleeve shirt.

"We're going to The Masonry. You have to actually look like you give a shit."

I stifle an annoyed groan. She's right. I would never even be let in the doors of The Masonry looking like this. I pull Rachel into my closet and grant her permission to play dress up.

Minutes later we're hailing a cab as I yank my mini skirt down over my ass—no bending this evening.

We're only a few blocks away from the club when my phone chimes from my clutch. Rachel rolls her eyes.

"Just this once. When we get out of the cab, that boy toy does not exist. You're mine," she says, gesturing for me to answer it.

> **Phoenix:** *You never answered my last question. Is everything okay?*
> **Ivy:** *Sorry about that. Rachel showed up and dragged me out for a night on the town.*

The past few days have been filled with playful rapid-fire questions back and forth getting to know each other better.

MONDAY …

Ivy: *Greatest embarrassment?*
Phoenix: *Hitting the side of Mom's house the moment I realized I couldn't drive manual transmission. What about you?*
Ivy: *If I told you I'd have to kill you.*

TUESDAY …

Phoenix: *Favorite song?*
Ivy: *Zeppelin's Trampled Under Foot. Yours? And answer carefully … I'm judging you.*
Phoenix: *Everlong by Foo Fighters. Greatest love song of all time.*

WEDNESDAY …

Ivy: *Cats or dogs?*
Phoenix: *Dogs. Cats are the root of all evil.*

THURSDAY …

Phoenix: *Ever get caught fooling around?*
Ivy: *Yeah. With BOB.*
Phoenix: *Capital letters? He must've been pretty good.*
Ivy: *Not exactly. Rachel walked in on me*

with my Battery Operated Boyfriend junior
year ...
Ivy: *Now I have to kill you.*

We've learned all sorts of charming—and mortify-ing—nuggets about each other this week. But strangely, I want him to know my ridiculous quirks.

I quickly flip back through his previous texts, won-dering what he asked. My first concert? Oh man, if I tell the truth I will undoubtedly lose all of my music cred with him, but I don't want to lie to him either.

> **Ivy:** *Hanson. But only because Rachel made me go with her*
> **Ivy:** *The first concert that I actually wanted to see? U2.*
> **Phoenix:** *Hanson? I never pegged you for liking girl groups ;) Mine was Radiohead in Grant Park.*
> **Ivy:** *OMG! I was at that show too!*
> **Phoenix:** *Remind me to tell you how I got backstage during the encore. Have fun to-night.*
> **Ivy:** *Same to you. I'll give you a call tomor-row.*

I make eye contact with Rachel and theatrically toss my phone back into my purse for safekeeping.

"Thank you!" she says with a smile.

The Masonry is the club where you go to see and be seen, and I would much rather hit up a dive bar in my pa-jamas than be dressed to the nines, but I do it for Rachel because she is the only one who puts up with my shit and doesn't complain. I couldn't ask for a better best friend.

The music is so loud that my ribcage vibrates and the visibility is near zero. Rachel grabs me by the hand and weaves us through the crowd up to the bar. It takes us nearly fifteen minutes to get the bartender's attention, then we each order two drinks and double-fist our way through the crowd to try and find a place to sit.

We're fortunate enough to spy an open table on the other side of the dance floor, so we quickly make our way over and saddle up on the silver barstools. I quickly toss back my first old fashioned and trace my fingers over the rim of the empty glass. The cool burn makes its way down to my belly and I feel warm all over instantly.

I zone out and let Rachel ramble about Eric and decorating her new apartment and job hunting. I'm not sure exactly what details she gives, but I look up when I feel the back of her hand swat my arm. A pair of attractive twenty-somethings approaches our table and gesture for us to join them on the dance floor.

Politely, I shake my head no. I'm not shy, and under normal circumstances I would have been on the dance floor fifteen minutes ago, but dancing with strange men just feels wrong right now. Like I'd be cheating. I'd much rather be dancing with Phoenix. Thinking back to the house party before I blacked out, I remember how in sync our bodies were as we moved to the music.

I try to shoo Rachel out onto the dance floor, but she insists on staying with me and takes a rain check with the guys before they leave, dejected.

"This is weird, right?" I shout over the music.

"What is?"

"This," I say with a shrug. "The way I'm feeling. We're sitting here in this club, surrounded by hot guys who want to buy us drinks and dance, and all I can think about is Phoenix." The truth is, it is taking all of my willpower not to pick up the phone and call him and curl up in his voice.

"You have got it so bad." She grins warmly as she plucks the olive from her martini and pops it into her mouth. Her smile tells me that she's genuinely happy for me right now. I look out over the mob of people dancing and stifle a yawn. As much as I'd rather not be here, I really do enjoy Rachel's company.

"You're really not feeling this, are you?"

I shake my head no and nurse my second drink. My heart just isn't in it.

"I'm sorry. I really thought getting you out of the house would help." Her lips form a straight line as I shake my head. "Come on, then. Let's go back to my place and order a pizza." Rachel grabs her clutch and pulls me out of the bar.

We take off into the night for a little girl time. No boys. No booze. No bars. Just us girls and Rachel's phone as she sends and receives texts and Facebook messages throughout our entire conversation. As we gossip into the wee hours of the morning I realize for the first time that maybe Phoenix is right. We spend far too much effort digitally connecting with other people when the person we should be communicating with is right in front of us.

THE BELLHOP OPENS THE DOOR and places my luggage underneath the window. I casually slip a few singles into his palm before he retreats back to his post in the lobby.

Deep in the belly of my purse, my cellphone trills the chorus of "Everlong." Last week when Phoenix told me that it was his favorite love song, I'd sat down and really listened to the lyrics for the first time, then quickly made it my ringtone for him. It makes me smile each time he calls.

My insides tingle in effervescence at the thought of Phoenix and I can hardly contain the perma-grin on my face. It takes me a few moments to dig my phone out from the loose change, receipts and lip gloss swimming in the bottom of my bag.

"Hey, Phoenix," I greet him in a lazy, cool voice, though I'm certain he can feel my smile beaming through.

"Hey, Ivy. Have a good flight?"

"I did. I never realized just how big New York City was until we were landing. It's insane." I pull the curtain back to admire the view and find myself looking at concrete wall. I should have expected that.

103

"I only have a moment to chat, but I wanted to make sure you made it in safely." Muffled voices and laughter fill the line between us, but he shushes them quickly.

"Thanks, that's so sweet of you."

"Hey, listen, are you going to be around later tonight? Around nine or so? I'd love to call back and talk longer."

"Sure. Seeing as I don't really know anyone in New York, I don't have any plans other than walking around the neighborhood."

"Perfect. Be safe when you go exploring. Chat soon."

"All right. Bye, Phoenix."

I end the call and toss my phone onto the bed. For the first time, I notice just how small the room is. It takes me all of five steps to cross from one end to the other. I open up the closet door only to find the bathroom instead. The space is no larger than a postage stamp. While the hotel advertised itself as "luxury boutique accommodations," the emphasis certainly was not on luxury.

On the back of the door, I find a hook to hang my clothes up for tomorrow's interview and organize my toiletries on the bathroom sink before turning the hot water on.

My shoulders finally begin to relax once the scalding water beats down my back. I wash away the grime of my travels, the stench of the cab, and let my mind loose as the heavy steam sticks to my skin. Gone are my worries from Chicago—no Genevieve to commandeer my free time, and no parents to try and submit me to their control. This trip is about me, my future, and nothing else.

I spend the next few hours pampering myself. I take my time getting ready and make my way outside right as the orange sky comes burning to life. Glowing clouds spiral the sky, echoing vibrant hues of red and pink before darkness takes over.

I take the long way by foot to Gallery 545, picking up a sandwich at a local deli to eat on my walk. The director said the gallery could be tough to find, so I want to make sure I know what I'm looking for tomorrow so I'm not late.

The Chelsea neighborhood is otherworldly and with each step I find myself walking further and further into a dream. *My dream.* It's a perfect blend of trendy and historic with fine restaurants, contemporary bars, and an appreciative nod to its past while flirting with the future. Street art meets sophisticated architecture. It's easy to see why it earned its reputation as the art gallery capital of the world. It's easy to imagine myself living here among the impeccably manicured tree-lined streets, thought provoking street art, and wrought-iron fences protecting the brownstone dwellings.

Eventually, I find myself staring up at a three-story building. It's a rehabilitated warehouse with frosted windows. The brick, presumably original, is chipping away into small piles of crumbs on the sidewalk below. There are no signs, and the door to the gallery is unnumbered. The only identifying marker is a small handwritten note above the doorbell that reads, "In art as in love, instinct is enough. – Anatole France." I can only assume Mr. Horesji intended it to be inconspicuous. You would likely pass it by if you weren't specifically searching for it. It's beautiful and unassuming; everything I want my life to be.

I cross the street and sit on a bench, studying Gallery 545 as I pull the sandwich from its bag. With each bite, I imagine its interior walls, clean and white. Exquisite paintings and sculptures, depicting a modern marriage of Western and non-Western styles. I'm so lost in thought I don't even realize night has fallen and I'm flirting with nine o'clock. I rush back to the hotel to settle in for the night.

THE UNFAMILIAR DEFAULT RING ON my phone startles me. I don't recognize the number. Normally I would send it to voicemail, but it is pulling up as a video chat request.

That's odd.

"Hey, gorgeous!" Delight tingles through my body as I find Phoenix smiling back at me enthusiastically. "I hate not knowing when I get to see you next, so I bought an iPhone so we can video chat."

His sweet gesture takes me by surprise. I can't help but find the irony in the situation. The very piece of technology he hates is the one that threads us together.

A quick rasp on the door pulls my focus away momentarily.

"Hang on a sec, someone's at the door."

I jump up and peer through the peephole to find room service on the other side. That's strange ... I didn't order anything. Opening the door, I welcome the young man, who places a tray of strawberries, sliced cheese, and a glass of wine on the end of my bed.

"Thank you," I say before returning my focus to Phoenix. "Well, this is nice. It must be from the gallery."

Examining the silver tray, I realize there's no note. I watch Phoenix's face light up as he brings a matching glass of white wine up to the screen as if to toast me.

"Or it could be from your date," he replies.

"My date?" I say inquisitively. "You did this?" He nods. I shouldn't be so surprised. Phoenix has always been so thoughtful. "Aww, you're so sweet. Thank you!"

I take a bite from a plump strawberry and the juice runs down my chin in what is arguably the most unromantic move of all time. I smile at myself, having the grace of a Mack truck, but I savor the sweet nectar as it brings my taste buds to life.

"I thought you weren't a fan of wine."

"I'm not. But I figured I'd make an exception on this special occasion. To you, Ivy. May tomorrow be the beginning of everything you've ever dreamed of." He takes a sip with a serious look in his eyes, and I follow his lead, taking a sip of wine. It's smooth and fruity and calms my nerves. I instantly recognize the taste.

"Mmmm … Moscato is my favorite. How'd you know?"

"Lucky guess, I suppose. I wanted to bring you a taste of Italy before your big interview tomorrow. I remembered you telling me that you had visited Piedmont during your travels, so I thought this would bring you comfort and smiles."

Is this guy for real? These are the kind of moves reserved for Harlequin fiction and romantic comedies. Drinking the wine, admiring the smooth, rich flavors, I can't help but wish I were drinking him instead.

"Guys like you aren't supposed to exist in real life."

He softly laughs as a light blush tints his cheeks. "I'm all real, baby."

Over the next few hours we talk about everything and we talk about nothing. We sit in silence, looking at the other as if we were in the same room, only two feet apart.

At one point I find myself reaching out to touch his face, but pull my hand back quickly, realizing just how weird it would be if I caressed my cell phone. I want nothing more than to climb through my phone and into his lap, drowning him in kisses. It is truly one of the best dates I've been on in my life.

But there is something to this distance thing we've got going on. Talking on the phone for as long and as often as we have, has allowed us to get close without ever being physical. There is never an opportunity for the "old Ivy" to rear her ugly head and fuck everything up by sleeping with him too soon. I don't have to worry about him thinking I'm a prude if I don't go home with him, or worse, what he'd think if I slept with him too soon.

"God, I wish I were there with you tonight." The look in his eyes pierces right through me. I recognize it from the moments before we kissed on Lake Mendota.

"Me too. You'd be able to keep me calm before the big interview." And what I really mean by "keep me calm" is keep me distracted in the most pleasurable ways possible. I glance over my shoulder and notice the clock. "Oh shit, it's almost midnight. I really should get some beauty rest so I can be on my A-game tomorrow."

"Okay. You're going to be brilliant. Just be yourself and remember to breathe. They'll love you. And if you get nervous, just imagine yourself as ten years old. Minus the fart jokes."

I snort at his ridiculous words. Talking to him for the past few hours had completely eased my nerves. I take a deep breath, feeling confident.

"Thanks, Phoenix. I appreciate it. Everything, really."

"No problem, Ivy." He pauses thoughtfully. "There's

one more thing I need you to do tonight."

Please God, don't let him ask me to flash him my boobs or something equally juvenile. I actually like this one.

"Before you fall asleep, but after we hang up the phone, look underneath your plate," he says with a shy grin. "Good night, Cubby Bear. Talk to you tomorrow."

"'Night," I whisper sleepily before he ends the video feed.

Curiously, I lift the corner of the china and find a simple note, hand-written on a napkin. I have no idea whose script it is, but that doesn't matter. What matters is he went through the effort to make this surprise happen for me.

He remembered! Maybe things with us don't have to be a complicated adult relationship after all. Perhaps things between us could be this simple and straightforward. I'm tickled that he remembered me saying this on our date a few weeks ago.

Quickly, I grab a hotel pen from the bedside table and put a checkmark next to "yes," then snap a photo of the napkin with my camera phone. Before I can second guess myself, I attach the picture to a text message and send to Phoenix.

As my head finally hits the pillow, I take a deep breath. They *definitely* don't make guys like him in real life.

LAST NIGHT'S WINE AND CONVERSATION was just enough to relax me into a deep, satisfying sleep. I wake up excited, refreshed and ready to conquer the day.

The interview, while nerve-wracking, went surprisingly well. Professor Whitman had warned me that any playful quizzing James might do would really be a test to make sure I was more than adept with my Art History knowledge. Whit taught me well, so I knew I would have no issues impressing him, but when we began talking about modern day artists, I really started to shine. Some of the connections I had made in the local art scene in Italy would prove to be invaluable to him and I left feeling confident that I would be offered the position. As he walked me out of the gallery, James promised I would know more in the next few days.

When he closed the door behind me, I examined the small piece of paper with the handwritten quote by the doorbell more closely.

"In art as in love, instinct is enough. – Anatole France."

I trusted my instinct with following my passion for art and things seem to be falling into place. Could I be so lucky for the same to happen with my love life? Can I let my guard down, follow my instinct, and reap the riches it could possibly bring?

I'm tempted to pull the quote down and hide it in my pocket like a secret treasure, but settle for a photo of it instead. Snapping the picture quickly, I save it to my photo stream and return to the hotel to pack up for my flight home.

My work here is done, and hopefully, it is just the beginning.

June

DRIVING DOWN LAKE SHORE DRIVE with Rachel is one of my favorite things to do in the world. It's like we're in high school again where life is carefree with no pressing obligations, and nobody matters but us. When she called this morning, asking if I wanted to grab brunch and then hit up the beach with her, it was a no-brainer plan to escape the torture of my parents' house. Only in Chicago does an air temperature of seventy degrees with frigid water temps of Lake Michigan constitute a beach day.

"Oh, I love this song!" Rachel squeals, turning the volume up to eleven.

I settle deep against the seat, a smile slowly pulling my lips apart. The lyrics roll over me in incandescent waves, filling the tiny crevices of my soul with sunshine that melts me from the inside out. Closing my eyes, I soak in the words as they describe the feeling of reuniting with a past love, both emotionally and physically.

It is as if every love song on the radio was written

with Phoenix in mind.

Life is in technicolor.

Flowers smell sweeter.

Colors glow brighter.

My senses are awakened from the empty slumber of the past few years and I never want to sleep again. What is happening to me? I'm losing my cynical edge. How does he have this effect on me? It's impossible to erase him from my mind. God, I'm *such* a girl.

I quickly pull my phone out of my bag and fire off a text message before Rachel notices my mind is five hundred miles away.

> **Ivy:** *Just so you know, I'm missing you like mad today. What are you up to? xoxo*

I twirl my phone in my fingers and look out the window to Lake Michigan. I wish I were on a different lake with a completely different person sitting next to me. I close my eyes against the headrest and daydream of Delilah's bench and the most magical kiss of my life.

We drive in silence a while longer, then pull off on a side street downtown to find parking. The beach is surprisingly crowded for a weekday.

"So how was the interview?" she asks as she lays out her beach towel in the sand.

Admittedly, I haven't thought much about the interview since I left New York. It's hard to focus on anything but Phoenix lately. "Fine … good, the interview went well. Really well, in fact."

I don't have it in me to gloat about inevitably having good news come my way; partly because I don't want to jinx myself, but also because I don't want to ruin her hopes of me staying in Chicago. I offer Rachel a timid smile and plop down next her in the sand.

"You're really not yourself, Ivy." She tosses her flip-flops to the side and shimmies out of her shorts and T-shirt. "Strip down, girly! Let's get some vitamin D on that pasty corpse of yours."

After a few hours of basking in the warm sunshine, I check my phone to see if Phoenix has texted me back. I frown when I see no new messages. He must be busy building a plan for some potential new client he has been trying to land for the past few weeks.

"What's with the freaked out bald dude on your phone case?" she asks pulling me from my reverie.

I glance down at Edvard Munch's famous painting and smile. It has always been one of my favorites because it's so misunderstood.

"It's called *The Scream*." It doesn't surprise me that she has no recollection of learning this in our Intro to Art History class freshman year. She slept through half the semester and cheated off me on during exams.

Rachel shudders. "He skeeves me out. He reminds me of Kevin McCallister screaming in *Home Alone*. Is he witnessing the zombie apocalypse or something?"

I snort at her comment.

"No. The painting is about love, actually."

"Love? Yeah, right." She scoffs.

"Yes, love." I sigh. "It's about despair being the inevitable outcome of falling in love. Nearly every single love you experience will encounter searing heartache on some level and that thought alone is terrifying."

"That's depressing, Ivy."

"Well ... that's art. Anyway, this piece was one of the first notable paintings in the Art Nouveau movement," I add, trying to at least give her an education since Professor Whitman apparently failed her.

"Blah, blah, blah ... art nouveau? You sound like you're in love nouveau," She mocks.

"Don't be ridiculous." I feel my cheeks flush and I suppress a smile.

"Oh. My. God. You totally slept with him, you slut monkey! You're in love at first fuck!" Rachel shrieks.

"No," I correct her. "I neither slept with him nor am I in love with him."

At least I don't think I am.

"Fine, maybe you're not, but you *are* in a long distance relationship," Rachel sings at me.

"I would hardly call one date a relationship." I give her a pointed glare. I mean, we're not in a relationship, are we?

Shit.

Maybe we are?

I don't know.

"But you want to be."

I smile as I close my eyes and absorb the warmth from the sunshine. I can't deny it ... *won't* deny it. Even after knowing Phoenix for such a short period of time, he has bewitched me. Without even looking at her, I know that Rachel is staring at me.

"After a decade of friendship, this is the first time I've ever seen you like this over a guy." She snickers.

"Let's not even go there." Because if we go there, I'm going to get excited. And when I get excited about a guy, that is the instant I allow myself to get my hopes up, which is the very same moment I position myself to get devastatingly hurt. As fucked up as it sounds, I would rather be the one who does the hurting.

Rachel sits up with a serious look on her face. "So you kind of like this guy, eh?"

If by "kind of like" she means completely and totally enamored, first and last thought each day, a single text setting me off with the urge to dance in the rainy streets without abandon, where I can't even think straight because he occupies every last fissure of my brain, then yes, I kind of like Phoenix.

"Yeah, I guess you could say that."

I turn my face away so she can't see the rising blush of my cheeks. Liking a guy to this extent is completely foreign to me, and it is absolutely killing me that the one guy capable of turning my insides to mush is a five-hour drive away. Why couldn't I like a guy in the same area code? I hate not knowing when I'm going to see him again. I don't want to call him or text. I don't want to video chat. I just want to be in his arms, kissing his lips, inhaling his breath, wrapping my legs around his waist, getting lost in his presence.

I just want to be with him.

I'm floating on uncharted waters, standing on the edge of the boat, warring with the decision of whether or not to throw myself overboard. If I jump, love will either chain itself to my ankles like a cement block, pulling me under, drowning me, or love will throw a life preserver and keep me afloat, the water lapping my skin in kisses. That's the thing about these kinds of emotions, they will either save me or kill me.

"For what it's worth, Ivy, you look like a girl in

love," she says with a pointed look. "But I would like to call out the best part about him being in St. Louis…"

"Oh?" I ask, squinting into the sun.

"You don't have to shave religiously."

Leave it to Rachel to find the silver lining in the distance.

AS I LIE IN BED that night, Rachel's words echo through the peaks and valleys of my mind.

Is this love?

I don't know.

But whatever it is, I know it's true because of the way he makes me feel. And I've never felt anything like this before in my entire life.

I toss and turn sleeplessly. I have to know if he feels this strongly too. Is he thinking of me nearly as much as I'm dreaming of him? God! These emotions are making me bat shit crazy. *Get a grip, Ivy!*

What we're doing simply is not enough for me. No longer do I want to just text or settle for video chats. I want nothing less than the opportunity to lace my fingers between his, run my hands through his hair and watch him in the morning light as it cascades through the blinds. I want to kiss him until my lips are swollen with passion. Rake my fingernails down his back.

I want him mind, body, and soul. I need to be with him.

I need to be his.

Fuck the distance. Phoenix should be here with me. Or maybe I should be there?

I don't know.

But I'm certain that we should be together. We were meant to be a couple.

There are art galleries in St. Louis, right? Perhaps I need to expand my job search there. Just because I get a job offer in New York City doesn't mean I have to take it. Could I be the kind of girl who blindly follows her heart? Sure, my heart lies in art, but could I truly be happy without Phoenix in my life if I'm living alone in New York?

Why must this be so confusing? Why the hell am I even entertaining shuffling my future for some guy I've just met?

My subconscious snarls at me, knowing exactly why I'm entertaining the thought.

I roll over and look at the clock. It's nearly four in the morning and my exhausted body refuses sleep with my mind running rampant. Grabbing my phone off the nightstand, I fire off a text, not caring that it's the wee hours of the morning and that Phoenix is likely asleep.

Ivy: *I have a problem.*

He responds immediately. I don't even feel bad about possibly waking him up.

Phoenix: *What's the matter? Are you okay?*
Ivy: *I'm fine. It's just that I'm here. And you're there.*

I look at my last message and take a deep breath. Rip off the Band-Aid, Ivy. Just tell him how you feel, no matter how terrified you are.

Ivy: *Do you know what this means?*
Phoenix: *?*
Ivy: *One of us is in the wrong place.*

When my text goes unanswered after several minutes, the severity of my pathetic emotions set in. I've probably scared him off. Or maybe he fell asleep? Or hell, maybe I've read into everything way too much and he doesn't like me as much as I like him. Shit, that would be the worst. I don't know.

Just as I close my eyes again to try and drift to sleep, my phone begins to sing the Foo Fighters's song that makes me giddy with anticipation and desire.

"Hi," I whisper sheepishly. My insides shift subtly, and I feel a bit lighter at the thought of him on the other end of the line.

"About that … what if one of us wasn't in the wrong place?" He wastes no time getting to his point. "What if we lived in the same state? Same area code, even?"

Any semblance of exhaustion is pulled from the room as I attempt to process what he's trying to tell me. I sit up immediately and search my brain for words.

"What do you mean?"

"I didn't want to say anything until it was finalized, but the proposal I've been working on the past few weeks is for a freelancing gig just north of Chicago," he says quietly. "We can actually see if this … if *us* could work."

A veil of silence presses over the phone as words escape me and I feel my heart rate spike.

"I mean, I know that you may be headed to New York soon, but even the opportunity to be around you for a few weeks is better than nothing."

Is this for real? He's making it crystal clear that he's interested in exploring whatever this is between us. My toes curl in excitement. It's a legitimate chance to be together. To see each other whenever we please. To hold hands and touch. To actually attempt to date without the assistance of wireless Internet and modern technology.

"Are you serious?"

"It's not in writing yet, but it's looking like it's a done deal. I spent my entire day on the phone with them presenting my revised plans. They are petitioning for approval on the budget to make it happen. I think they want me to come up in a few weeks to meet in person, and I'd love to spend time with you again if you're free."

I bring my fingers up to touch my lips and trace the emerging smile.

The job would be a six-week project, commissioned by a national telecommunications firm for their new satellite office. That could mean six glorious weeks together. And if we accomplished as much as we did in one night in Madison, imagine what we could do in six weeks.

Somehow the distance has only made us closer, and I'm eager to discover just how in sync we are when we're finally within each other's grasp again.

"Sleep with me tonight." His voice is so soft, I almost miss his request. "Just stay on the line, close your eyes and fall asleep with me. I don't want to say goodbye yet."

My insides melt at the thought of listening to him breathe through the night. I curl up on my side, throwing my arm over a spare pillow to hug it close to my body, imagining it's him. Burying my nose into the fabric, I inhale fresh linen instead of his defining scent.

"One day, Ivy, you're going to roll over in the morning and find me there next to you."

I can only hope, Phoenix. I can only hope.

As a delicate snore comes through the line, I give a knowing smile and close my eyes.

GLANCING AT MY CELL PHONE, my heart races when the 212 area code flashes.

New York. It's the call I've been waiting for.

"Hello?"

"Hello, Ivy? This is James Horejsi from Gallery 545."

My hands grow clammy and I wipe the sweat against my linen pants as I barely register anything that James Horejsi says.

"There is an official offer letter in the mail, but I wanted to call and offer you the position personally. Take some time to consider the opportunity and the implications of moving to New York. It's a tough town and not for everyone. The offer is on the table for two weeks from this Friday. I will give you a follow up call at that time."

Holy shit.

I got the job. I have an open door to get to New York and start a life for myself. To make a name for myself. To proudly stand on my own two feet and think *I* did this. I can hardly contain my excitement and find myself jumping on my bed like Genevieve and I did when we were little, pumping my fists in the air while I dance to imaginary music.

James ends the call abruptly and I immediately dial Phoenix. He answers on the first ring.

"Why hello there, Cubby Bear!"

I am so overjoyed I nearly fall off the bed.

"I got it! I got the job!" I squeal into the phone like a giddy schoolgirl.

"There was never any doubt in my mind that you would. Congratulations, Ivy. I'm really happy for you." Pride rings through his voice, veiled with a hint of sadness. The moment is bittersweet. Telling him that I'm headed to New York is the definitive answer that we are not getting any closer in proximity, but in spite of this revelation, he still seems happy for me.

More than anything I wish that he were here with me to celebrate. I don't think there is anyone in this city who will be happy for me. Certainly not my parents who are probably secretly holding out that I'll take the LSAT and head off to law school, Genevieve won't give a damn, and Rachel will just be in denial about me leaving her again.

WHEN I RUN DOWNSTAIRS FOR dinner, my stomach is in knots. It is nearly impossible to gauge my parents' reaction to the news I'll be sharing tonight. Will they be excited that I'll be out of their hair and on the East Coast? Will they reiterate their disappointment for my career choice? Deep in my bones, I think I already know the answer.

"I have some news," I announce as we finish passing the pork chops around the table.

"Oh! Me, too!" Genevieve chimes in. "I heard from

the florist today and it turns out they *will* be able to get the tiare apetahi for the centerpieces."

Mom delicately pats the back of her hand. "That's great, dear. When does CJ get back? We would love to have him over for dinner sometime soon."

I should really be annoyed at the fact my mother is ignoring me, but I'm used to being glossed over in favor of Genevieve.

"His trip was extended so he could get a few more contracts signed while he is overseas. He should be back next week," Genevieve says proudly as she sits up a little straighter in her chair.

"Well, we would love to have him over for dinner again before the wedding. Wouldn't we, Stephen?"

My dad grunts in acknowledgment.

"Besides CJ still needs to meet your sister, you know," my mother points out and Genevieve releases a huge sigh.

"So what's your news, Ivy?" Genevieve asks, spearing a delicate French green bean on her fork and popping it into her mouth.

I choke back a smile. I'm not sure if I'm excited about leaving these kind of moments behind or if I'm simply proud that I nailed an especially challenging interview and found a job that's perfect for me all on my own.

"Well, the gallery in New York called me this afternoon."

My mother's fork clanks as she drops it on the plate and temples her fingers in front of her mouth.

"They offered me the position." I try to hide my elation.

The glance my parents exchange is impossible to

miss. After a quarter century of marriage, they have perfected the art of silent conversations. Clearly my interview has been a point of closed-door discussions for them and they have already come to some kind of decision on the matter.

"Oh, that's nice, honey," she deadpans before picking her fork back up and continuing with her meal. There were no congratulatory words, no emotion in her voice. Just *that's nice*.

I hate that word. 'Nice' should be reserved for mundane bullshit things like tea parties, perfectly pressed linen pants, and precisely arranged bouquets of flowers.

Genevieve doesn't acknowledge my news, too self-absorbed with her *nice* wedding details. I look toward my dad and he's giving me a stern, disapproving glance.

"Before you make any decisions, you should know that I had lunch with Juan Ramirez earlier this week. You remember Mr. Ramirez, don't you?"

How could I forget him? He's the family friend who always comes off a little too friendly. From the day I got boobs he's been salivating over my developing body.

"Well, Juan said they are hiring for an Associate Director position at the Museum of Contemporary Art. I told him about your studies and your time in Italy and he was quite impressed. Apparently, the job has your name on it. All you have to do is call and it's yours, no interview necessary. The position comes with quite a bit of notoriety and a healthy salary. Certainly more than what you'd make holed up in some tiny no name art gallery in New York."

Unbelievable!

I cough, nearly choking on my food. I cannot believe the audacity of my family. I've always known how backhanded and manipulative they can be, but this is reaching a whole different level. The depths my parents will go to try and control me truly know no bounds. The Museum of Contemporary Art is within walking distance to my parents' home on Astor Place and they would expect me to live here if I took the job. My father's childhood friend is Vice President on the board there so, of course, my parents would use their contacts to keep me leashed close to home.

"I'll give you his number after dinner. Just give him a call in the morning and firm everything up," he says as if I have no choice in the matter.

I slap my hands down on the table and stand up, outraged. "You're kidding, right? The one great thing in my life right now, the thing that I worked hard to achieve on my own without the Cotter family name, you're trying to take that away. I just ... I just cannot deal with you people right now." I throw my napkin onto my plate and turn on my heel. I need to get away from my family and just be happy with myself for once. I need to be in New York. This whole exchange only validates my desperation to get out of town.

Quickly, I grab my house keys and storm outside heading downtown on foot. I need to remove myself from their hold and just walk. Clear my mind and rid myself of my family's bad energy.

That exchange went about as well as I suspected: zero support and enthusiasm. Although, I definitely did *not* predict my dad playing the Museum of Contemporary Art card. Why can't they just be supportive of me for once in my life? I want to be in New York. I *need* to be there. There is nothing holding me to Chicago.

Except a small sliver of possibility named Phoenix.

I've never been anything like Genevieve. Why do they think they can just buy me off? Why can't they accept me for who I am? Would it really be *that* bad to have a daughter who works in a New York art gallery for a living? Shit, I am more cultured than all three of them combined. They should be kissing my ass at the doors I could open with connections in the industry I'll be making.

I'm walking down North Avenue to no place in particular, grappling at my options, when a firm hand grabs my arm and spins me around.

"Ivy! Why are you ignoring me?"

It's Matt. Of course it's Matt because God obviously has a sense of humor and really just wants to fuck with me today. I swallow a groan and pull my arm away from him.

"I've been trying to get your attention for two blocks. Are you okay?"

"I'm fine, Matt," I say curtly with a sigh. I really don't have the time or patience to deal with him right now. I silently remind myself that when your past calls you don't answer since it will have nothing new to say. "What do you want?"

He throws both of his hands up, feigning innocence. "Calm down, Ivy. I'm not stalking you or anything. I live just around the corner, next to the pet store. I saw you crossing the street back there and wanted to say hi. But when I noticed how out of it you looked, I got worried." He stuffs his hands shyly in his pockets. "I'm sorry. I didn't mean to piss you off."

I stop to look at him. His crooked smile is still charming, just no longer charming enough to get into my pants. The light in his eyes tells me he still cares, which really should not come as a surprise. I remind myself that I'm the one who stopped caring a long time ago. To be honest, I'm a bit surprised that he's even standing here talking to me considering I was the catalyst for his theatrical departure back in Madison. I've been nothing but a bitch to him for the past year. I hate that he goes out of his way to be nice. I'm not worthy of his kindness.

"Do you want to grab a drink? Some coffee, maybe?" he asks, shuffling his feet.

I want to ask him what he's playing at, but he seems genuinely interested in just catching up. My mind flashes to Phoenix and guilt sinks its vicious teeth into my neck. Even as an innocent offer, assuming that's what this is, it wouldn't feel right. Plus, I've hit my annual allotment for drama and nothing good could possibly come out of *just* coffee with Matt.

"Thanks, but I don't think that would be a good idea."

He bites his bottom lip and looks away. "Okay. Well, if you change your mind, you know how to get a hold of me."

I nod at the offer, even though there is no way in hell that will ever happen. "See you around, Matt." I turn back to the direction I was walking and slowly exhale, releasing tension I didn't realize I had been holding in my shoulders.

"Ivy?"

I turn back around to look at him. And, for the first time in all of the years I've known him, I *really* look at him. When you strip away the alcohol and the parties and his family's money, Matt isn't so bad. During this year apart, he seems to have gotten his shit together and has turned into a guy you can just sit down and talk with.

"You look different. Good … happy. Well, not in this moment, obviously. Just in general." He nods at the sight of me. My soul melts ever so slightly at his kind words and the reason behind them. "I'll talk to you later."

I reach into my back pocket to grab my phone to call Phoenix and erase this whole exchange from my mind, but there's nothing there. My phone is on my nightstand. Charging. *Damn it.*

I continue to aimlessly wander the streets, without concern for my safety, as thoughts about my future plague my soul. When I walk through the front door a few hours later, my dad is waiting up for me, whiskey neat in hand. He tilts his head slightly, inviting me into his office. I shouldn't feel awkward in here, but I do. I look at the rows of thick books that line his dusty shelves and see a small picture frame tucked into the side, hidden from view. It's an unusual sight as our family was never one for hanging photos throughout the house. I pick it up and find a faded picture of the two of us at Wrigley Field. I couldn't have been older than six with my sweaty pigtails and cotton candy smeared across my mouth.

"Ivy," he begins, "about earlier, I was only trying to be helpful. Your mother thought it would be a good idea."

Helpful. Right.

I place the frame back on the shelf and turn to him.

His eyes plead with mine. "I did not mean to make you upset. Honestly."

There is nothing else to do but nod. I'm not going to argue with him, but I refuse to let anyone make this decision for me. Even if this gesture of handing over a job I didn't earn on a silver platter came from a good place, I couldn't accept it.

"Sleep on it for a night or two," he says as he hands me Mr. Ramirez's business card with his cell number written on the back. "then give him a call and just hear him out."

I spin the card mindlessly through my fingers. The thought of working with such a skeezeball sends shudders down my spine. Surely my dad picked up on Mr. Ramirez's affinity for his daughters over the years?

"Please don't be angry with me," he says with a heavy sigh. "I just know how hard it can be to find a job after graduation. I thought you'd be relieved knowing you could get your start at such a reputable place like the MCA. You could really make a name for yourself there, Ivy."

The more he speaks, trying to justify his actions, the angrier I become.

I reach out and take my dad's lowball of whiskey from his hands. Never breaking eye contact with him, I throw back his drink in one swift gulp and relish in the burn as I feel it move through my body. I place the business card inside the now empty glass and slam it down on his desk.

Then I leave without saying a word.

THE NEXT MORNING, I DECIDE to lay low in my bedroom, desperate to avoid my family and their disapproving looks. I have no intention of calling Mr. Ramirez. My dad can fill him in, or leave him wondering for all I care.

I find myself mindlessly flipping through the TV stations looking for a distraction, and put down the remote when an image of Baby carrying watermelons with cousin Billy fills the screen. I love this movie. *Dirty Dancing* always makes me think of Rachel and the night we reenacted the Mickey and Silvia *Love is Strange* sequence in our living room after a few too many vodka tonics on a random Tuesday night. We laughed until our bellies ached. Then our bellies ached so much we both threw up. Ah, the memories.

I'll never understand why Patrick Swayze said "Nobody puts Baby in a corner" in the film. First of all, she was arguably in the best seat at the table since it faced the stage head on. Secondly, it's not like anyone forced her in that chair. Baby probably chose to sit there knowing her sister was about to make an ass of herself onstage and she wanted the best possible view so she could partake in a lifetime of mockery. Hell, if I knew Genevieve was about to partake in something ridiculous, you bet your ass I'd pay top dollar for the best seat in the house. And let's not even attempt to count the times that Baby willingly seats herself in a corner throughout the entire movie. The iconic line is so ridiculously flawed.

As the credits roll across the screen, I look at the clock and decide it's late enough in the morning to call Phoenix. I want to unload about my dad's job offer, but I don't want to give him any false hope about me staying local while he's up here. I decide to keep this news a secret for now.

I turn my TV off and grab my phone with a smile.

"Good morning, gorgeous!" Phoenix croons into the phone. He's in an awfully good mood today.

"Hey, you! How's it going?"

"Not too bad. What do you have going on today? Any absurd wedding duties to fulfill?"

"I'm excited to report that I have absolutely nothing planned. In fact, I may not even bother putting on pants."

"That's kind of hot, Ivy."

I grin, liking playful Phoenix.

"Yeah, well a day like today isn't worth putting on a bra, either, Mr. Wolfe," I reply, trying not to come off too much like a phone sex operator.

"So … what *are* you wearing?" he purrs seductively. I try hard not to laugh into the phone. He sounds absolutely adorable.

"Just a tank top and underwear," I say, my voice laced with hunger.

"Lucky tank top. Do you have any idea what you're doing to me right now?" The smile in his voice radiates through. "So really, what are your plans today?"

"Nothing, actually. I think I'm just going to lounge around and watch eighties movies." With any luck, Jake Ryan or Lloyd Dobler will show up at my house and save me from my family. Johnny Castle was a welcomed distraction already, though I found my mind drifting off to Phoenix and the memory of doing our own dirty dance throughout most of the film.

"Well … I've got an idea. But it would require you leaving the house and actually putting clothes on."

"I'm listening," I say, encouraging him to continue.

"Can you be ready in an hour? I need you to go somewhere for me."

What the heck? Am I running errands on his behalf like a personal secretary? Could he be more vague?

"Oookay?"

"Go get dressed. I'll text you the location in a minute. Do you think you can be there in an hour?"

I want to put up a fight and be lazy, but his boyish charm and excitement win out. "As long as it's not across town, sure."

"Perfect. I don't think it's very far from you. I'll call you in an hour."

I'm intrigued by the prospect of this mystery location and what's in store for me today. Wouldn't it be amazing if he were there waiting for me? I quickly shut down that thought, knowing he needs to be in St. Louis this week to complete his plans for the prospective client.

By the time I'm done pulling my hair up into a loose ponytail and changing into my favorite yoga pants and a well-loved, Depeche Mode shirt, my phone chimes, notifying me that I have a text message.

Rather than sending me an address, Phoenix has texted me directions to follow to my destination. I instantly recognize the place he's referencing as it is walking distance from my parent's house. Tossing on a baseball cap, I grab my keys and my phone and head out the door toward Lake Michigan.

It is truly a magnificent day. It makes me wonder why I'm so content spending so much time inside. The sidewalks are crowded with families enjoying the sunshine as cyclists and runners weave in and out of the crowds. I follow the lakefront running trail south toward Castaways, a beachfront bar and grill designed to look like a beached cruise ship. On beautiful days, like today, it turns into a meat market for all of the local trixies.

His directions take me right along the lake to a remote section of land that juts out from the main shoreline on the backside of the restaurant. For being so out in the open, it sure is secluded.

I check the time and sit down on the ground, listening to the sounds of the waves and distant laughter while I wait for Phoenix to call. I extend my arm and take a quick photo of myself with the lake in the background and send it off to Phoenix so he knows I'm here.

Minutes later, "Everlong" fills the air and my heart skips a beat. I quickly answer.

"This spot is beautiful!" I melt into the phone. I'm thankful that no one is around because I am certain I sound like an overeager goofball.

"It looks like you found the place easily. I'm glad you got there," he says, the smile in his voice evident.

I look out over Lake Michigan and watch a sailboat, full mast, dipping with the waves in the wind. It reminds me of Monet's *Sailboat* series and the serenity it brings. I want to reach out and place this image, this moment in a frame.

"So why on Earth did you have me come here?"

"Do you remember what you told me the night we first met?"

We talked about a lot of things that night. I rake through my mind and don't recall mentioning Lake Michigan at all.

"No, but in fairness we talked about a lot of things and there was a good amount of alcohol involved. So while some things are foggy, I definitely remember meeting one of the hottest, sweetest guys I've ever known." I bite my lip, figuring a little flattery will do him some good.

"Well, the night we first met, you told me that the Gateway Arch is your favorite place to be in St. Louis. So that's where I'm calling you from. And right now, you're sitting in my absolute favorite place in all of Chicago. So rather than call each other from the confines of our own homes, I thought this afternoon we could share our favorite places with each other while we talk."

My heart sighs in delight. This boy. He does things to me I never imagined possible. He makes me feel emotions that I've fought to shut out for years. It's almost too much.

I'm rendered speechless as I listen to him softly breathing into the phone, his breaths falling into the pace of the soft lake waves. It's calming and rhythmic. A soft smile plays at my lips as I realize that this moment by myself, with him on the line, is the epitome of perfection. Or about as close as perfection can get without him physically here with me.

"Thank you," I finally muster in a whisper at his

thoughtful gesture. Even though we're hundreds of miles apart, he has found a way to connect us on a deeper level. I have no idea what I've done to be deserving of such a wonderful man, but I want to claim him as mine.

"The landing today is stunningly beautiful, Ivy. I can't believe I've never actually been down here before. It's not nearly as touristy as I thought it would be, although you couldn't pay me to go up in that thing," he says, suppressing a nervous laugh. I would never have guessed he was afraid of heights.

"The arch towers to insurmountable heights and there is a blinding reflection at the top where the steel begins to curve back down toward the Earth…"

I close my eyes and listen to him describe his surroundings to me in great detail, my imagination becoming his canvas. I can feel the height of the arch above me, soaring up and over and down. I can see the family attempting to fly the kite on the windless day, with little success. And I can almost smell the flowering bushes along the path in the park at the foot of the arch. But when he tells me about the elderly couple sitting hand in hand on a nearby bench, I smile. And I can hear the smile in his voice too.

"They have to be eighty years young," he says. "And after all this time they are still so in love."

I smile thinking back to Delilah's bench in Madison and I suddenly feel overwhelmed with emotion. We both release a quiet sigh at the same time.

We're fortunate to be sharing the same blazing sun, with nary a cloud in the sky. I imagine Phoenix sitting in the shade of a large oak tree, shoes off, digging his feet in the soft, damp grass. What I would give to be sitting there beside him.

"Tell me about the lake. What do you see?" he asks.

I look out across the lake and admire its vast beauty. It's hard to believe that living here for two decades I've never come out to these break walls. It's so close to my parents' home and such a welcomed escape. As I look into the green waters, I suddenly feel as if I am in a gallery, looking at a painting. Not examining it objectively, but focusing on how this moment, like artwork, makes me feel.

Sitting here on the edge of the city, it's like I'm sitting on the edge of the Earth with my feet dangling off the side. I feel small and insignificant. Not in a bad way, though.

I notice that no matter what, the water always returns with each and every delicate wave. Even after being repeatedly pushed away from the shoreline, the water always comes back, beating its rocky edges, smoothing them out, wearing them down over time. It's kind of romantic—after an infinite number of rejections, the water doesn't give up. Nature wills it to return. Beyond its control, it just keeps coming back. It's a bit like love.

My eyes focus on a small stone a few feet away from me. I crawl over and reach out to pick it up, feeling the smoothness of its sides between my fingers. While on my hands and knees, I catch a glimpse of myself in the water's surface. I look completely different, happy even.

"I … I see the work of persistence. Forces beyond our control breaking down the sharp edges, making the hard lines soft."

I realize this wasn't the response he was anticipating, and that he has no idea that I'm holding the result of innumerable years of work by Mother Nature in my hand. That I'm looking at myself in an entirely different light due to the intangible work of Cupid's arrow. My eyes examine the stone more closely and I can't help but realize how perfectly insignificant it is, how insignificant I am.

How can something so incomprehensibly great have such a profound impact on something so insignificant?

We both fall silent and our breathing falls into pace with one another.

It amazes me that this spot exists right in the heart of the downtown bustle. It's so calming and peaceful and humbling. It's not a place that you would think to come to either and it makes me wonder how Phoenix stumbled upon it.

"How did you discover this place? I grew up less than a mile from here and never once followed this path out this way." I close my eyes and lie down against a large rock, listening to the waves gently lap up against the break wall and feel the cool air slowly warm as the sun spills over the horizon.

"It had to have been three or four years ago. I was in Chicago for the weekend with …Annie, my girlfriend at the time." There is an uneasiness to his voice when he mentions her name, and I realize this is the first time since our date in Madison that he's talking about his past. "I was training for a marathon and—"

"Wait, what? You run marathons?" This comes as a surprise. I know he frequently runs, but it seems a bit silly to run a stupidly far distance for fun. Maybe he *is* insane.

He softly laughs. "No, I don't run marathons, Ivy. I was training to run the Chicago Marathon, but ended up getting injured during a long run and never made it to the starting line."

"Oh. I'm sorry." I don't know why I'm apologizing, but I imagine having a lofty goal and falling short is nothing short of frustrating. Or heartbreaking. Both, really.

"Anyway, I was out one morning for a long run along the lakefront path. The sun was just coming up over the horizon and the sky was simply electric. It was my first and only time I have ever witnessed a sunrise. And it was breathtakingly beautiful—a kaleidoscope of blinding light in shades of gold, fiery orange, and magenta. It was unlike anything I had ever seen before. It was also the moment I decided to break up with Annie.

"That sunrise was so exquisite it begged to be shared with someone. But I didn't want her to know about it. She just wouldn't have appreciated it. So I kept it a secret. It wasn't worthy of being shared with her. A lot of moments weren't worthy of being shared with her, but I was too blind and too comfortable to do anything about it. It took some time, but I finally realized during that run that staying with Annie for as long as I did meant I was sitting idly and not spending time with my soul mate. Sitting on the curve of that breaking wall, I realized that by staying with her I was doing a disservice not only to myself, but also with the woman I was meant to be with and share sunrises with…" His voice trails off in a reflective moment before he adds, "you."

The gravity of his words hit me like a freight train, fast and overwhelmingly powerful. Our connection is unmatched. I never imagined anyone could genuinely feel this way about me. Heck, I never imagined I could genuinely feel this way about anyone else. Or genuinely feel, period.

I have no words for him. Just feelings. And I know we need to talk about the implications of what he just confessed, but I don't know where to even begin. Even at this distance, even with only knowing him for such a short period of time, my heart is tethered to his. He believes he's meant to be with me, and I want to believe that he is right. I want to believe that this emotion we share is strong enough to overcome the odds. That together we can prove that distance is no match for us.

That sometimes people are just meant to be together.

THE REST OF THE WEEK passes in a blur as I'm kept busy helping Genevieve complete all of the final wedding preparations. And by helping I really mean doing her bitch work. It is exhausting. I address envelopes for her thank you cards from her bridal shower. We go to Bloomingdale's four times to add more items to their wedding registry. And we even have her makeup trial done three times, because we left the first two appointments wearing the wrong shade of champagne eye shadow. In case you are wondering, champagne comes in thirty billion shades.

If I ever get married, I'm just going to elope because all of this fanfare doesn't matter in the grand scheme of things. Genevieve is so focused on her wedding day that she's forgetting it's the years that come after that are the most important.

It's nearing midnight and Phoenix hasn't seemed himself all night. He wasn't playful in his texts throughout the day and now there is a sadness looming in his voice that I just can't decipher. My mind grazes over the past hour, thinking back to anything I might have said that could have rubbed him the wrong way. I felt like I've carried most of the conversation, and on the whole tonight's call has felt a bit … strained.

Maybe he's pulling away from me because he knows that there is no way for us to be together. An 'us' is simply not in the cards given our very different futures and the physical distance between us. I wouldn't blame him. It's already going to be so hard to end whatever this is that we have when the time comes.

"Are you sure you're okay, Phoenix? You just seem so sad tonight," I ask with a frown. I don't want to push him to talk, but something is clearly weighing on his mind and it's going to chew at my insides until I know what it is. When he hurts, I hurt.

The whoosh of his lungs as he exhales is startling. "No, I'm not okay. I'm not sure what I am right now."

Shit. This is it. This is the part where he tells me we can't be together. But truthfully, I'm so thankful for the little time we shared. I no longer believe in coincidence. Rather, I believe in my instinct. Trusting myself to follow what I'm drawn to. I have faith that my intuition will not steer me in the wrong direction, but instead, guide me to the exact place I need to be at just the right moment in time. I refuse to regret opening myself up to him, and I brace myself for the blow that inevitably is going to come as I wait for him to continue.

"I got a voicemail from my Uncle Tom while I was in the shower this morning."

And exhale.

That's certainly not what I was expecting. And Uncle Tom? That's not a name I've heard before. Then again, he's never really talked about his family. From what I've gathered, his father is estranged and he's an only child, which really leaves him with no one of importance in his life. *Except for maybe me.* I nervously chew on the tip of my thumb and listen intently.

"That's my dad's brother," he says with a heavy sigh. "He called … he called to tell me that my dad is sick."

Oh, no. Even through their relationship is strained, I can't begin to imagine how much this must hurt. Now, more than ever, I want to crawl through the phone and into his lap. I want to be able to reach out and comfort him. Damn this distance.

"Oh my gosh. I'm so sorry, Phoenix." There are no apologies I can offer to help ease his weary mind, but that doesn't stop me from trying. "Have you tried calling him?" I ask, my voice thick with sincerity.

"My dad? No," he says sharply, and in the silence on the line, I swear I hear him whisper, "*I'm scared.*"

"I did call my uncle back though…" His voice trails off and I hope the silence will encourage him to open up. "He has an aggressive case of non-Hodgkin lymphoma," he continues after a few minutes of silence. "It sounds like they didn't catch it early enough, so even with treatment his prognosis isn't good."

I feel the air get sucked from my lungs and my heart physically aches for him.

"I've spent the past few weeks avoiding phone calls from my dad," he confesses. "He has reached out at least once a day since the end of April. I've sent each and every one of those phone calls to voicemail and never once checked his messages."

"Maybe you should call him back?" I suggest gently. "I'm sure he would find comfort in talking to his only son."

143

"No! I'm far too angry," he clips. His voice is steel and I know there is no changing his mind. At least not today. "I just thought I would feel different. I've always thought that he was the one who should have died. He should have been in that car wreck, not my mom. So, in a way, this disease is just karmic retribution. But now ... him dying isn't going to bring my mom back. It's just going to make me an adult orphan. And it pisses me off."

He doesn't have to explain himself—I know exactly what he means. The notion of bad shit happening to good people is something I've grappled with most of my life. So when bad shit happens to bad people, you expect it to feel much more satisfying. Except it never does.

"I'm sorry that I'm being such a downer."

"No, you're not being a downer. You're just sorting through it all." I bring my knees up to my chest and wrap my free arm around them, hugging myself tightly. "I wish I were there with you."

"Me too," he says with a sigh. "But I get to see you in what, three weeks?"

"Less than three." I'm half tempted to skip Genevieve's bachelorette party this weekend and head to St. Louis to be with him. He sounds like he could really use a friend right now.

No.

Actually, I'd like to believe that he could really use *me*.

"I can't wait. There have been a few times I've wanted to just jump in my car and drive up there to see you," he confesses.

My heart feels lighter at the thought of him dropping everything to road trip it to Chicago for a visit.

"Well, you know what they say, good things come to those who wait, but great things come to those who are patient." Though my patience is wearing thin these days.

I much prefer instant gratification, and I would do anything to make time move faster so we could be together again, but I know the wait will be worth it.

Jesus Christ on a cracker, I sound like a walking ad against premarital sex.

"Can I make a suggestion?" I ask.

"Sure, Ivy," he says with a sigh.

I take a deep breath, knowing that I am about to overstep an unspoken line and probably tick him off.

"Reconsider calling him. I know things between you two are strained, but I don't think they are irreparable. When your mom died, he lost two of the most important people in his life. And he's been trying to reconnect with you. That has to count for something," I suggest softly.

The only sound I hear is that of his thoughts processing my words. Nothing. At least I hope that's what he's doing and not reveling in the calm before the shit storm. My heart races in anticipation when he finally begins to speak again.

"I can't promise you that I'll call him. But I can promise that I will at least think about it … for you."

"Thank you," I whisper into the phone. I know that I'm totally the wrong reason for him to see it through, but I want him to want to call his dad, so I'll take whatever he is willing to offer. "Try and get some sleep tonight. Okay?"

"I will."

"Sweet dreams, Phoenix."

"Only if I'm dreaming of you, Ivy."

THE NEXT DAY MY OFFER letter from Gallery 545 arrives, at least I think it arrived earlier that day. My parents left it on the console table in the foyer in a stack of junk mail and never said a word about it to me, so for all I know it could have been sitting here all week.

They simply are the epitome of thoughtfulness.

I sit down on the stairs and rip it open in lackluster fashion. Don't get me wrong, I'm truly excited for the opportunity, but as I scan the words on the pages I'm unable to process anything it says. My mind is too absorbed with the pain that Phoenix is deflecting. My soul aches to comfort him.

Estranged or not, his father and his uncle are Phoenix's only living relatives. And I know on some level it will be painful to lose him. Even through hate, we still find comfort knowing someone is there just in case we ever need them. I just hope that Phoenix is able to push his pride aside and pick up the phone to connect with him before it's too late.

When the front door slams abruptly, I nearly jump out of my skin.

"What?" Genevieve barks at me, her arms overflowing with Louis Vuitton, Neiman Marcus, and Barney's shopping bags. "Don't just stand there, Ivy." My name is sour off her tongue and she rolls her eyes in disgust. "Help me carry my stuff upstairs."

I look at her briefly before returning my eyes to the paper that details my future. Sighing, I fold it a few times before stuffing it in my pocket and reach out to take part of Genevieve's load. The offer isn't going anywhere and I am certainly not in the right mindset to dive into my New York plans just yet, especially when part of me yearns to stay here knowing that Phoenix is coming for several weeks.

"What is all this stuff?" I ask, not really wanting to know the answer.

"Most of these are clothes for my honeymoon. CJ and I are headed to the Intercontinental resort in Bora Bora for a week before chartering a yacht to Tahiti the second week."

"Oh, that'll be nice," I say, feigning excitement for her. Mostly, I think I'm looking forward to her becoming someone else's problem day in and day out, though I doubt she'll ever stop trying to boss me around.

"Yeah, it will be. Mom and Daddy are giving us our dream honeymoon as a wedding gift."

I struggle to keep my jaw shut though their grand gesture really shouldn't surprise me at all.

"So about this weekend," Genevieve begins, "I need you to get to the hotel early to set everything up for my bachelorette party. I've already taken care of just about everything since I know exactly how I want things. I just need you to actually step up and execute."

Read as I don't want to lift a finger and it will be much easier to just make you do my bitch work.

"Do you think you can handle that?" she snaps.

"Sure, Gen," I say with a sigh, dropping her shopping bags onto her overstuffed down comforter.

"I'm serious, Ivy. I'm trusting you to make this night perfect for me. If you don't think you can take care of it I need to know now. I can have one of the other bridesmaids do it or I can just get there early and do everything myself."

I barely hear her mumble *I probably will anyway* under her breath. Genevieve is being unnecessarily sharp, but we're only a week and a half away from her big day where she'll walk down the aisle and hopefully out of my life.

"I'll take care of it. You just relax," I tell her, pressing my lips into a tight, fake smile. I'm sure my feeble attempt to reassure her doesn't do much to ease her stress. I watch as she examines her face closely in the mirror, pulling her skin to study her pores.

"So what were you looking at on the stairs?" she asks, her eyes never leaving her reflection.

"Nothing, really. Just my offer letter from the gallery."

"Oh?" There is a surprise in her tone that rubs me the wrong way. "How much will you be making?"

Of course that's the *one* bit of information she's craving. What my pending salary has to do with her is beyond me. My income is of no concern to her. I could be making pennies an hour and that would be more than enough for me to uproot my life and leave my family behind.

"I, uh … I didn't get that far before you came home."

"I highly doubt you'll get paid much of anything. I mean, it's *just* art. It's not like you're curing cancer or something."

There's a pang in my chest at her comment as I'm reminded of Phoenix's father. I couldn't care less about her disregard for the fine arts, but her complete lack of tact is downright disgusting.

"You're right, Genevieve. It's *nothing* like curing cancer," I deadpan. I shake my head as I turn toward the door.

Pulling the letter out of my pocket, it is clearer than ever.

I have to get out of this hellhole.

"I WANTED TO LET YOU know that I plan on looking for work in New York after this project outside of Chicago wraps."

Wait. What?

We've been on the phone for more than two hours tonight, talking mostly about the stupid shit we did when we were younger, so his declaration completely catches me off guard.

"Does that scare you?" he asks softly. I swallow my uncertainty as his question echoes through my head. It makes me *something*, but not scared. I search for the words but find myself at a loss. "There is nothing keeping me here in St. Louis."

"First of all, that's not true," I quickly interject. My mind goes to his father, and however little time he has left. It pains me that he still hasn't spoken with him. I know his dad's condition is weighing on his mind, even if he refuses to admit it. I can hear it in his voice. As the only child, he should stay close and help him, no matter how strained their relationship may be. I think sensing that his father isn't all that bad is what softens my insides.

"Second of all, you can't move just for me," I lie. Secretly, I want him to move for me. I want him to want to move mountains to be with me, to bend his life to fit perfectly into mine. But that is something I could never ask of him. Especially since he only recently popped into my life.

I mean, who moves for someone they only recently met? For someone they've only shared one date with? That's just crazy.

Love makes you do crazy things, my subconscious nudges.

But love is suicide, my mind refutes, laying the foundation to build another wall and guard me from the inevitable pain that is coming. But love? I am most certainly *not* in love. I need to get a grasp on my life.

"I know it sounds crazy," he says, reading my mind, "but the thought of you being halfway across the country when I know you should be right here next to me makes me … well, it just makes me angry. It's not how things are supposed to be. This is so fucking unfair."

There is no disagreeing with his comment. Life is so stupidly unfair. These miles, these phone calls, these late night conversations are not how our relationship should be defined. For some reason, right now, it works for us, but we both know it can't work like this forever. One of us is going to have to throw away our life plans and dare, or we will have to be apart in every sense of the word.

I pale at that thought.

There is another option, though. My father's offer nudges my mind. Sure, it's not my dream job, but I could *probably* be happy at the Museum of Contemporary Art. I could learn to enjoy life in a museum rather than my dream of working in a prestigious gallery.

No doubt my father would hold things over my head indefinitely if I stayed in Chicago. And if things didn't work out between us, my family would never let me live it down.

But is it selfish to leave and run down my dreams? Or is it more selfish to take the job here so I can have Phoenix close to me?

I still can't bring myself to tell Phoenix about the offer. I couldn't bear the aftermath if he ever actually expected me to take it so we could be in the same place. While deep down I know I could never take it, I can't bring myself to completely discard the opportunity just yet.

Phoenix shakes me from my wandering mind. "I just want to be with you any way that I can. If that means that you're mine with two thousand miles of land between us, then so be it. I am willing to walk those two thousand miles barefoot just to see you."

A soft laugh escapes my lips. "Uphill both ways?"

"And in the snow." He pauses thoughtfully for a moment. "I know it's not fair to ask the same of you, and I never would, but I have never been so sure about anything or anyone in my entire life. And I'm certain that you feel it too."

The beating of my heart simply stops.

Our whole relationship is comfortably terrifying. Having grown so close to him over the past month, I'm absolutely sure of my feelings, but that little nagging voice deep down says that this is all too good to be true.

Damn it! Sometimes I wish I could just turn off my brain.

"You realize in a little over two weeks I get to hold

you in my arms again?" I can hear the smile in his voice.

A soft moan passes my lips as my soul is soothed at the thought. I lick my lips, remembering how sweet he tasted. The next few weeks cannot pass by fast enough. I wish my life were a DVR machine so I could fast forward through all this mundane bullshit and get focus on the feature presentation.

"While I'm in town, I'm going to take you out on a real date. Wine and dine you like you deserve. Anywhere you want to go, we'll go there. I don't care where it is, as long as I have you on my arm. But Ivy, we've talked so much the past few weeks, I honestly don't know how much talking I can do face to face with you. So be ready because I plan on kissing the fucking shit out of you on every last inch of your perfectly soft skin. I need to explore each and every tender curve of your body. The inside of your body will be jealous of the outside," he says slowly, seductively.

Fuck. I realize I'm panting at his words. If I have anything to do with it, the outside of my body will be jealous of my insides because that is exactly where he is meant to be.

"I want to be with you in every sense of the word. I want to take my time with you. I want you to beg me, possess me. I want you in my hotel room and I don't want to see the light of day until the entire building knows my name."

My mouth goes dry and my fingers twitch at his words. Desire courses my veins and I need to reel in the pooling heat before I turn into a phone sex operator. God, the things I would do to him if he were right here next to me. I would ravage him ten ways to Sunday. The blissful thought of being thoroughly fucked heats me from the inside out.

"Ivy…" The way he exhales my name practically brings me to my knees here on my bedroom floor. "I need to be with you more than I need to breathe."

When I close my eyes, I can almost feel him sitting here beside me, whispering his wishes and promises softly in my ear. A pleasurable shiver races down my spine and I take a deep breath. I *do* feel it. This feeling is impossible to ignore as it wraps itself around myself and holds on for dear life. I never want to feel it go. My heart aches for his touch. My body thirsts for his skin on mine. There are so many things that I want to do with this man … to this man. I can't simply tell him how I feel about him. I need to show him with my body what I'm incapable of putting into words.

"I'm yours," I breathe into the phone. "My body, my soul … it's nothing without you. Every last piece of me is yours for the taking."

I say the words without thinking, knowing that it's true. My desire to be with him in every sense of the word wins out over logic. It doesn't make sense to be with him, given our circumstances. My head relentlessly reminds me that distance is simply too great. But when your heart and instinct team up to scream at you, you had better just shut up and listen.

One week until the wedding

WELL, THE GOOD NEWS IS Genevieve was right—I didn't have to plan one lick of her bachelorette party. The bad news is that the stupid party is tonight—well, more like all day, tonight and tomorrow morning, and I don't feel like spending my time with Gen and her single-minded minions. My body is still exhausted from staying up until five in the morning chatting with Phoenix.

I arrive at the Four Seasons just off of Michigan Avenue in the early afternoon to get everything set up. Awaiting my arrival is a case of the finest pink champagne already chilled, fresh flowers for our suite, gourmet chocolates at ten bucks an ounce that no one will eat, and the boxes of decorations and gifts that Genevieve had delivered ahead of time.

Our room for the evening is completely and utterly ridiculous. Of course, she reserved the most magnificent suite the hotel had to offer, the very same room that rock royalty stay in when they have a tour stop in the Windy

City. It's outfitted in sleek monochromatic tones with polished dark silver crown moulding and a grand chandelier casts rainbows across the floor and walls. It's ornate and ostentatious, and even though it shouldn't, it makes me highly uncomfortable.

Pushing those feelings aside, I quickly unload the boxes and stack the gifts on top of the baby grand piano in the center of the room. Genevieve has pulled out all the stops for tonight. Each of the fifteen party guests will receive a ballerina pink Kashwere bathrobe with their monogram stitched in silver. I adjust the white satin ribbon on each bundle of fabric, tying each bow to perfection. These are just the start of Genevieve's grandiose gesture, thanking everyone for celebrating her special night as a nearly married woman in an alcohol-induced haze.

A beauty day at the ritziest spa in the city is just the prelude to a drunken night. I call down to the spa and confirm that the nail technicians and massage therapists are primed and ready for our arrival in two hours.

I hang a sparkly banner that reads "Cheers, Bitches!" in the archway leading into the main living space. I want to ask why I'm making such a fuss over everything, but if I'm being entirely honest, it's because some tiny, miniscule part of me does care. Even though Genevieve drives me bat shit crazy and I have zero tolerance for her drama, she's still my sister. While I don't particularly like Genevieve the vast majority of the time, I do love her. *Kind of.* She wasn't always so bad. We used to be best friends back in the day when things were B.G.—before Glen. I have a tiny flicker of hope that maybe someday we can capture that again, but I don't hold my breath.

After the confetti sparkles on the table and the sweet

scent of flowers fill the air, everything seems to be in order for the grand event. I grab my cell phone and settle into the couch to wait for the guest of honor to arrive and approve of my setup work.

A smile plays at my lips while I scroll to Phoenix's name and hit the call button. Just the sheer thought of this boy makes me feel all giddy inside. The sensation never gets old.

The phone rings twice before going to voicemail. I hang up abruptly, unsure of what to say on the message. That's odd, but I'm sure he's just busy. I call back a few moments later, prepared to leave a message to let him know I'm thinking about him and that I'm counting down the days until I see him … eight to be exact. This time my call is answered after the first ring.

"Hey, handsome!" I flirt into the phone.

"Oh, Ivy. Hey there." There is a hint of surprise in Phoenix's voice.

"Did I catch you at a bad time?" I have to fight the stupid smile off of my face. Every time we talk it makes me feel incredibly girly deep inside. I can't believe I'm turning into *that* kind of girl. I sort of adore him for it.

"No, you're all right. I just, uh, I have some friends over." I hear him pull a door shut for privacy.

"Oh. Well, tell Sully and whoever else is there I say hi."

"Yeah, sure. I will." His clipping tone catches me off guard and I feel like I've interrupted something important.

"Well, I won't keep you long. I just wanted to let you know that I'm thinking about you. And I can't wait to see you soon." I bite my lower lip, deep in thought of all the delicious and inappropriate things I want to do to him.

God, I hope I don't sound overeager and desperate.

"I know. Next weekend can't get here soon enough."

I smile. It is so good to hear his voice and know that he's on the same page as me.

In the background I hear a female. I can't make out what she says, but he quickly muffles the phone so his response is warbled. My stomach hits the floor and every nagging demon and insecurity I've been fighting to ignore the past few weeks rears their ugly head.

"Who-who's that?" I have to ask even though I don't want to know the answer to my question. Deep down, I know the real answer will crush my soul.

"No one," he hesitates. "Just my friend Hailey."

I think back through the dozens of conversations and texts we've shared, and this is the first he's ever mentioned of a Hailey. He's obviously never mentioned her because he doesn't want me to know about her. And I just interrupted something.

Fuck.

"Hailey?" My voice cracks as her name leaves a bitter taste on my tongue.

"Yeah…" He lingers just a beat too long in silence. "I, uh, need to get going, Ivy. Have fun tonight, okay?"

"Wait, Phoenix…"

"Yeah?"

I want to ask him about her, put my paranoia to rest. But instead, I sigh softly, feeling my heart sulk and start to crumble in a dark corner of my soul.

"Never mind. I'll talk to you later."

I end the call without giving him a chance to respond. The monsters in my head viciously taunt me. What goes around, comes around, Ivy. This is the universe paying you back for what you did to Genevieve all those years ago.

An internal war wages and logic tells me I'm simply jumping to conclusions because of the distance between us. I have to be. My past has no bearing on his present.

I *must* be reading into things. I *am* reading into things. Fuck.

I can't possibly be reading into things.

I choke back the tears to avoid ruining my mascara and my eyes focus in on the bottle of Gosset Grand Rose on ice in the corner. I quickly rip off the foil, pop the cork, bring my lips to the rim, and chug.

A PAIR OF GENEVIEVE'S SORORITY sisters are the first to arrive. They find me dry and fully clothed, lounging in the oversized bathtub, feet dangling over the side of the porcelain rim, and near-empty bottle in hand.

"Woah," the red-haired girl drawls, looking at me bug-eyed. Her animated expression and subtle gap between her two front teeth remind me of Pippi Longstocking, minus the braids. "Are you okay, honey?" Her southern accent is as soothing as a hot mug of chamomile tea on a snowy afternoon.

As I sit up, the fizziness warming my chest shoots straight to my head. "S'alllllll good!"

The no-name blonde in tow with Pippi rolls her eyes. "Clean this up, will you? The others should be arriving soon." She shakes her head and returns back to the living room of the suite.

Pippi puckers her lips in thought. "You're the sister. Ivy, right?"

"Yep," I state, popping the p. It's hard not to wonder what terrible things Genevieve has told her friends about me. I'm certain I cannot make it through this evening with Little Miss Hailey running rampant in my mind while being judged by my sister's friends for someone I once was.

Ugh. Hailey. The name lingers on my tongue like spoiled milk. With a name like that she probably came into his life bare-breasted and riding on a unicorn that shits rainbows. She's probably lying naked underneath him right now. She's probably perfect.

And beautiful.

And easy.

And everything I am not.

Except for easy. No use in denying that now.

Fucking asshole. Why did I even bother? I knew all along it would end in disaster and I'd get hurt. I just thought it would take longer to get to that point.

New York cannot get here fast enough.

"I'm Mimi. Can I get you anything? A nap? Some water, perhaps?" Ah, Pippi has a name! *Mimi.* It's just as trite. I'm sure it's short for something … Amelia or Mariah or something equally irritating. Pippi is a much better fit for this chick.

Her perfectly plucked eyebrow arches up at me, but I can see the amusement in her eyes. She isn't judging me at all. She finds me funny. A welcomed change from the rest of the world.

What do I need? Other than a fork to stab Phoenix's eye out for making me feel and then hurting me like this?

Breakfast food. I need breakfast food.

"Waffffffles!" I practically sing my request before the hiccups take over. Mimi's giggles sound like wind chimes.

It's delightful and I can't help but smile.

"You are certainly nothing like your sister."

Thank goodness for that.

"Okay. Let's get you up and outta this tub. You should really try to sober up before the bride gets here. Genevieve will blow a gasket if she sees you like this."

She's right about that. Genevieve would shit bricks knowing that I drank her bubbly before she ever arrived. *Thunder stealer*, she'd likely call me. And tonight of all nights it's the Genevieve show, starring, produced, and directed by Genevieve Cotter with her name strung up in lights. No, really … it is. Her name is lit up on a welcome sign downstairs in the lobby. Everyone with us tonight is just an inconsequential extra in the performance.

Mimi tugs at my arms, pulling me to my feet, and I step out over the rim of the bathtub, but my legs give out from under me and I find my cheek kissing the hard, cool marble floor as I stare at the intricate scrolling on the over-sized claw foot tub.

I flop onto my back and laughter boils over. Mimi can't help but join in finding hilarity in my clumsiness. Eventually, I manage to sit myself up straight and rest the back of my head against the ledge of the bathtub.

"What's the matter, darlin'?" Mimi fills a cup of water from the bathroom sink and sits down next to me on the floor. She offers a warm smile like an open invitation but doesn't press me for details. I really don't want to talk about it, especially with someone I just met. Plus, this isn't exactly my finest moment.

"Guys suck." I exhale in a huff.

And they do. Why is it that they always seem to have a hidden agenda and secrets? Damn them all! I thought I had found a good one. All of his sweet acts of kindness are meaningless. Null and void. And now he's somewhere out there gallivanting with some trixie whore named Hailey.

"Oh, honey! I know they do." Mimi passes me the water and I down it in one large gulp. She reaches out and smooths a few strands of hair behind me ear. Her touch is comforting. And even though I only met her a few minutes ago, it feels as if we've been lifelong friends. But that could just be the champagne talking.

"I don't want to talk about him."

If I talk about him, I'm going to spiral into even more of a wreck than I am right now. But if I don't talk about him, it'll eat at my insides and *then* I'll spiral into even more of a wreck. It's a no-win situation. I'll be far better off cutting my losses and moving on before I allow myself to actually feel something serious for a guy I've known all of five minutes.

Stop lying to yourself, Ivy. You already do feel something for him. Damn my nagging conscience.

Mimi offers a knowing nod and we sit there in silence. The buzz from the champagne is heavy and I feel as if my limbs are light.

My mind wanders to my sister and this ridiculous wedding. How the hell did *she* manage to find a guy? Her personality is as sweet as acid. Genevieve is *so* not deserving of love. She is a horrible person. My parents are horrible people. Nearly everyone in my life is horrible. And just when I think I find a nice guy, he turns out to be horrible too.

After a few minutes, Mimi begins to speak. "You know, all of us are shocked that Genevieve is the first to get married. I've always felt her relationship with CJ was synthetic. Hell, even her friendships feel forced. Amy had to practically drag me here today."

She'd read my mind.

I offer her a consoling smile. "You should try living with her."

Mimi scoffs. "I did. We roomed together for a semester at Chi Rho Gamma. Her nose was so high in the air I thought she would drown in a rainstorm. Her sense of self-entitlement was just unbelievable. Let's just say it was short-lived and I moved out at the end of the fall semester. I like to claim artistic differences."

"Mm-hmm." I know exactly what she means. Genevieve has never been easy to be around. Her self-centeredness knows no bounds and she always found a way to play the victim. Although I assumed this was a side she reserved just for me and not her friends. Interesting that her friends have experienced this firsthand. She can be such a manipulative bitch.

"Why don't we get you lying down? You can sleep off the heartache and the booze. I won't tell Genevieve you kicked back one of the bottles by yourself and I'll make sure Amy keeps her trap shut."

Mimi pulls me to my feet again and leads me into the bedroom, tucking me under the overstuffed comforter gingerly. The last thing I remember is a blur of a fiery red hair closing the door before darkness took over.

I WAKE FROM MY NAP about two hours later with a splitting headache and a quiet suite. Mimi left a note on the nightstand letting me know that everyone was headed down to the spa for some much needed pampering and that she'd told Genevieve I'd eaten some bad maki rolls for lunch and wasn't feeling well. I roll over to grab my phone off the nightstand and the urge to call Phoenix and give him a piece of my mind creeps into consideration. Instead, I force myself to put my phone away and make myself presentable for the afternoon's festivities.

The living room is filled with gifts and the overnight bags of all of Genevieve's alleged close friends. If they share the same attitude as Mimi, I can't help but wonder if my sister ever feels truly lonely. Or truly loved. Or if she has any clue how much she is despised. Probably not, but I doubt she'd care much if she did know.

I quietly sneak into the spa, hoping to avoid a scene with Genevieve. Mimi spies my entrance from the end of the pedicure chairs and nods me over. I take a seat on the stool next to her chair.

"How are you feeling?"

"Slight headache and I think I may still be a little tipsy, but much better overall. Thanks again for helping me out earlier."

"No problem, darlin'." Her twang strangely makes me happy. "I know a broken heart when I see one."

"So how pissed is she?"

"She seemed fine. Not really concerned that you were *ill*, but certainly not angry. Maybe she wanted to avoid a scene? Anyway, she's getting her massage right now, so I bet she'll be pretty mellow."

I hope that Mimi is right. There is always a risk for whiplash with Genevieve's mood swings and I definitely don't want to deal with any of her potential extremes that could come out to play. The pedicure chair next to Mimi opens up and I hop onto it, slipping off my kitten heels.

By the time the nail technician applies a second coat of charcoal grey polish to my toes, Genevieve emerges from a massage suite all-aglow, looking blissfully relaxed. She kindly accepts the lemon water from her massage therapist before spotting me across the room.

"Oh, Ivy!" she exclaims, rushing to my side. "I heard you ate some bad sushi. Are you feeling better now?" I lean over the side of the chair as she pulls me tightly into a hug.

This is a surprise. Clearly she's putting on a show for her so-called friends. Her fakeness knows no bounds. Thank goodness there's still a bit of alcohol in my system or else this moment would be even more painfully awkward.

"Yes, I'm feeling quite a bit better. Thanks, Gen." I give her a timid smile before she flits back to some of her other sorority sisters. On the other side of the room, Mimi bites back a giggle and shakes her head in disbelief.

"Genevieve makes it seem like you two have been best friends your entire lives. I don't know how you put up with that nonsense," she says once Genevieve is out of earshot. I'm appreciative of Mimi's sympathies.

For as long as I can remember, Genevieve has always been two sides of the same coin. You never know who you're going to get on any given day, but it usually depends on who surrounds her. Fortunately for me, her friends are providing a cushion so she is sweet as strawberry pie that is secretly laced with arsenic. Had she walked into the hotel room instead of Mimi and Amy, we would all be dealing with a raging bitch right now.

Upon returning to the grand suite, everyone frantically begins to get ready for the night. The bride-to-be has informed everyone to dress in black with bright pink high-lights to coordinate with her official wedding colors. I've decided to pair my favorite fitted black jeans with a black leather corset top. I feel hot. And confident. But there is simply not enough makeup in the world to disguise my broken heart.

"Screw Phoenix," I whisper to my reflection as I finish applying my mascara.

Oh, how I wish I could.

Genevieve stands out from our crowd—she is wearing a shockingly short white mini dress that barely covers the good china. And based on everyone else's attire, I'm apparently the only one who believes your vagina should not be longer than your skirt. Hopefully Genevieve has no reason to bend over tonight or else everyone is in for a free show. Fortunately for all, there is not one sash or light-up neon penis in sight. Apparently the unspoken theme for our group is classy sluts as we look like a pack of high-end escorts.

Our gaggle of girls heads out toward the Viagra Triangle, a prominent area downtown on Rush Street. The stretch gets its name for the older, wealthy men who come to flash their worth to younger trixies like ourselves. It doesn't matter if they're married or not; these men aren't looking for anything serious, just a quick lay, and the girls are just looking for attention. It's an easy match for everyone involved.

After dinner at one of the most touted Italian joints in the city, we stumble down a dimly lit alley to a door hidden from view just off of the main strip. A built man sporting a sleek black suit and earpiece stands behind a plum velvet rope. As we approach, Genevieve begins to dance her way down the alley like it's her own personal catwalk. The man says something into the lapel of his jacket and steps aside, allowing us access to what appears to be one of the most exclusive hot spots in all of the city.

"Welcome to Nuit Noir, ladies."

The lights dimly glow a striking electric blue and the DJ, perched on a stage behind the bar, is blaring a loud techno re-mix of a Yelle song I heard all the time in Italy. Oversized concrete posts line the perimeter of the room. I imagine that the space may resemble something more along the lines of a bomb shelter than a dance club when the house lights are on. Long strips of plum fabric billow from the ceiling, softening the harsh, cold feeling from the cement.

Most of the tables are empty, but that is because the dance floor is a wall of human bodies gyrating in time with the heavy bass line. I see young, leggy socialites tempting wealthy businessmen, a couple rolling on E on the edge of stripping down naked, and in a booth behind another set of purple velvet ropes I spy Hollywood royalty in town for filming. I know for a fact they're not of age, but as they throw back shot after shot, I realize that this club is above the law.

I motion my head over to the bar and our group follows. Mimi and I saddle up next to a salt and pepper forty-something in a three-piece suit. He eyes me up and down, spending a little too much time focusing on my ass. *Yes, I know it looks exceptionally good tonight. No need to ogle.* I offer a tight smile and turn my attention to the bartender.

"I need a round of cosmos and lemon drop shots for sixteen!" I shout over the din.

"Sixteen?" he asks, showing me one finger and then

six, just to make sure he gets the order right.

I nod.

As the bartender begins flipping the shot glasses up onto the bar pouring the vodka, the salt and pepper three-piece leans into me. "Let me get that for you." It's confirmation of what I already know. When you look as hot as we do tonight, it will be fairly easy to score free drinks all night long.

"No, we couldn't possibly ..." I refute demurely, delicately batting my eyelashes.

"It's not up for discussion." Raising his hand to stop me from finishing my rejection, he slides his black American Express card onto the counter and pushes it toward the bartender.

All of the girls huddle around me as I begin to pass the shot glasses back to our party.

I raise my glass in the air and proclaim over the music, "May we never regret this night! Cheers, bitches!"

Everyone hollers in wild fanfare and simultaneously we all throw our heads back and drink. The tart vodka burns my insides and I instantly feel warm all over. I'm surprised by how smoothly it goes down. There's only one shelf in this place and it doesn't get much better than top shelf vodka.

Genevieve drapes her arm around my neck and shoves her empty shot glass in the air before shrieking a powerful, "WOO!" in my ear before addressing our little crowd. "I'd like to thank my sister, Ivy, for planning such an awesome party for me tonight!"

I make a mental note to remember this moment in time, when my sister actually felt an iota of appreciation for my existence, fake or otherwise.

Placing my shot glass upon the bar, I begin to pass the cosmopolitans back to the rest of our group. The mystery man next to me gives me a knowing smile and signs the receipt. He leaves it face up, presumably for me to see his generosity.

Holy fuck. The tip alone is triple digits. For that price, I'd expect these drinks to give me a massage, an orgasm, and a victory lap.

Suddenly I feel obligated to keep him company for a little while. I hop onto the bar stool next to him and sip my drink. It tastes infinitely better than any other cosmo I've had before. I suppose top shelf liquor will do that.

I lean into his ear. "Thanks for doing that." I look over his shoulder and see half of the girls ogling at us and starting to hit the dance floor.

"My pleasure." A flirtatious smile plays at his mouth and his tongue traces along the bottom lip. I look down to his left hand which is holding a scotch and soda and see a wedding ring. *What an asshole.* I know I'm no angel, especially with other people's relationships, but helping a married man carry out an affair is something I'm simply not capable of anymore. Even I have standards. Maybe once upon a time I would have, but not these days.

As I politely sip my cosmopolitan, the sugar from the rim of the glass sticks to my lips. He reaches out and wipes his thumb across my lower lip, then sucks the sugar off, looking at me with hooded eyes.

My mind drifts to Phoenix and I can't help but wonder what he's doing right now. If he's still with what's her name doing who knows what. For the first time since we've been out partying, my heart starts to ache. It physically throbs and I bite back the tears. I need to keep my mind off of Phoenix tonight. Cut my losses and move on. I refocus my energy on this handsome gentleman in front of me, even though there is surely nothing gentle about this man. Maybe I do have it in me to hook up with a married man if it gets my mind off of the hurt I'm feeling?

I lick my lips provocatively and take a slow, polite draw from my cosmo. "What's your name?" I ask, trying not to shout into his ear. I bite my tongue, wanting to ask what his wife's name is instead.

He puts a single finger to my lips and shushes me. "Don't ruin it," he responds softly. As he leans into me, he runs his nose down the curve of my neck and into the dip of my collarbone, inhaling deeply.

I shiver and steel myself for a little mystery. There's no way in hell this is going anywhere, but I find myself desperate for his distraction.

He takes my hand as I quickly toss back what's left of my cosmo and I let him lead me to the dance floor. The drinks paired with the alcohol consumed during dinner set my insides afire. I pause to admire the way his finely tailored pants accentuate his tight ass, and I clench my teeth, fighting the urge to bite it. Mister Mystery pulls up a chair and sits along the edge of the dark wood dance floor. The lights, smoke and noise that fill every fissure of the room assault me.

"Dance for me," he says seriously. There is an evil, mischievous glint in his eye. He leans back in the chair, hooking his ankle over the opposite knee. He watches me, expectantly, waiting for me to move. His hands meet in front of his mouth like a prayer, fingers templed at his lips. I instantly go from feeling like a high-end socialite to a cheap hooker in a matter of seconds.

Surely he can read the discomfort on my face as I make no effort to hide my uneasiness. He gestures his fingers in a "carry on" motion.

I need more alcohol to deal with this and grab a shot glass from a waitress working the dance floor. I most certainly cannot put on a show for him. To me, dancing is a two-way street, bodies acting and reacting to the motion of the other. Not me, gyrating solo on the dance floor so some guy can get his rocks off. If he wants a private dance, there's a strip club not too far from here that he should go check out. I'm sure there are plenty of vixens willing to flash him their fine china for the right price.

Standing in front of him, I lean over and put my weight in my hands on his thighs. No doubt he's getting a good view of my breasts in this corset.

"Come, dance with me." I flutter my eyelashes and give a flirtatious tug on his striped silk tie. I watch his eyes drift down to my tits and his Adam's apple bob as he presumably swallows down his guilt.

His eyebrows arch with amusement and I see a tiny spark light up in his eyes. Stripping his jacket from his shoulders, he allows me to lure him onto the dance floor and we begin to dance together, a little too intimately for my liking. Through the alcohol haze, I focus on his roaming hands and silently applaud myself for wearing pants and not a mini skirt tonight.

He loosens his tie and slowly paws down the side of my corset from my breasts to my waist until he's caressing my hips. He moves his hips lower, pushing one of his knees between my legs. He looks, but doesn't dare touch me further even though it's evident he wants more.

I can feel his hard-on through his fine dress pants and

I close my eyes, taken back in time to a junior high dance where poor Carl McLaughlin got an erection while we slow danced to Seal's *Kissed from a Rose.* I choke back a laugh. Guys, at any age, are all the same really. Even so, his reaction makes me feel powerful—like a snake charmer coaxing a lethal python on command.

As we dance, I keep my head down in the crook of his neck and chest, inhaling the mixture of sweat and expensive cologne. His smell is not nearly as enticing as Phoenix's. Any other girl in this club would be flattered by his obvious display of affection, but I'm so embarrassed *for* him I can't even look him in the eyes.

Over his shoulder, I see the rest of the bachelorette party watching me intently. Genevieve is eyeing me jealously and giving me an approving nod as she dances with Amy and a few other girls from Chi Rho Gamma. Mimi is slack-jawed and giving a questionable nod. I think she's asking if I need to be saved. I smirk and shake my head. In spite of everything being wrong in this moment, the mystery man is providing a welcomed distraction from the painful blow Phoenix delivered earlier today. Already it feels like that was light years ago.

The man leans down, taking his index finger to my chin and lifting it up so I'm forced to look him in the eyes. He slowly licks his lips as he studies my face. I can't help but notice how his bottom lip juts out seductively, inviting to be bitten. A shiver runs down my spine when he runs the tip of his nose down my neck. His dark features could easily lure a young woman into his lion's den, but I know he's hunting the wrong prey tonight.

My sweat builds in time with his growing erection. I am nowhere near drunk enough to continue to allow myself to be in this situation, but before I'm able to break away, he makes his move quickly, taking my face in his hands and shoving his tongue into my mouth before I'm able to protest. His lips are rough, possessive and I mentally note how even the clueless first kisses I experienced as a young teen were better than this. He is all tongue and saliva.

Oh, hell no.

I fist my hands on his shirt and push back against him to break this mess of a kiss. Another round or two and I can do this. I can get lost in him for a little while and forget about Phoenix. I'll just act the part until I'm drunk enough to forget.

"I need another drink," I feign seductively.

I drag him back to the bar to order us another round of drinks and I stop dead in my tracks at the sight before me. Genevieve is leaning face down over the counter; standing next to her is a middle-aged Asian man dressed in all black, with Amy on her other side. Genevieve quickly snaps her head up and touches up the side of her nose. I watch her glassy vacant eyes as she rubs the powdery white residue across her upper gums.

Are you fucking kidding me?

I can hardly believe the scene unfolding before me as Genevieve continues on with her evening like she did not just take a line of coke off the bar.

I back away quickly, trying to remove myself from the situation before Genevieve realizes I saw her. I stumble into my mystery man and I simply shake my head before he releases me and I retreat to the bathroom.

Quickly, I push the door shut and lean against the back of it, taking a calming breath. Mimi emerges from one of the stalls, straightening out her skirt. I'm amazed that she's managed to avoid snapping an ankle—*those heels must be at least four-inches.*

"Ivy! You have to tell me your connection. How did you get us in this club?"

My eyes scan the floor for answers.

"I, uh. I didn't. Genevieve coordinated everything."

"But she said—"

"I know what she said, but I had nothing to do with getting us in here." I snap back. Too much is happening too quickly and I need a few moments alone.

"Whoa. Kitty got claws!"

"Sorry, Mimi," I pause, debating just how much I want to tell her about our evening. "I just saw my sister do a line off the bar, Phoenix is probably off fucking that whore on a unicorn, no doubt, and that douche bag back there is trying to get into my pants. I'm just freaking out a little bit."

Mimi reaches out and touches my elbow. I'm not sure if she's trying to comfort me or check her balance. Perhaps both.

"A unicorn? Honey, how much have you had to drink?" she asks, kindly. "And not that it's worth anything, but your sister has been a cokehead for as long as I've known her."

My only reaction is to blink. How have I never known this? What other secrets is she hiding? I know we haven't been close since before we were kids, but I feel like I would have caught onto *something* over the past handful of years.

"You okay?" she asks, genuinely concerned.

I nod my head, not even caring that it's a lie.

"Good. And don't worry so much about Phoenix. It'll work out like it's supposed to. Boys are dumb and your mind is probably just playing tricks on you. I'll see you out there." Mimi blows me a kiss and snakes out the door back into the din.

Digging into my back pocket, I grab my phone to see just how much longer of this hell I have to endure. My heart seizes when I see a missed call from Phoenix nearly two hours ago.

Shit. While he was thinking about me, trying to get a hold of me, I was parading around the club with the tongue of some guy whose name I don't even know trying to give me a tonsillectomy. My insides sink rapidly, guilt weighing me down.

I hit the return call button, not caring that it's so late right now. I just need to hear his voice. I need his comfort.

I wince when it goes straight to voicemail and hang up quickly.

There is so much I want to say to him. I want to wrap myself in his velvet voice. I want to apologize for shamelessly flirting with the mystery man. I want to yell at him for hurting me. But does he even know that he hurt me?

This boy has got me so tied up and twisted emotionally. We're not even a couple and yet I'm terrified of losing him. Everything about him makes me feel too vulnerable.

I choke down tears and hit redial one more time. It doesn't even ring and I immediately hear his voice in the speaker, "Hey, it's Phoenix. You know what to do."

"Hey… it's me. I … I'm sorry. It's just … I just miss you." I linger on the line longer than I should, unsure of what I'm apologizing for. For my insecurity-induced drinking binge earlier? For my shameless flirting and grope session with the salt and pepper man? For being the most ridiculous mess of a young woman who should never be given the opportunity to be with a nice guy because I will inevitably self-destruct and ruin everything? Perhaps all of the above?

Eventually, I hang up, pull myself together, and return to the bachelorette party to fulfill my maid of honor duties with a sinking feeling resting deep inside. When I emerge, the douche bag is long gone. I can only assume he has returned home to his unsuspecting wife to shower her with horrible kisses. What a pathetic waste of a man.

After grabbing another shot and an energy drink mixed with vodka, I approach Genevieve to check up on her and make sure she is having a good ole' drunken—and high—time. Because if she doesn't, I will never hear the end of it. What I find is Genevieve sloshing a martini around in one hand and attempting to apply a coat of electric crimson lipstick to her lips with the other while she dances. The mess she leaves in her wake is mine to clean up.

She makes eye contact with some attractive thirty-something a few feet away on the dance floor. Her intoxicated attempt at sex appeal is nothing short of hilarious, and I know I have to intervene before she makes more of an ass of herself. Horrifying images like this are what the socialite section in the newspaper thrives on.

"Whoa, relax on the lipstick, Genevieve. Less is more," I gently reason with her like she's a child. I pull the tube away from her lips since she can hardly keep it in the lines of her mouth.

"Whatever, Ivy. Whoever said less is more *obviously* never had more in the first place."

Gah! I cringe at her comment. She knows I hate it when she makes remarks like that. Genevieve lives to give the impression that our family is so rich we buy a new boat whenever our old boat gets wet. And while that may not be far from the truth, it's sickening how she parades it around. In reality, my sister and I aren't the ones with money—our parents are.

Genevieve tends to get caught up with the competitiveness of life. She wants to be more successful than her colleagues, own more things than her friends, and carry the illusion of a happy relationship when in truth none of these things actually make her happy at the end of the day. In reality, the only person any of us should be in competition with is ourselves. And even then, the only competition should be trying to be better than the person you were the day before.

I know we're getting close to the end of our evening since Genevieve, the mean drunk, has come out to play. I throw back the rest of my drink and grab a glass of water from the bar.

"It's vodka, straight up." I shove the new glass in her palm and watch her tilt her head back, allowing the clear liquid to slide right down the back of her throat without even swallowing. She is so wasted she doesn't even realize that she just tossed back water.

Yep, it's time to go!

Mimi helps me rally the girls and we head back to the hotel on foot, hoping the fresh air will help sober us up a bit.

"You know, Gen always tried to make us all believe that you were busier than a two-dollar whore on nickel night," Mimi says, her accent thicker now that she's had a few too many drinks. I love learning all about myself from the rumors that get passed around. Though, in fairness, that was probably true once upon a time, but I don't dare confirm that for her. Instead, I offer her a tight smile of understanding.

"Yeah. Well, Gen here manages to bring out the best in me," I say, sarcasm riding thick. In between us, Genevieve stumbles over her own feet and we simultaneously lunge to keep the bride upright. I instantly regret my reaction and wish I would have let her fall flat on her face. She is so far gone she has no idea we're even talking about her.

Back in the hotel suite, I put our unconscious bride in the oversized California king bed and rejoin the rest of the girls to polish off what's left of the champagne. I zone in and out of listening to their mundane chatter as I twirl my cell phone in my hand. I fight the urge to call Phoenix, knowing that he has to be passed out since it's past two in the morning. My mind drifts, imagining all of the horrifying and provocative situations he could be in at this very moment with Hailey's sugary voice singing in the background.

After a while, anxiety takes over. And when the room begins to spin and stars fizzle in my brain, I drag my drunk ass to the bedroom to sleep away the heartache.

THERE IS NOTHING WORSE THAN being completely incapable of shutting your brain off so you can sleep. Given the volume of alcohol I've consumed, I should be dead to the world for a good ten hours. But no. The combination of hard liquor and champagne appears to have had an adverse effect on me and sleep simply will not come to this exhausted body.

I roll over angrily, and suffocate my thoughts by pulling a pillow tightly over my head. It doesn't work. The synapses in my brain are dancing in rapid-fire succession and all efforts of subduing my soul are useless. And to top it all off, Genevieve is snoring to the tune of a marching band. At least everyone should start waking up sometime relatively soon so we can clear out of the hotel and I can go back home to sulk in solitude.

My mind continues to replay last night's events at Nuit Noir, and I can't help but feel guilty about my rendezvous with the handsome man with no name. I catch a whiff of his cologne on my skin and my stomach curdles in disgust, although I'm not sure if the guilt is rooted in the fact he was a married man or if my heart still completely belongs to Phoenix even after he was trying to keep that girl a secret from me.

I am *so* not cut out for this long distance thing. My mind plays too many games with me and I don't know if I can ever trust anyone completely. And to play devil's advocate, I haven't always been the most trustworthy person either. In hindsight, allowing the man at the club to kiss me was something the old Ivy would have done. I really should have stopped him.

Today, there is a come to Jesus talk in store for Phoenix and me. If we're not on the same page, if he's canoodling with someone else down in St. Louis, then we need to get this all out now and decide where to go from here. Because if we're not aligned, I don't think we can successfully have this relationship … if that's what this is. If that's what he even wants still.

My subconscious is shouting at me to stop reading into things. Just because I never knew about Hailey doesn't mean there was anything worth hiding. Factor in his estranged father's illness and the amount of stress he's under with work, it is no wonder Phoenix hasn't been his usual, happy self. In fact, I think I'd be more worried if he were carrying on as if nothing was the matter.

I roll over and grab my cell phone off of the nightstand. As I flip through past text messages, I'm torn on whether or not our interactions have been genuine all along. My instinct says yes but my mind continues to inject doubt. I guess I shouldn't be surprised if last night he'd called to tell me that Hailey is his girlfriend and cut ties with me. I flip over to my recent call list, willing it to light up with a call from Phoenix at this very moment to put my mind to rest. I know I won't be able to function until I get to the bottom of this. There is nothing I need more than to put my heart at ease one way or the other.

Exhaling slowly, I remind myself that the old Ivy would have dropped him faster than a popsicle melting in hell. My track record for screwing things up and running away is quite impressive. For better or worse, he makes me feel emotions that I thought only existed in books. But the hurt and confusion I feel is far worse now that I'm sober. But that could just be this wicked hangover talking.

We *will* get to the bottom of this.

I *will* not run.

We *will* talk through this.

We *will* be better for it.

I steel myself and fire off a text to him.

Ivy: *We need to talk.*

As much as I hate those words, it's simple and to the point. I put my cell phone down on the nightstand and crawl out of bed, leaving Genevieve to continue sawing logs. I run to the bathroom to brush my teeth before calling the concierge to make arrangements for breakfast to be brought up to our suite. I'm desperate for coffee and breakfast carbs. Some greasy sausage and biscuits to soak up the leftover alcohol in my stomach sounds especially appetizing this morning. Although I'm certain most of the food will go uneaten by this particular crowd. Most of Genevieve's sorority sisters look like they'll have a slice of grapefruit with a side of laxatives to start their day.

When I hear Dave Grohl singing "Everlong" from the other room, I practically sprint to pick it up before it wakes anyone up. Phoenix's bright and smiling face lights up the screen of my phone. I didn't expect him to actually call me right now. It's barely after sunrise.

"Hey," I whisper softly into the phone and quietly creep toward the glass door, stepping out onto the balcony for some privacy. I'm taken aback by the beautiful view of Michigan Avenue. It's vacant with the exception of a few random cabs searching for an early morning fare. The late spring sunshine pours through the buildings, and in the distance I can see blinding reflections jumping off of Lake Michigan.

"Hey, what's going on?" Phoenix asks as he stifles a yawn. "Everything okay?"

"Um, yeah. I just thought we could talk later." I swallow my racing heart back into my chest where it belongs.

"Well, I can talk now. What's up? How did the bachelorette party go? I figured you'd be asleep until noon." I hear him rustling in his bed. It's difficult not to imagine him sitting up with a sleepy smile, perfect bed head and pajama bottoms hanging low on his hips. I'd happily give up all of the breakfast food in the world for a chance to see him lying next to me in pajama bottoms one morning.

I don't even know where to begin this conversation. I want to confront him. I want him to comfort me. I want to lift this cloud of guilt that is pushing me into the ground. Inside I am a melee of emotions and I really don't want it to become evident in my voice.

I hesitate and decide to rip the proverbial Band-Aid off as quickly as possible.

"Who exactly is Hailey? And please don't lie to me."

Even when the truth is a cold-hearted bitch, I would rather be hurt with honesty than soothed with a lie.

"Shit, Ivy. That's what this is about? I saw your text message and completely panicked. I thought something bad happened last night." The relief in his voice is evident and it warms my heart. Though the tone combined with his assumption of me doing something bad is disheartening. He doesn't trust me. But in fairness, he probably shouldn't. My subconscious screams obscenities, reminding me that something bad did happen last night. I know I should tell him about the kiss and the wayward thoughts that followed, but I don't dare ruin this moment.

He takes a deep breath. "I've known Hailey since we were teenagers. There's nothing romantic going on between us. She's practically a sister to me."

I exhale all the air in my lungs and thank the sweet baby Jesus. I *was* reading into things. I seriously need to get a grip and simply tread carefully.

"It's just … I don't know. I have trust issues. I'm messed up." And it's true. I have never let a guy in like I have with Phoenix. And with him seemingly light years away, my mind automatically goes to a dark place with each and every doubt. It is as if I've been unwrapped, bitten, and left to bleed out. Allowing myself to be vulnerable and actually feel something is scary as shit. It makes me feel weak and out of control. And I don't do that emotion particularly well.

"You're not messed up, Ivy. I meant it when I said that Hailey was just a friend. She's been going through a lot these past few months and your call yesterday interrupted a rather *heated* discussion we were having."

Heated? While my curiosity is piqued, I know it's none of my damn business to even ask what it's about, though I'm certain he'd tell me anyway. But I don't even know the girl. Whatever issues she has, she has a right to hash them out with her friends.

"You promise?" I ask, my voice barely audible.

"Yes," he says in a heavy exhale. "I swear."

In this moment, I want nothing more than for him to be standing in front of me, wrapping me tightly in his arms and reassuring me that everything will be okay. I want to look him in the eyes and just know that we are meant to be.

Internally, I struggle with coming clean about the sexy exchange with the salt and pepper man and him forcing his lips on me on the dance floor. But it's not like *I* was the one who kissed him, and I certainly did not kiss him back. So there's no reason to feel guilty. Right? But would I have wanted Phoenix to walk into the club and catch me in a moment like that? No, absolutely not. So these feelings of guilt are totally justified right now.

"So tell me, how'd it go?"

"Ugh. It was something else," I begin. "I learned my sister is a closet cokehead. No amount of alcohol could have prepared me for her bullshit. At least she was halfway nice to me, even if it was just all for show." I leave out the part about him making me feel so paranoid and heartbroken that I broke out the booze before anyone even arrived.

"Could've been worse, right?"

It was. It was way worse than that. "Yeah, I suppose," I say coolly.

"I picked up your three voicemails around five this morning when I woke up to use the bathroom. It sounded like you guys were having a good time."

Voicemails? Plural? Oh, shit. That must have been

the vodka calling. I know I left him that awkward one from the bathroom at the club, but there were two more messages? Fuck, this is not good. I cannot be held liable for anything I said in my overly emotional state. Why doesn't the technology exist to prevent drunk dials to hot crushes halfway across the country? Those calls could have gone one of any number of ways. Suddenly, I find myself thankful that I'm alone on the balcony where no one can read the mortification in my eyes.

What on earth did I say to him? Please, oh please, tell me I didn't yell at him about Hailey. Or lay into him about needing to call his father. Or tell him off because I had a moment of insecurity.

"Oh?" I play coy. Maybe if I don't say anything, he'll just bring it up in discussion?

"Mm hmm," he hums playfully into the phone. "Do you really think that?"

Do I really think *what*? My heart begins to jump erratically in my rib cage and my head pounds. The only thing I'm really thinking right now is that I'm an idiot, but I can't tell him that. I probably mindlessly rambled to the point of mortification. God, I hope he deleted those messages.

"Well..." I say, trying to hide the uncertainty in my voice.

"It's okay. I know that you were drunk when you said it, so I'm going to let you off the hook if you didn't mean it. But, for what it's worth, I more than like you too."

I feel my face flush scarlet and I bite my lip to tame the ridiculous smile forming between my cheeks. Even in a haze of guilt and liquor, my heart still won out and gave a confession of the feelings I'm too afraid to admit in sobriety.

"I am connected to you in ways I never dreamed possible. As much as we both hate this distance, it's giving us
a unique opportunity to build trust and really get to know
each other without the physical shit getting in the way. Not
that it'd be shitty to be physical with you. It'd be anything
but that I'm sure. I mean, I'm sure you're amazing and …
I … damn it! I'm just going to shut up, now."

As he stumbles over his words, I giggle in relief, ignoring the continued creeping sensation of guilt on my
soul.

"Well, you're right about one thing," I say with confidence. "I *am* amazing."

Phoenix lets out a low groan on the other end of the
line and I can only imagine the path his mind is taking.

"Well, the good news is I'll be in Chicago a week
from today. After Sully's wedding, I have a meeting with
the executive team just north of the city on Monday to present my designs to them. I thought I could see you on Sunday? Who knows, perhaps I can get there in time to bring
you a late breakfast? We could spend the whole day together." I can hear the smile in his voice. "And maybe part
of the night?" he adds with a hint of playful curiosity.

"I'd like that. I'd like that very much." I tuck some
loose hair behind my ear and smile just thinking about
spending time with him in person.

"Perfect," he whispers.

Yes, it *is* perfect. Everything about this man is perfect. Why I deserve his attention is beyond me, but I'm not
going to question it anymore. I *can* do this distance thing. I
can and I will give it everything I've got.

"And Ivy, I want you to know I meant what I said

about Hailey. She's just a friend. I've been yours since the moment I first saw you and you had no idea I even existed."

His words take my breath away and I feel my eyes start to fill with tears. I can't recall anyone ever saying something so sweet to me.

"There is no one else," he whispers into the phone, assuring me.

"Good." The word falls out of my mouth before I can even process what I've said. *Good?* Of all the things I could possibly say right now, 'good' certainly is not one of them. I am such an idiot.

"All right, well I need to get going. I'm meeting up with a few guys for a morning run."

"Okay," I softly say.

"Later, Cubby Bear."

"Have a good run."

I end the call and sit back in the Adirondack chair on the balcony, absorbing the breeze rolling over my body. For having barely slept a wink, I find myself feeling refreshed and downright giddy. His words echo in my soul...

I've been yours since the moment I first saw you and you had no idea I even existed.

This.

This is surely what that "L word" feels like.

Tuesday

I DAB CHERRY RED GLOSS on my lips and tousle my hair one last time. Surprisingly, I look and feel beautiful. The deep plum cocktail dress perfectly hugs my curves and complements my skin tones. Hopefully no one notices the bags under my eyes from my late night phone call with Phoenix.

My insides burst at the thought of him. I've got it bad. I snatch my phone off the bed and blow a kiss at the camera as I take a photo of myself. I attach the picture and fire off a text.

> **Ivy:** *Wish you were here! Is it Sunday morning yet? XO*

We are only a few days away from being reunited and my mind is racing with excitement. Within seconds, my phone chimes.

Phoenix: *We need a fast forward button. I'm about to have dinner with some friends and I could explode after seeing that photo.*

Explode? Oh, I can make him explode.

Ivy: *Is that so? Then we probably shouldn't video chat tonight. I'd hate for your cause of death to read spontaneous explosion upon viewing my unmentionables. XO*

After tonight's party, I'm planning on modeling my latest purchase from the intimates department at Saks during a video chat. You know, a tempting preview of what will be waiting for him this weekend. I can't wait to see the look on his face. Even more, I can't wait to see the look on his face this weekend.

Phoenix: *You are such a tease. And a vixen. I look forward to my demise. Wink.*

I laugh as I toss my phone into my purse and give myself one final glance in the mirror. Only three or four hours until we can reconnect on the phone tonight. Just thinking about Phoenix brings my face to a glow and I feel gorgeous from the inside out.

AS MAID OF HONOR, GENEVIEVE expects me to dote on her every move. And knowing that my days here are numbered, I focus more on keeping the peace, so I oblige. When I walk into her bedroom and she baits me with a cheerful, "What do you think?" I know to plaster my fake with a look of awe and respond with, "Perfect." She's clearly going the virginal look this evening with a knee-length ivory dress complete with lace overlay and ballerina pink ribbon around her waist. I don't know who she thinks she's fooling. She lost her virgin status well over a decade ago.

To kick off the wedding week festivities, our parents have rented the Signature Room, towering ninety-five floors into the Chicago skyline and boasting a dramatic 360-degree view of both the city and lake. It was a strategic move to flaunt our status and impress upon CJ's parents that the Cotter family is un-fuck-with-able. Leave it to my mother to ensure that every detail is conducted in a flair of superiority.

It is all incredibly ridiculous, in my humble opinion.

"Mom and Dad left about twenty minutes ago. I told them we'd come over together. Besides, I wanted to chat with you," Genevieve says. I eye her suspiciously. "You know, girl talk," she adds with a shrug.

Girl talk. Sure. I can't wait to see where she's going with this.

"Well, we'd better head out, Gen. The guest of honor shouldn't be *too* fashionably late for her own party."

Harold opens the back door for us and we slide across the leather interior of the Lincoln. I sneak a peek at my phone, hoping for another text from Phoenix. I frown when I realize he's probably already with his friends for the night.

"Expecting a call?" Genevieve asks with a bitter taste in her mouth.

"No, just checking the time," I say casually. "I'd hate

for you to keep your public waiting." I intend to be teasing, but I can tell that my comment grates across her skin. Genevieve's eyes roll so far into the back of her head I'm certain she's looking at the void where her brain should be.

"God, you don't have to be such a jealous bitch, Ivy," she says as she pulls out her compact to admire her reflection. I bite my tongue. The metallic taste of blood fills my mouth and I look out the window, trying to ignore her. Just a few more days and I will be out of this place.

The Hancock building is a little more than a mile from our home, but in this evening traffic it takes us nearly twenty minutes to get there. Leave it to Genevieve to keep her adoring fans waiting.

Pulling up to the side of the skyscraper, I climb out of the car and follow Genevieve into the sleek lobby where an open elevator awaits us. The doors shut and she immediately begins checking her make up again in the reflection of the door, admiring her shiny, plump lips.

"Ivy, I just want to let you know that I forgive you."

"Thanks, Gen. I shouldn't have been so rude in the car." The lie rolls right off my tongue. I couldn't care less about my sister in this moment. The list of things I *do* care about is short—Phoenix, my best friend, and this job in New York.

"No, I don't care about that," she pauses for a moment. "I meant about Glen. I know you were young and you made a mistake. I forgive you." Her voice has an heir of dominance that sends a shudder down my spine.

I'm left completely dumbfounded. Glen got off easy. So easy, in fact, that he was the one to break up with her.

"Besides, it's not like you could ever get a guy like Glen or CJ on your own," she spats, flipping her auburn curls over her shoulder. "Try as you may to take all of the good things away from me, you will never succeed."

She plasters a smug smile to her hideous mug just as the doors open, then sashays toward the live jazz quartet that is playing in the Signature Room.

"Bitch," I mutter under my breath.

This is definitely going to be a long night.

I walk into the restaurant and scan the room, looking for Rachel. Long ago she'd agreed to be my date for all of these asinine wedding functions. When Mom and Dad learned I had no intention of allowing Matt to escort me, they voiced their disapproval. And when they realized I'd be bringing Rachel with me they blew a gasket, convinced that all of their well-to-do friends would think I was a lesbian. If my parents ever found out about my girl on girl experimentation, they would keel over and die on the spot.

There is no sign of Rachel yet so I shoot her a text to let her know I'm here as I make my way over to the bar to order a gin and tonic. The bartender hands me my drink with a lazy, playful wink.

The world moves in slow motion when I turn around, and I find myself in the zero gravity hesitation of peace just before the roller coaster hurls you back toward the earth.

The first thing I hear is his laugh.

After so many late nights on the phone with him, I'd recognize it anywhere. It comes from deep within his belly as joy erupts from his soul.

My eyes follow the sound of his voice and zero in on him. A smile plays on my lips and my heart grows ten sizes in anticipation.

He's here.

Phoenix is actually here. He came to surprise me and help me deal with my family and get me through all of this wedding bullshit! I couldn't ask for anything more in this moment. Now, more than ever, I'm certain he's the one. He's so thoughtful and selfless and unlike any guy I have ever wanted to be with.

As I begin to make my way over to him, I'm walking on clouds, floating through the air.

Until my crosshairs focus on his hand tenderly stroking the small of her back. A gesture so impossibly subtle and so fatally intimate that it brings me to a halt.

On the other end of his hand is a petite blonde thing in a seductive little red number. I can't see her face, but you can tell by the way she carries herself that she is truly a sensational beauty. And even worse, she knows it.

The feeling of my heart collapsing in on itself is suffocating. I can't breathe with the weight of this reality crushing down on my chest. My mind blanks, my insides twist, and my stomach bottoms out as I slam into the Earth's surface from my walk in the clouds.

I want off of this ride.

Desperately.

I cannot believe what I'm seeing as I force my feet to continue moving toward him. Acid bubbles in my stomach, and anger takes over.

Phoenix throws his head back in laughter again, shaking the floor beneath me with each hearty bellow. Smiling, he tilts his head down to whisper something to the girl, and she bites her lip seductively, undressing him with her eyes. I feel like a voyeur spying on a private moment between two longtime lovers.

I'm halfway across the room when he locks my gaze.

Those piercing eyes stop me in my tracks.

"Ivy," Phoenix calls out to me. He says my name as if it's a statement, but his face reads question and surprise. It is clear that he was not expecting to run into me this evening. We were not intended to cross paths today.

No, no, no.

This cannot be happening to me.

I quickly start to back away and trip over an ottoman in a sitting area by the grand windows. It's evident that I look wasted as the contents of my drink have now ruined the silk of my bandage dress. Pushing myself to my feet, I grab my purse off the floor and run to the elevator bank.

My heart rips from my chest and flies down the hallway, far away from here. I do all that I can keep up the chase in its pursuit.

The pain of letting the wrong someone in is crushing. What's worse is thinking you've let the *right* person in only to discover you've been played a fool.

I look over my shoulder and see him trying to catch up to me. He's fast, but I'm faster as I pull myself away from this hell. I feel like Cinderella fleeing the ball. But in this fairytale, Prince Charming is a lying, two-timing sack of shit. In fact, this is no fairytale at all. It's a nightmare.

By a stroke of luck, the doors open right as I approach and I crash into someone just as they are walking out into the party. I slip into the box and obsessively push the close button, forcing the doors shut, cursing them to close faster so I can escape.

Just as the doors are sealing their last final inches, I catch a panicked look on Rachel's face as she calls out my name.

Shit!

How could I be so stupid?

I slam my fist against the elevator wall.

You would think plummeting toward the earth in a tiny elevator box would go by quickly. It doesn't. I'm trapped in a cage that is defying the laws of gravity. Visions of Phoenix flash in my mind: his smile, his laughter, his whispers ... *his date*. His beautiful, buxom, blonde date. His lies.

God, I am an idiot.

I stumble out of the building and onto Michigan Avenue before the sobs take over. Hopping out of my heels, I hail a taxi and slam the door shut before anyone has a chance to come after me.

"The corner of North and Wells please," I say, trying to catch my breath, not even thinking about the destination. The cab driver gives me a stern nod and heads north, taking me away from my own personal hell.

I STARE UP AT THE weathered brass numbers on the door and take a deep breath before pounding it three times. This is where my gut told me to go.

Matt pulls the door back in surprise. I force my way through the threshold, falling into his arms and clutching the chest of his shirt. It's soft. Familiar. An intoxicating combination of soap and sage. He wraps his arms around me tightly, smoothing my hair.

Instantly, I unravel at his touch. As I cry, he coos softly in my ear for several minutes, a feeble attempt to calm my stormy soul. There's no need for words right now, only a yearning to lose myself, if only for a little while.

It's hard to process everything I feel in this moment: self-loathing, curiosity, anger, sadness, hurt. The past few weeks I've fallen for every lie that Phoenix fed. He made me believe that I was special, that things in my life could be different, *would* be different. That in spite of distance, circumstances could never keep us apart. That distance would actually bring us closer together. Not in the physical sense, but rather connect our souls more strongly. That I was his.

But it was all a ruse.

I look up from my mascara-stained cheeks. Matt's blue eyes incinerate me and for a moment, I hesitate. I sense he's silently inviting me in, luring me to his mouth. Stretching up on the tips of my toes, I deftly press my lips against his. He turns cold, stone, and I slowly reacquaint my tongue with his mouth. Pushing back, I realize he's resisting my advances.

Fuck.

Mortification takes over as the leading emotion in the drama that my life has become.

"I … I'm sorry. I shouldn't have come here." I break free and race back to the door. It's evident I can't stay here. He's probably moved on. The sensation of being un-wanted guts me.

Matt grabs my hand quickly and yanks me back against his strong chest, pulling me further into the living room. "No. Stay."

His voice is husky and his breath is hot against my neck. He looks confused. And eager. "I was going to meet up with some of the guys for a couple of drinks. But … change of plans …" he trails off with a shrug.

Silence passes between us, but novels are written in-side our stare. Our history allows us to pick up right where we left off, even though nearly a year has gone by. Faith-fulness was never our strong suit, but none of that matters when we're together like this.

Matt grabs my face and kisses me roughly, frantical-ly.

Full of haste.

Full of hatred.

Full of longing.

I'm desperate to erase Phoenix from my mind, and I know that being under Matt's touch will allow me to disconnect from Phoenix and from myself. We treat this fleeting moment as if it will disappear without warning. Liquid peppermint rolls off his tongue as I inhale it deep into the back of my throat. A tingling sensation burning smooth like alcohol, races through my insides and pools in the depths of my belly. His fingertips squeeze their way down my body, digging in my hips, leaving red hot indentations.

Matt kicks the door shut with his foot and guides me into his living room. Easing me down onto the couch, the weight of his body blankets me before pulling back. He looks into my eyes, teasing a glimpse of sincerity as he thumbs away the trail of tears on my face. His five o'clock shadow scratches my cheeks as he traces his nose against my jawline. His breath is sticky hot against my neck. My nerves are on end, live wires charging his touch with electricity.

Gradually, he picks up the pace and his hands pull furiously at my arms as he searches for a way into my dress. All evidence of tenderness now gone, he is much rougher in this moment than he ever was when we dated.

He is eager to possess me again.

And I am eager to let him.

Eager to forget.

Matt's touch is nothing like what I imagined Phoenix's would be like. Phoenix would take his time, tasting me slowly, being deliberate and thoughtful with each brush of skin. Matt is hurried for his fix. And frankly, I'm desperate for him to hurry up and erase the pain from my memory. I push Phoenix's specter to the back of my mind and clench the belt loops on Matt's jeans.

My fingers fumble with his belt and a long groan escapes his mouth as my hand brushes up against his length. Matt was always eager and willing. *Good to see some things never change.*

The button on his jeans is impossible. Matt takes his hands off of me to rip his pants off in a hurry. Our clothes are obstacles, standing in the way of what we want. I need his skin on mine. *I need his escape.* I need it more than I need oxygen.

If only for a little while.

Like this—a mass of furious limbs driven by desire— we were always good together. And this moment proves we still are.

Matt pulls his shirt up over his head in one swift move. His body is the same as it ever was: carved, lickable, and soft and firm in all the right places. I trace my fingers over his chest, examining a new tattoo just below his collarbone. It's a keyhole in the center of an antique skull and cross bone. Hauntingly beautiful.

I rattle my head. Sex first. Questions later.

Urgently, Matt pushes my dress up around my waist and I feel his nails squeeze the inside of my thighs. Trailing his tongue up my leg, he nips his teeth on the outside of my panties, the elastic snapping my hips with a sharp, pleasurable sting. I squeal in surprise or anticipation of what's to come, I'm not sure which.

Eagerly, he rips my underwear down off of my legs and pushes two fingers deep inside to find me wet and ready to go. I buck my hips hungrily to meet him as he gives me a wicked, knowing smile. His eyes meet mine as he lowers his mouth to the heat between my legs and teasingly sucks on my clit, nipping it with his teeth. I throw my head back, forgetting my own name.

"I need you inside of me. Now," I command.

He sits up and pulls his wallet from his pants on the floor, grabbing a condom. I fight the urge to tell him no, he doesn't need to use one because I'm pathetically desperate to feel him inside me and erase everything. But even in my foggiest of mindsets, I'm not that stupid.

I take the foil from his fingers and peel back the wrapper, taking control of the situation. His head dips back, exposing his long neck as I roll the condom down his firm length. Matt whispers obscenities under his breath as his eyes roll back into his head. I take in the sight of him as desire pulls my insides.

He guides himself to my opening and presses himself inside with a throaty moan. It has been nearly a year since he was last inside my body, but he still stretches me, filling me to perfection. Hurriedly, he begins to thrust himself in and out my body and I can feel the thrumming of my heartbeat echoing inside my ears as I roll my head back. A gasp escapes my lips as his roughness takes me by surprise.

Suddenly, Matt stops and hovers above me. His angry face stares down at mine and I can read the mixed emotions in his stare. "I knew you'd come to your senses," he seethes. "I've been waiting too fucking long for you to come back to me." He slowly withdraws himself before violently plunging back into me over and over. I close my eyes at his words and know that this is wrong, that I shouldn't be here. In my mind I see Phoenix's face.

I feel nothing.

I feel everything.

I feel …

I feel like I'm going to be sick.

Frantically, I push Matt off of me and race to the bathroom, grabbing the toilet before unleashing the contents of my stomach. With each heave, acid burns me from the inside out. It is as if my subconscious knew exactly what I was doing and intervened to expel the demons I've been harboring within.

"What the fuck, Ivy?" Matt says. He hangs his naked body from the doorframe and glares at me with his eyes full of enmity.

I wipe my mouth with the back of my hand and give Matt the side eye. My world has just flipped onto its side and he's pissed about blue balls. This asshole is incapable of change. I couldn't care less if he has to screw a box of tissues tonight.

"Just go and get me some fucking water, Matt."

He wrings his hands through his hair in exasperation before disappearing down the hall. I listen to the echo of his heavy, pissed-off footsteps. My insides are on fire as my body cramps in misery. Matt slams a glass of water on the floor next to me, and I watch it slosh over the slide, making a mess on the cold tile beneath me.

"Pull yourself together and I'll drive you home." The anger in his tone is intimidating.

I don't want to go home. I'll go anywhere but home. But apparently, I'm not staying here tonight. Then again, I'm certain my presence would merely cock block him from whichever conquest he would be bringing home after last call.

"Don't bother. Just give me a few moments and I'll call myself a cab." Matt closes the door and I hear him mutter obscenities through the walls. Slowly, I compose myself. I'm nauseated and crampy and my head is pounding to the beat of a thousand staccato drums.

With a shaky hand, I raise the glass to my lips and the cool water helps bring me to my senses as I wash my face and rinse out my mouth. Leaning against the sides of the sink, I stare at the reflection of a woman who is broken and lost. It's the same reflection I've seen staring back at me the past few years, but this time I'm actually cognizant of how empty I am, and how hollow my life has become. Hours ago, I was so sure of what I wanted, and now? Now I have no idea *who* I even am.

Matt is nowhere to be seen when I emerge from the bathroom so I let myself out. I walk aimlessly through the Old Town neighborhood before folding myself over on a bench when the pain of my broken heart becomes too much.

THE CABBIE PULLS ONTO ASTOR and stops in front of my parent's estate. "This it?" he asks, eyeing me from his rearview mirror. I don't recall getting into the cab, but I throw a wad of bills into the front seat and slam the taxi door shut.

The house is dark and I find comfort knowing that no one is home. As I expected, and wanted, their night continued on without me. Undoubtedly, excuses were made for my theatrical exit and I'll probably never hear the end of it, but for now, I've found solitude.

Peace.

Climbing the stairs, I stop and look at the walls. In a happier home, you would find photos from family vacations and school portraits, freezing that moment in time. But not here. Here the walls are covered in oil paintings hung in gold leaf frames; meaningless and void of any emotion. I ache for that sense of family before I make my way to my childhood bedroom. My shoes are kicked to the corner and I leave the stained dress in a pile of ruins on the bathroom floor. In a drawer I find one of my old high school T-shirts, so soft and threadbare it's like a second skin.

I take one final glance at my phone before I crawl into bed. Seventeen missed calls—three from Rachel, the rest from Phoenix. Some text messages from the pair, but I don't dare read any of Phoenix's bullshit. I'm not in the mood for his excuses or truths tonight, so I turn my phone off and chase a few sleeping pills with a sip of vodka, willing myself to sleep before the rest of my family returns home from their perfect, happy Norman Rockwell dinner.

17

Wednesday

MORNING COMES ENTIRELY TOO SOON. And the void where my heart once was is overwhelming.

I open my eyes and get lost in the patterns of the textured ceiling. Last night was an absolute nightmare and my body is still reaping its assault. I'm sore, undoubtedly bruised from Matt's angry hands, crampy, emotionally wrung out and seemingly hungover in spite of not even drinking last night.

The pieces are finally fitting together. CJ ... Sully ... Cortland James Sullivan III is marrying my sister. Phoenix is in the wedding. The very same wedding I'm standing up in as the maid of honor in a few short days. And on top of it all, Phoenix is with some other girl. The thought of seeing him with that girl this weekend is torturous. I've spent the last however many weeks playing right into his lies. I am arguably the stupidest, most naïve person in the history of time.

I can't believe I've allowed myself to start to feel

something for him. He is no better than my parents. All that deceit … I wonder if there was any truth to the things he told me over the past few weeks.

Surely there was. The connection we had was so real.

But how could that connection possibly be real if he could blatantly lie to me like that? Phoenix is no better than anyone else in my family.

Seriously, I cannot get over that this is my life. That last night actually happened to me. Rachel is right, I'm an absolute mess. I should have just waited downstairs for her in the lobby or called her when shit first threw down between me and Genevieve on the way to the dinner.

Oh, crap.

Matt.

The indiscretions of the night are slowly returning to the forefront of my mind. I slept with Matt. Kind of. Who knows how many people have heard his version of last night by now.

Fuck.

Just kill me. He is never going to let me live this down. I have undoubtedly opened the door for him to try and weasel his way back into my life. Why can't I just lock him in my past where he belongs and throw away the key?

Between stumbling upon who Phoenix really is, throwing myself at Matt, and then falling ill on top of it all, I've had enough drama to last me until I turn thirty. I haven't physically felt this terrible since I woke up at that house party in Madison when I met Phoenix. My heart breaks a little more at the thought of him.

My insides give me another lowly gurgle. Just as I'm about to pull the sheets back to start my day, my door cracks open. Genevieve pops her head through the frame.

"Hey, are you okay? I didn't see you at all last night after we arrived. You're not pissed off at me about what I said, are you?" There is a hint of sincerity in her voice, and for a fraction of a moment I'm reminded of how things used to be between us when we were little, when we were actually friends. But the moment is overshadowed by her obliviousness to the drama that threw down at her own party. Her level of self-absorption is truly astounding.

"Yeah, I'm fine. Just..." I trail off. "Something came up and I needed to get out of there. Sorry I bailed. I hope I didn't put you in a bad spot," I lie, not really caring about her dinner last night.

Genevieve plops down on the side of my bed. Her warm eyes contradict the sour look on her face. "Oh, Ivy. If you're jealous about me getting married, it's okay. Your day will come eventually."

And there it is! Her tone is mocking and I bite my tongue, fighting the urge to reach out and bitch slap her. Only another week or so and this will all be behind me.

"But until then, we have to go to the seamstress this morning. You need to learn how to bustle the back of my dress!" She bounces ever so slightly and claps her hands. The squeal that escapes her body grates against my skin like nails dragging along a chalkboard.

I sigh, realizing that there is no use in fighting her this morning. We're so close to the wedding day that I just need to get through the next few days.

"All right, I'm getting up. Just let me hop in the shower and I'll be ready to go in thirty minutes." Genevieve stands up to leave as I toss the sheets aside to start my day.

My heart stops.

Red.

I see red everywhere. It's covering my sheets, my clothes. Everything.

"Oh my god," Genevieve says with a genuinely concerned gasp. "Is that blood?"

"I … I … I don't understand."

My mind goes straight to Matt. What the fuck did he do to me last night?

Genevieve stands, frozen in shock. "Are you hemorrhaging? That's too much blood to be your period. We need to get you to the hospital," she says, rushing to my side.

This is the first caring gesture I've experienced from my sister since we were little and she gave me her teddy bear after I left mine at Nana and Pop Pop's house. "Mom and Dad are both out running errands with Harold right now. I'll get us a taxi. It'll be faster than calling an ambulance." She grabs my purse from the armoire as she races out of the room.

My soul bottoms out from my insides and I can feel my pulse behind my eyes and in my fingertips. Confusion is not an emotion I'm familiar with, but my mind fogs over as the dizziness sets in. I quickly change into fresh clothes, ignoring my need to shower, and allow Genevieve to lead me outside to the taxicab.

"Northwestern Memorial Hospital. And step on it," she commands, and the next few hours happen in flashes of vignettes, moments stringing together.

Genevieve gnawing on her thumbnail to the brink of bleeding.

The overwhelming lightheadedness upon my shoul-

ders.

A needle piercing my forearm flesh with a bitter sting.

The cool liquid pumping into my body from the IV drip.

Hushed whispers questioning surgery.

The concerned faces of nurses, doctors, and orderlies.

I'm lying on a thin, uncomfortable bed in the emergency room, focusing on the melodic beeps of a machine monitoring my health.

"Ms. Cotter?" a phantom voice calls out. A man in a white coat at the end of the bed comes into focus. "Ms. Cotter … do you understand what I'm trying to tell you?"

"I … I'm sorry?" My face contorts in confusion.

"Ivy," Genevieve says gently, placing her hand delicately upon my arm. "This is Dr. Porter. He's been the one ordering tests for you." She looks from me to the doctor, then back nervously, again playing into the illusion of the doting sweet sister.

"Ms. Cotter," the doctor begins again, "it appears that you've had a spontaneous abortion, more commonly known as a miscarriage."

His words take me by surprise. *Abortion?* I didn't have an abortion? There's no way I could be pregnant from last night.

"I … I don't understand. I'm not … I … I wasn't pregnant. I haven't had sex since last year, and I've had my period since then."

With the exception of Matt last night, my subconscious scolds, but I push that thought down.

"Your blood tests show traces of human chorionic gonadotropin, the hormone indicating pregnancy." He tries to place a comforting hand on my ankle, but his face is vacant before looking back at my chart. "Without baseline blood work, we cannot confirm for certain, but given the clotting and amount of blood expelled, we believe this to be the case. There will be no need for a dilation and curettage as your body is expelling the fetus on its own. Can you remember the start date of your last period?"

I rake my brain, trying to remember. "Um, it was back in Italy so ... eight or nine weeks ago? But I've always been irregular, so there was never a reason for me to be alarmed," I explain softly.

Dr. Porter nods and makes a few notes on my chart. "Well, your blood test also indicated that you have an infection. It's difficult to say if the infection is what caused the spontaneous abortion. It would be a rare occurrence, but certainly possible."

I cringe, wishing he would stop saying those two words. I know they can't be true. The doctor keeps talking, but his words wash over me in waves. The word 'pregnant' echoes through my mind, like a pinball, incapable to coming to a standstill. Unless I'm the Virgin Mary, his prognosis is incorrect.

"We'll need to have you on intravenous antibiotics for the next forty-eight hours so we can monitor your progress. We'll move you up to recovery shortly so you can get more comfortable, but you'll need to let the bleeding run its course." He gives me a single nod and a sad, tight-lipped smile. Without a second glance, Dr. Porter turns around, leaving Genevieve and me alone with the sound of the beeping monitor.

"You little slut," Genevieve says, trying to come off as teasing and playful. "Who have you been sleeping with? Spill it! It's Matt, isn't it?"

No, this is impossible. There is an irrefutable look of shock on my face as Genevieve glares at my suspiciously.

"I'm serious, Gen. I haven't slept with anyone." *Except for Matt last night, which you are never finding out about. But that is completely irrelevant and has nothing to do with what's going on right here, right now.*

She rolls her eyes at me. "Well, then who have you been obsessively texting and secretly calling at night? I know you're hiding something. Or should I say, someone?"

It takes all of my energy to not reach out and smack that condescending smirk right off of her face. But her comment makes me think about *him* and instantly I feel sick to my stomach. He looked so happy in that moment last night, until panic and dread overcame him when he realized that he'd been caught red-handed.

Might as well come clean here. I have absolutely nothing to lose at this point anyway.

"It's a guy I was sort of seeing." *Was* being the operative word. "But that's nothing, really. I've recently realized it just is not going to work out between us. I thought I could do the long-distance thing, but I'm just not into him enough to put that kind of effort in."

The lies have become easier and easier to dispel. The image of Phoenix and the blonde-haired beauty from last night flash into my mind again, and my heart clenches and emptiness ensues once more.

Genevieve doesn't say a word, but I can tell she doesn't believe me. A digital chirp breaks our stare down and she pulls her phone from her purse to read her latest text.

"That's Mom. She and Dad are on their way."

Great. That's just fucking great.

I have no idea when she even told them we were at their hospital, but their presence is exactly what I don't need—loathing parents to look down their noses and silently scold me for something I didn't do.

Just kill me now.

WHEN I WAS LITTLE, I could fall asleep anywhere. Oh, how I wish that were still true. Now it feels like each time I blink my eyes the demons of the unknown begin to creep into the forefront of my mind. The thought of falling asleep petrifies me, but at the same time that is the only thing I want to do, need to do—shut my eyes and dream this nightmare away. Lying in this hospital bed, I pretend that I'm on an airplane, eyes closed, so no one will talk to me.

When my parents arrive, I stay eerily still, faking sleep. I'm not in the frame of mind to explain myself to them, to anyone actually. It wouldn't even matter; they'd only hear what they wanted to believe.

I listen intently to Genevieve recounting the morning to our parents. The blood, the panic, and the trip to the emergency room and everything that Dr. Porter said. I'm secretly thankful that she is the one doing the talking. I'm not sure I could speak if I even tried. At least she has the decency to call it a miscarriage and not a spontaneous abortion. Medical terminology or not, that is such a vile thing to call it.

My dad gasps faintly, and I feel his rough palm take my hand and squeeze. The sudden jolt of emotion slowly starts to melt away the ice inside.

"Well, I can't say this is a huge surprise," my mom exalts. After all of these years, she still sees me as a pariah. "I raised my daughters to be better than that. I'm glad you have at least grown into a dignified young woman, Genevieve."

I'm not sure whose reaction is more heartbreaking. I'm tempted to stop faking sleep and expose their perfect little princess for the cokehead she really is, but my dad interjects before I have the chance.

"Hey!" my dad snaps at her. "Enough of that. Like it or not, Ivy needs us." He's gripping my hand so tightly I fear he may break a finger. Softly, he adds, "She's our baby girl."

I hear my mother scoff, dismissing my father for taking my side.

A quick knock on the door interrupts their conversation.

"Hello, everyone. My name is Karen and we're here to take Ms. Cotter up to her recovery room on the sixth floor. If you will all just clear the way, we can get her upstairs quickly and settled in for visitors. You'll all be much more comfortable up there."

Several pairs of feet shuffle across the floor, and I hear the orderlies fidgeting with my equipment.

"Come on, honey. Let's get going. We should still be able to get in with the seamstress if we leave now," my mom says to Genevieve.

"You can't be serious, Margaret," my dad says.

"I don't know what you expect me to say, Stephen. The wedding is this weekend and there is so much left to do. We can't waste a full day doting on Ivy." Her haste washes over me in waves.

212

"Am I allowed to go with her?" my dad asks, concern tracing his voice.

"Of course, sir," an unrecognizable voice confirms.

"Give us a call later," my mom says. "I can send Harold back here to pick you up if you'd like. But I hope you don't stay here and waste the entire day, Stephen."

I listen to the clicking of my mom's high heels as she exits the room, presumably with Genevieve right behind.

There is no request to call with updates. No comforting words as they part. I'd venture to say they never even touched as she left the hospital room. My mother and sister, cut from the same cloth, too cold and self-absorbed to comprehend the pain of anyone else. My dad mutters something indecipherable under his breath.

Moments later, I'm traveling down long hallways and elevators, but my dad keeps his hand in mine the entire time.

My bed stops moving and the metal side rail drops. Feeling a sense of safety in the absence of Genevieve and my mom, I slowly open my eyes. My dad looks down at me with so much love that I'm overwhelmed to the point of tears. I open my mouth to speak, to tell him my side of the story, that this can't possibly be true and that it has to be a mistake, but I can tell he already believes me without ever hearing a word.

"Shh, you don't have to say anything, my sweet Ivy." He leans over and kisses me softly on my forehead. This is the most physical affection he has shown me since I was a little girl, and the gesture is quite welcome. When it's just my dad and he's free of my mother's influence, he is an entirely different person. A person I actually like.

He pulls me so I'm sitting upright and a nurse helps

move me from the gurney to a more comfortable bed in a private room, careful not to pull the IV out from my arm. Once everything is settled, the nurse hooks up an antibiotic drip along with a fresh saline bag and my dad sits in the recliner next to me in a comfortable quiet. My mind races, asking questions that could never possibly get answered. I reach to the side of the bed and grab the TV remote, desperate for some kind of distraction. I flick the television on and hand Dad the remote. I frankly don't care what's on. I just want a noise other than the humming and beeping of machines, and *anything* other than the dialogue in my head.

He begins blindly flipping through the channels, instinctively stopping on WGN where the Chicago Cubs are playing the St. Louis Cardinals. Of course this is the match up. I can't help but wonder if Phoenix is watching the game, hand in hand with that girl. She's probably a Cardinals fan, too. *The bitch.*

It's a beautiful Wednesday afternoon game at Wrigley Field. We can see the clouds rolling by in the outfield against a powder blue sky. It's the top of the fifth and the Cubs are up two to one.

"Do you remember when I took you to your very first Cubs game? It was against the Kansas City Royals." Dad's eyes actually sparkle at the memory. "You had to have been about three years old."

I shake my head. I only remember being at a handful of games, most of which were during my high school years, and those were purely social affairs. I didn't really start paying attention to the games until I started watching them on satellite TV from Italy, a welcomed taste of home.

"Well, we had these really great tickets in a private

214

suite. Expensive, too, not that it mattered. You insisted on bringing my old baseball glove, even though there was no way we were going to be catching any foul balls tucked up in the rafters with the boxes. By the end of the first inning, you'd had a meltdown about wanting to be in the plants. It took me another two innings to realize you meant the bleachers," he recalls with a chuckle under his breath. I don't try to fight my growing smile.

"We left the front entrance, walked right up to the box office, and I bought us a pair of bleacher tickets. You were so excited you practically sprinted around to the back side of the field."

That sounds like something I would do. The bleachers are certainly where the fun is at in that stadium. You're close to the action, the people watching is nothing short of phenomenal, and, of course, the odds are that much better for catching a fly ball.

"You loved it back there. We ate cotton candy until our tummies ached, and you antagonized some drunk fans from Kansas City. Even as a child you knew how to ruffle feathers." He laughs. "Well, by the time the seventh inning stretch hit, the skies opened up and it poured down rain. Mother Nature really let us have it. Everyone ran for cover, but not you. You refused to leave. You told me that you wouldn't melt in a little rain."

I smile at his recollection of his memory. Even though I don't remember it, it doesn't make those moments any less special. It's nice to know that my dad and I weren't always so strained.

"Do you know why I wanted to name you Ivy?" he asks with an arch in his brow.

"Because Wrigley Field is your second home, right?

You are the eternally optimistic Cubs fan."

"No." He looks at me with a serious face. "I wanted to name you Ivy because I knew from the moment I laid eyes on you that you needed a name resembling strength. A constant reminder of just how tough you are. Ivy is a plant that flourishes in abundance, it's a tenacious little thing. Every time you cut it down, it manages to come back faster and stronger than before."

Oh.

We sit in thoughtful silence, looking at the television for an immeasurable amount of time. I finally glance over at him, only to find him staring at me.

"Thank you, Daddy," I croak in a hoarse whisper. I thank him for the stories, his company, my name. But most importantly, I thank him for seeing value in me, even when I feel I don't deserve it.

He simply pats his hand on mine a few times.

"It's time to rest now, Ivy. That's the only way you're going to come back stronger from all of this. You've never been one to let a little rainstorm ruin your life."

I heed his request and close my eyes, cautiously un-afraid.

Eventually, I succumb to the welcoming numb arms of sleep. This horrible, confusing, and frustrating world as I know it, fades away.

And I disappear completely.

I STARTLE AT THE SOUND of a metal cart crashing into my sorry excuse of a bed. Beside me, a nurse has dropped some supplies on the top of the cart. I have no idea how long I've been asleep, but I so desperately want to crawl back into hibernation.

"Oh good! You're awake," she chirps. "My name is Julie and I'm your night nurse. You've been out for quite a while, but I need to draw some blood so the lab can run a few more tests and check your progress."

Julie busies herself with raising my bed, making a few notes in the computer and pulling the needle from its packaging. Grabbing my arm, she ties an elastic tourniquet above my elbow and waits for the blue rivers to pucker. Why she can't pull from the IV is beyond me.

"Let's see what we have here," she mutters under her breath, examining the bend in my arm.

I squirm at the sight of the needle. I've hated needles ever since junior high when I had to have a premature tetanus shot after John Sheridan accidentally hammered a nail through the palm of my hand while I held his project together in woodshop. I walked around for months proclaiming I was literally Jesus Christ, stigmata in hand. You'd think that after feeling a nail go through your body a teeny tiny needle would be easy to handle. But, nope.

"Your father left just as my shift started at eight. He seems really nice. Very concerned about you. It's nice to have people who care in your life." She offers a weak smile.

I refrain from telling her she's got it all wrong; that I come from a lineage of truly horrible people and some-how, save for my best friend Rachel, most everyone around me is horrible too. Being in their presence awakens all of the horrible parts of myself, which is why I'm so desperate to leave them all far behind. Although my dad hasn't been so bad these past few weeks. Then again may-be he hasn't been so bad all along and I've just been too jaded to notice?

I wince as I watch the needle pierce the pale flesh of my forearm, expecting a burning sensation. I should feel something, anything, but I don't. There is no physical pain. Or maybe there is and it is simply overshadowed by the internal emotional pain coursing my veins.

Another syringe of antibiotics push through the IV bag and my arm instantly feels cold as the drugs infect my system.

"I'll get these down to the lab quickly and have the doctor stop by in the morning with the results." Her face is illuminated by the soft glow of the computer screen. She continues to make a racket with mindless busywork in my room. I just want to fall back asleep.

"Your brother will be happy to know you're awake. He left a few minutes ago to find some coffee. Your friend Mimi stopped by for a little bit, too, but your brother took her number and promised to keep her updated on your progress. I imagine he'll be back shortly."

My brother? I furrow my eyebrows and feel the air from my lungs rush past my lips. I have no idea who she's talking about and I'm not about to ask. She smiles weakly at me, the corners of her mouth turning down ever so slightly, as if she were offering silent condolences for the loss of a child I never knew. Or wanted. Fuck, this is so confusing. I know she's judging me. The internal dialog is evident in her facial expressions. She thinks I'm a slut.

"Would you like water or perhaps something to eat? The kitchen is closed through the night, but I can steal something from the secret stash for dads-to-be in the labor and delivery ward."

Did she really just say that? I tilt my head at her quizzically, slack-jawed. I'm still incapable of processing this miscarriage, but her comment sears me to my core.

"Oh, I'm so sorry. I wasn't thinking." Julie busies herself organizing the tray again, shifting her focus from her obvious lack in tact. She bites her lip and looks to the side. "You know, it's okay if you need to shut down or cry or scream. Or even feel confusion, or maybe even relief."

Thank you, Dr. Phil.

I open my mouth to respond, but words fail me. When people spend their energy telling you what to feel, it's hard not to feel anything but nothing at all. How do I even start to grieve a life that never started? That I never even knew existed? How the hell am I even supposed to feel? Because right now, I simply don't feel anything.

My eyes drift beyond her and I see Phoenix's silhouette appear in the doorway. Why the hell is he even here? He's listening intently as his fingers trace the rim of his styrofoam coffee cup. I eye him suspiciously as he raises a single finger to his lips in the shadows. My insides soften ever so slightly at the sight of him, but my instinct sounds a foghorn in warning.

Visions of him lingering all over that girl flood my memory. What the hell is he doing? How long has he been standing there? Why isn't he with his girlfriend? I roll the word around in my mind and instantly find myself jealous. The emotion is relatively foreign to me.

I want him to run next to me and hold me in his arms. I want to slap him into the next time zone. I'm not sure I can deal with my current situation *and* him at the same time. Jesus, how much other shit can I possibly deal with right now?

I can only assume he has passed himself off as family to gain access here. Admittedly, he's the last person I thought I'd see, but relief washes through my core and, for the first time, I feel like a little more than a hollowed out shell of a woman.

"Can I get you anything to make you comfortable?" Julie asks. I return my attention to her again quickly.

"May I have some pain killers? Maybe something to help ease the cramps?" I ask softly.

"That shouldn't be a problem. I'll be back with something shortly." Julie finally leaves me to my thoughts and Phoenix approaches the edge of my bed.

We evade each other's gaze. I can't help but feel like I've betrayed him somehow, but he wouldn't be here if he didn't care, right? He'd be off with that girl. Do I even want him here right now? Yes. Yes, I think I do. As angry as I am, I need answers. And he has them.

Seconds, minutes, hell even hours could have passed

with tensions rising high, electric currents curling through the air, charging the space between us.

Eventually, I will myself to lift my eyes and gaze over him. Light from the hallway accents his mussed up hair and an unfamiliar scruff traces his jawline. His eyes are like sinkholes, studying the floor as if he were committing the pattern to memory. It's clear that he is at war with himself. I have never seen him look more beautiful and honest than he does in this very moment. There is a beauty to his darkness. And a darkness to his beauty.

"What time is it?" I croak in a whisper.

He looks down at his watch. "Just after three in the morning." His eyes finally find mine and together we release a collective breath. "Sully mentioned there was a family emergency, that Genevieve's sister was in the hospital. Your last name is Phillips and I always just assumed Gen was short for Jennifer, so it took me a while to put two and two together," he admits softly with a frown as he rubs the back of his neck.

"I took my grandmother's last name while I was in Italy," I explain faintly, trying to control my conflicting emotions.

He absorbs my words with a silent nod. "What happened?"

Oh, that's rich. What happened? Is he really asking me this right now? I shut my eyes tightly to quiet the screaming in my head and take a calming breath before I respond.

"Are you freaking kidding me? What happened? *You*, you lying conniving asshole. You and that girl. *That's* what happened."

So much for that calming breath.

"Jesus Christ, Ivy. Is this about the girl I was with the other night? Do you even know what you're talking about?" He looks at me in bewilderment. "That was Hailey, Sully's ex. Months ago, before I ever even met you, she begged me to be her date to this stupid wedding. Anything you *think* you saw between us was nothing more than me being a supportive friend to her."

I pause, taking his comments in slowly. Even with his truth, it still doesn't explain all of the other lies.

"Why didn't you tell me that Sully's was the wedding in Chicago? And what the hell kind of name is Sully, anyway?"

Phoenix sighs. "Cortland James Sullivan III. Our group of friends growing up always called him Sully since his name is so damn pretentious. It just stuck."

I nod my head, thinking back to every detail he's ever confided in me about his friend. The infidelity. His asshole tendencies. The need for money to help his family climb out of bankruptcy. It all starts fitting into place.

"As for the wedding, I knew that if I mentioned it, you'd expect me to bring you as my date. And trust me, that was what I wanted more than anything. To get to spend time physically next to you, kissing you and dancing until our feet were blistered. But I promised Hailey months ago, before I even met you, that I would be her date for the night. I couldn't go back on my word, especially with their fucked up history. She deserves closure and a shoulder to get through it all."

Phoenix runs his hand through his hair, clenching his jaw. "I never in a million years expected us to be standing up in the same wedding, Ivy."

Neither did I.

His admission, while painful, makes sense. More than anything I would have loved to stand up in this wedding with him as my date instead of Rachel. He cautiously approaches the side of the bed and pulls his chair close. Instinctually, I turn my hand over and he cautiously reaches out and grabs it, his thumb tracing the inside of my palm. My soul softens ever so slightly.

If what he says is true, I made a huge mistake running away from him and into Matt's arms. He didn't lie to me time and time again as I had assumed. My guilty conscience grows and I close my eyes, wanting to vomit from my royal fuck up. I can still feel Matt in me and on me. And I can only hope that Phoenix doesn't sense my unease.

"I'm sorry if I've hurt you, Ivy. I'm so, so sorry. I should have been honest with you about the wedding from day one." He takes my hand in his and plants a soft kiss upon it.

Shit.

I'm the one who should be apologizing. Not him. I have screwed up in ways he never thought possible. Well, given my track record, maybe he did see the possibility all along. But there is no way he would forgive me for what happened. Ever. I know I need to tell him the truth, but I can't. At least not right now.

I close my eyes, swallow slowly and give a tight nod. "It's okay. I understand."

The stillness between us weaves a thread, tying us together once more.

"So do you want to tell me why you're hooked up to all these machines? Are you all right?" He scoffs under his breath. "I mean, clearly you're not. But are … are you going to be okay?"

The way he stumbles over his own words is adorable. It pushes my insides beyond butterflies. There is a whole damn safari raging a stampede in my ribcage from that single look of love in his eyes.

"I … I don't even know where to begin, Phoenix."

"You can tell me, Ivy." I focus on his fingers as they trace the lines of the palm of my hand.

Can I really tell him? I don't know. I doubt he wants the truth of just how damaged I am. I take a slow, deep breath. The kind of breath where you take in so much air you feel as if your lungs will burst right through your rib cage. I know that what I'm about to tell him will change everything. A piece of radical honesty that will tell me exactly everything I need to know about him.

I swallow hard.

"Yesterday morning I woke up bleeding," I begin slowly. "When they admitted me to the hospital, blood tests came back positive for infection. Apparently the infection could have … could've caused a miscarriage." I can feel my heartbeat quaking in my ears as my hands begin to shake.

"Wait. You're pregnant?" His face blanches and he withdraws his hand. My palm and fingers hurt with vacancy and my pulse churns fast to the point of nausea. And if I'm being entirely honest with myself, the sting surprises me when he speaks in present tense.

"No. Well … no. I'm not," I say, trying to capture his eyes in mine. "Truthfully? It has to be a mistake as I haven't slept with anyone in about a year."

It's an over-share, but I don't want Phoenix to think that I'm still prone to reckless nights with strangers like the old Ivy would do. Even so, I can see it in his eyes that he thinks I've been sleeping around behind his back for the past two months. He thinks that I'm incapable of change just because I used to be a whore. While that may be partially true, I elect to leave Matt out of the equation. Bringing him up now will only complicate matters, and there is too much at stake to risk bringing up that mistake in a moment of self-hatred and desperation.

The look in Phoenix's eyes is wounding. I can't tell if he believes me, but I'm worried that he doesn't. Everything I've allowed myself to feel for Phoenix over the past few weeks has been so terrifying and fulfilling. I'm determined for him to see the truth in my words.

"I swear to you, Phoenix," I plead. "Since I met you, there hasn't been anyone else." I sit up and try to reach for his hand, but the tug of the IV tubing pulls me back.

Please believe me. Please believe me. Please believe me.

If I think it hard enough, perhaps I can will him to understand that I'm telling the truth.

I watch the light leave his eyes as he is at war with himself. My pulse beats deep within my toes, and I'm suddenly very aware of everything—the hushed childlike humming of my monitors, the flickering light shining under the bathroom door, a distant car alarm resounding the night air, the soft hiss of Phoenix's breath as he exhales between his teeth.

He opens his mouth to say something, then promptly snaps it shut. My vision starts to blur as tears begin to pool in my eyelids. "You've never given me a reason not to believe you." He takes my arm in both of his hands and traces his fingers down my forearm to the palm, squeezing it ever so slightly. The memory of his kiss lingers in my hand. "Rest your eyes, Ivy. You need your sleep."

We fall asleep, just like that, with his head against the side of my bed, holding me the only way he physically could.

Phoenix has breathed hope back into my life.

19

Thursday

JUST AS THE MORNING LIGHT spills into my bedroom, I hear a soft knock and my mom pushes her head through the cracked door.

"Hey, sweetie, how are you feeling today?" She rushes to my bedside, fawning over me. She is clearly putting on a show since I'm not alone. Her actions say one thing, but her eyes tell a completely different story. Phoenix exhales heavily and squeezes my hand before slipping into the en suite bathroom. My mom's eyes follow his path, a questioning look on her face.

She opens her mouth, presumably to comment about Genevieve's groomsman in my hospital room at such an early hour, but I beat her to the punch.

"I'm fine, Mom," I deadpan. "You must remember meeting Phoenix the other night?" I give a nod in his direction, unwilling to share our deep history and how I've known him for a few weeks now.

She smooths the blanket at my sides and plucks a few

tiny fuzz balls, casting them to the floor. There is no way I'm going to dive into a monologue about my inner emotional turmoil eating away at my soul. Or how I'm so beyond confused that I could be this generation's immaculate conception. And I sure as hell am not about to explain who Phoenix is or what he means to me. Especially not to her.

My mother pulls her sweater set tighter around her arms. She's acting like my presence in this confined space makes her uncomfortable. "We need to see about getting you out of here today. There's still so much to do before the rehearsal dinner tomorrow night and you need to be helping your sister with the last minute details, not caged up in here like an injured animal."

Are you fucking kidding me?

My life has been thrown upside down without a safety net and she has the audacity to act like *I'm* the inconvenience. Never mind her blatant concern for my health and wellbeing. Surely she can't be serious, but the stoic look on her face tells me otherwise. I've been walking through a nightmare with my eyes wide open the past few days and Genevieve's wedding is the least of my concerns. For once, *just one fucking time*, I would like for something to be about me and not my sister.

As if on cue with my thoughts, Genevieve appears in the doorway, blowing over the top of her styrofoam coffee cup. Her hair is pinned up in a perfect messy knot and her designer ivory sundress screams here comes the bride. I want to claw her perfect little face off.

"So what's the plan? We're busting you out of here today, right? You still have to learn how to bustle my dress. And I need your help rearranging the seating chart to accommodate a few late guests. People can be so rude sometimes," Genevieve says.

Her comment is humorous and the irony is not lost on me. Her self-centeredness is not a shock at all. I don't have the energy to tell her where she can shove that bustle because having both her and mother in the room with me has put me on edge.

"I don't know. The doctor should be here soon with my latest labs," I reply sweetly. I know it would take a miracle to be released today, and I find relief knowing that I have at least one more day of reprieve here in the hospital. I close my eyes and silently wish my mom and sister out of my room and out of my life.

When Phoenix emerges from the bathroom, he senses my unease and returns to my side, tucking a loose strand of hair behind my ear.

"Do you want some water or anything?" he asks, ignoring my family. I can see how deeply he cares for me with his knowing glance.

Any frustration or anger I've held for this man has washed away. The tenderness in which he touches me tells me everything I need to know, giving me strength and reassurance. He's not going anywhere and I don't want him to.

I shake my head no. "I'm okay." I examine his face a little more closely. He looks like hell. "You must be exhausted. Why don't you go back to your hotel and get some sleep for a little while?" I whisper, recognizing that he needs some rest. But while he's wearing his weariness on his face, I selfishly don't want him leaving me alone with my family. I say a silent prayer, begging him to stay.

"I'm not going anywhere without you today." He gives my hand an encouraging squeeze.

This man.

This man is my savior.

He can sense my desperate need to keep him here by my side and he's refusing to go. With all of my recent screw-ups, what have I done to deserve him?

A sharp knock on the door breaks our focus, and I watch Sully strut in and wrap his arm around Genevieve's waist, pulling her in for a kiss.

"Hey, babe," he croons. "Can you believe parking is fifteen bucks an hour here?"

Standing at the edge of my bed, Sully's eyes flash recognition then horror when they finally register on me. He studies my face intently and I watch his Adam's apple protrude from his neck as he swallows hard.

This is the first time since that night in Madison we've actually laid eyes on each other, the pieces of the jigsaw puzzle firmly fitting into place.

Phoenix looks from Sully to me and then back to Sully again. Phoenix's face shifts from concerned to wild and outraged and protective in a single blink. He mutters a string of profanities underneath his breath and squeezes my hand so hard that I start to lose circulation in my fingers.

The air in the room shifts again and discomfort oozes from Sully's every pore. I swear I see him cower for one fleeting moment.

"Hey, you okay?" I ask Phoenix, tugging back on his hand. I need him to look at me. I need him to calm down. I don't know what is going on in that head of his, but he has to chill out.

Phoenix continues to glare at his friend. He clenches his jaw and I notice a sheen of sweat over Sully's brow as he shifts his weight back and forth nervously.

"You know, I really want to be wrong about this, Ivy." He looks to the window before pushing the heels of his hands into his eye sockets, opening his mouth in an angry muted scream. The uneasy feeling apparently justified.

"What do you mean?" I tug at his shirt, trying to bring his attention back toward me.

"You did this, didn't you?" Phoenix seethes at Sully, animosity winning the war of emotions. His friend says nothing. Does nothing. Just shifts his eyes to the floor. "You sick son of a bitch."

"Hey, calm down." I pull on Phoenix's hand. "What's your problem?"

Phoenix rises defensively on his haunches, and I find myself frightened by his reaction. What the hell happened to cause him to go off the deep end?

"I knew it," Phoenix says to himself in disbelief. "Why don't you tell Ivy what you did to her? Why don't you explain to Ivy and her family and her sister—*your fiancée*—why we're here right now?"

What the hell? What does he mean? Did what to me?

Stunned, my mom and sister look at one another in confusion, trying to paint the answers.

"Excuse me?" Genevieve snaps defensively, moving to stand in front of Sully.

I steel myself and challenge him. "Phoenix, I haven't seen him since the night we first met. In fact, I've never even been formally introduced to him as my sister's fiancé."

My eyes shift to Genevieve, offering her a quiet apology for the scene unraveling before us. Her eyebrows rise inquisitively as she drops her jaw, realizing that I've met her dashing groom before today.

"Come on, Sul," he spits. "You remember meeting Ivy before, don't you?" Phoenix moves Genevieve aside and gets up in Sully's face, a predator sizing up its prey.

His reaction makes me second-guess myself. Maybe Sully has no clue who *I* am, after all, we were all pretty drunk that night, but that look he gave me when he first walked in. It was one of guilt. Of knowing. Of recollection. Of...

"Are the pieces finally falling into place for you? Genevieve told you Ivy had a miscarriage, right?" Phoenix is practically screaming now as he enunciates each word slowly so they sink in. "A. Mis. Carr. Iage."

"I fail to see what this has to do with him, Phoenix," I say pragmatically.

"CJ? What is he talking about?" Genevieve shoots me an anxious look. I can't tell what Genevieve is thinking, but she looks like she is about to kill me. Sully and Phoenix's eyes are locked in a heated stare down, silently challenging each other, neither of them backing down.

"Ivy was there that night. In Madison. The weekend of your bachelor party. You practically introduced me to her," Phoenix spits at his best friend. "Don't pretend like you don't know what I'm talking about. I know you brought the roach with you that weekend. I suspected it all along. I told you *no.* And I tried everything I could to keep her protected from you and your fucked up antics. And somehow ...somehow you still managed to fuck everything up. I said no! I actually like her, Sully!" he shouts violently.

The weight of Phoenix's declaration sits upon my

chest. My mind can't get there fast enough. I watch as Sully's eyes grow wide, piecing the puzzle together, two steps ahead of everyone else. He opens his mouth to say something.

"Just what are you insinuating, young man?" my mother barks at Phoenix.

"Jesus, you are such an asshole," Phoenix says, shaking his head in disbelief, still ignoring my mother. By his hip, I spy Phoenix's hand stretching and contracting into a fist. One by one he pops each of his knuckles as anger boils through his chest.

"What the hell is he talking about, CJ?" Genevieve asks again cautiously, tugging on his arm.

"Your fiancé!" Phoenix shouts. "The night I met Ivy, he drugged *your* sister. *My* ... my ..." He can't finish his thought, defining what I am to him. Phoenix rakes his hand down his face as my insides tumble like the melee of a washing machine. I swallow the rising bile as my pulse quickens to the point of nausea.

"Tell the woman you're about to marry what you did to her sister while she was passed out," Phoenix dares him. "Tell her!"

I wince as he shouts.

Sully's silence is his confession.

We all sit there in stunned stillness, trying to process the implications of what was just said. All eyes are on Sully as we wait for some kind of response. Something to be said to prove Phoenix wrong. I *need* him to be proved wrong. The thumping of my heartbeat deep within my ears gets louder, faster, frenzied, and I feel like I'm going to throw up.

My mind recalls a conversation I had with Phoenix

233

where he told me how Sully would go to all lengths to help his friends get laid. Paying a prostitute for his cousin, slipping drugs to a girl at a bar for his brother. I never would have guessed that Sully would be capable of drugging unsuspecting girls and that I would be involved in his fucked up charades.

"How *dare* you, you piece of shit!" Genevieve shrieks. She charges at Phoenix and starts slapping him across his face and chest.

Phoenix grabs her wrists with force and stares right through her. The look he gives dares her to keep challenging him, to think of the implications of what is happening. He says nothing, gently pushing her to the side.

The next thing I know, Phoenix unleashes a guttural sound and my mom is trying to pull him off of Sully, but Phoenix is just too angry. Too strong. Too overcome with hatred. I watch his shoulder snap, throwing the weight of his body into his childhood friend's cheek. His nose. His eyes. He continues drawing his fist back, pummeling into his face over and over and over again.

I'm not sure whose it is, but blood covers Phoenix's knuckles and it stains Sully's shirt. The scene unfolding around me is complete chaos. I can't think over Genevieve's wails as my mother tries to calm her. I can't breathe with the gravity of this situation on my chest. I can't process with this truth infecting the air. The room has become a whirlwind of motion, emotion and sound. And here I sit in the middle of it all, the quiet one, the eye of the storm.

I have no concept of how much time passes before security finally rushes into the room and pries the pair apart. Genevieve fumes as she casts daggers at me eyes and coddles CJ. In an unsurprising move, my mother is right there beside her, inspecting the damage done to the groom.

I look at Phoenix as his chest rises and falls rapidly. His wild eyes soften at the sight of me. Tears fill my eyes, blurring his image in a kaleidoscope of color. I want to tear his face off as my mind races with too many unanswered questions. But I know he's just fucked me over on a level I never imagined possible.

"Why?" Why what? I don't know. I don't even know who I'm addressing with my question. I just … I just can't process Phoenix's accusation.

"Ivy," Phoenix says with a pained expression, "I was only trying to help."

Help? What he is doing is certainly not *helping* me. For the past few months, he has led me to believe that we had something real. Something not based on lies. A legit connection. But all this time he knew, or at the very least suspected that Sully had done something to me the night we met, and he never said a word.

Who the hell does that?

If he has been harboring this shit the entire time, how can I even begin to trust him with anything else? Is Hailey really who he says she is? Is *he* really who he says he is?

Is nothing sacred anymore?

Well, fuck Phoenix and the righteous horse he rode in on.

"You think you can come in here and expect me to be okay with all of this? Expect me *not* to hate you? You can't come in and save me, Phoenix. I'm not a fucking princess and I most definitely don't need rescuing. Especially not from you," I bite back, seething acid. "You are unbelievable. Just get out!"

The security guard grabs Phoenix and removes him from my room and presumably the premises. I can't stand the sight of him right now.

As he leaves, Phoenix gives me a tearful, apologetic look. He understands that, truth or not, he has hurt me on levels unfathomable. The pain within his eyes could write volumes. I feel numb as I watch him walk out of my room and out of my life.

Sully ... CJ ... Cortland ... whatever the hell his name is, has brushstrokes of blood painted across his jaw and chin and nose. A piece of living art in front of me, features rearranged in Cubist fashion. A Picasso, to be precise. The pretty boy isn't so pretty anymore. *Good.*

"That means you, too!" I hiss at Sully in disbelief.

The shuffling of his feet sounds like a death march toward the door.

My heart lurches at the silence in the room. My mother and Genevieve exchange a mortifying look. The one thing Phoenix never wanted was to bring me pain. But for the truth to be told, the pain is inevitable. His heart aches for me, and mine for his, but my mind spits in his general direction as rage sets in.

Phoenix knew. He fucking knew. He admitted he suspected Sully had done something and he never once said anything. What kind of despicable human being does that? The asshole kind, that's who. I feel my veins surge with anger and hurt, then my insides fall through my body and to the floor when I recognize the look on my family's faces is one of contempt.

"You slept with him?" Genevieve gasps, tears filling her eyes. "How could you?" Her eyes plead with mine.

Of course she believes that I'd do this intentionally. That I would bring this upon myself, upon her. That I would find a way to fuck things up beyond repair. Genevieve is so far beyond delusional that she is incapable of registering what all of this actually means. That her beloved husband to be isn't who she thinks he is. That he's a rapist.

"Are you fucking kidding me?" My voice cracks as emotion takes over.

My mother barks at me. "Ivy!"

The look in her face tells me everything I need to know. It doesn't matter what happened, or how it happened, they will always see me as the daughter who screws everything up for everybody else. The one who whored herself out to her sister's boyfriends and now her fiancé. The one who pursued a career not worthy of their approval. The horrible one bringing the demise of the Cotter family name.

Round and round we go. I will never be able to get off this carousel of disappointment. And this time, I never even punched my ticket to ride. I was dragged on kicking and screaming. Without my knowledge. Without permission.

This ends…

Right here.

Right now.

I cannot handle the loathing they continue to unload on me. Their loathing turns into self-loathing and no longer will I allow hatred to have a vice grip on my soul.

I am done.

"Just get the fuck out!" I scream in a fit of rage at Genevieve.

"Watch your tongue, young lady. Don't you dare spit profanity at us!" My mother says as she glares at me in disgust, antipathy evident in her body language.

Of all of the moments to step up and pretend to be my mother, this is the one she chooses. I find the look of horror on my mother's face highly amusing, but she is no longer allowed to scold me like a petulant child.

I take a calming breath and collect myself, calculating my next move. "I'm not spitting profanity at you," I say in the most pleasant tone I can summon. "I'm enunciating it. Loud. And. Fucking. Clear. Like a goddamned lady."

The conviction in my voice surprises me, and the terrible parts deep within proudly wear a sinister smile. I watch my mother as shock and horror replace the smug look she wears upon her Botox-filled face.

Genevieve is the first to leave wordlessly, likely to go find Sully and examine the damage done to his face. I don't dare justify myself to her, but he got off easy as far as I'm concerned. If I could kill him myself, I would. Phoenix should have killed him with each punch, though Phoenix has another thing coming if I ever see his sorry ass again. My stomach turns at the thought of him.

It takes effort to not laugh under my breath as I imagine how the supposed love of Genevieve's life will look in their wedding photos, assuming she is stupid enough to still marry him. I can't help but wonder if the thought of her husband-to-be being a rapist has registered in her mind. I want to tell her all of the awful things I've learned about him through Phoenix, before we realized how we were connected, but that won't change anything. Nothing I say will help the situation, so I don't even bother. Plus, she won't want to hear what I have to say. Genevieve and I will never recover from this, I'm certain.

My mother eyes me with such abhorrence that I don't even have to wonder what she's thinking. Her glare says it all. Hate pierces right through me. I've never noticed how her mouth puckers with displeasure like she just sucked a lemon dry whenever she looks at me with disgust. But if looks could kill, I'd be dead. Actually, I would've been dead about eight years ago. I guesstimate that's around the time she emotionally disowned me.

"It's one thing to be a complete bitch, Ivy, but it's another to be a disgrace of a daughter." Her words, while true, still sting, but I don't flinch. I don't dare give her the satisfaction of seeing how she affects me.

I watch as she collects her purse and turns toward the door. I allow her the last word in this conversation because I refuse to give her the last word in my life. If I have my way, this will be the last time I see her for a very long time.

My eyes return to the vacant wall across from my bed. Ever so slowly, I breathe in through my nose, fill my lungs beyond the point of capacity, and exhale through my mouth. Deep, cleansing breaths, trying to release the tension I've been carrying for years.

A few quiet minutes later, the day nurse returns. "Is everything all right in here now?"

"I'm fine," I respond numbly as I stare through the white sterile wall. I know that I'm really not fine, but I also know that wasn't what she was asking. She doesn't care about my personal bullshit. It's not her job. She only cares about getting me cleared so the next patient can be wheeled into this room.

"From here on out, no visitors. Let security know the

only one allowed in this room is Rachel Meyers." I don't intend to come off brash, but that's the thing about emotions—it spoils all sense of rationality.

"Rachel Meyers?" I give her an affirming nod. "Sure thing. I'll let the desk know. Anything else?"

"More pain killers."

And make them strong, I silently ask. I don't want to feel anything again for a long time.

20

The next day... or two.
Who knows, really?

INHALE NUMBNESS.

Exhale apathy.

Repeat involuntarily.

When you think about it, involuntary behavior is fucked up, really. Our bodies just take over without thinking. Without permission. Without control. Without cognizance. And even when we try to resist, to hold our breath or keep our eyes open, our conscious eventually relinquishes control and our body involuntarily takes back over. It's really quite obnoxious, being forced to do something you don't want to do. I could really do without breathing right now, and yet my lungs continue to expand and contract without my permission.

At some indiscernible point in time, the stark white, sterile walls of the hospital room involuntarily turn into the beige, standard rooms of Rachel's apartment.

I don't remember coming here, but I'm thankful to be

sitting among her moving boxes, mindlessly watching her unload her belongings, listening to her fill the air with her thoughtless thoughts.

Inhale numbness.

Exhale apathy.

Repeat involuntarily.

The scent of fresh paint assaults my nostrils and churns my stomach. I'll never understand why anyone would paint an empty apartment beige with all of the colors available in the spectrum.

Beige is where color goes to die. Is there a shade out there that could be more horrible than beige? Some might say black, but black hides secrets and haunts and conveys anger and emptiness. On the other hand, white is stark. It brings cleanliness. Godliness. Purity. And pearly white gates.

But beige? Beige is emotionless. It is the shade of lifeless contempt.

My mother is beige. Genevieve, too.

And now, after Phoenix coming clean with the truth, *I am beige.*

Involuntarily, I laugh under my breath and take notice of how fitting my surroundings are. Condemned to a life of beige.

And so again, I inhale numbness.

Exhale apathy.

Repeat involuntarily.

"I STOPPED BY YOUR HOUSE on my way home. Gen was none too pleased and nearly didn't let me in but your dad saw me at the door. He asked me to have you call him … he's worried about you," Rachel says, placing an old duffel bag at my feet. "Anyway, I thought you might like a few of your things."

"Thanks," I whisper with a tight smile and make a mental note to call my dad sometime soon. Even though we've come a long way the past few days. I'm just not ready to talk to him. I have no idea what day it is. Surely Genevieve is getting married today or tomorrow, but I don't even feel bad for not being there. As far as I'm concerned, they can all go to hell.

Friends like Rachel are rare. She is indefinitely the first person to go to bat for me. But she never fails at being the first to give me a high five in the face with the back of a chair when I act like a raging bitch. Since leaving the hospital, Rachel has opened her home to me. It's a humble apartment in the Wicker Park neighborhood, which is full of quasi-hipsters much like my dear friend.

Rachel stands there, looking at my intently. She clearly wants to tell me something but hesitates.

"Out with it already," I say.

She sighs and pushes her hair back out of her face. "Genevieve was really wrecked," she begins. "I think it has finally hit her that her fiancé did the unthinkable."

I look at Rachel, vacant and unfazed.

"She didn't look good, Ivy," Rachel informs me. "Maybe you should ca—"

"No," I snap at her sternly. Hell will freeze over before I call my sister. I know Rachel means well, but I do not have room for toxic people in my life anymore.

She unloads a heavy sigh in the space between us. "Well, you are welcome to stay as long as you need to, Ivy. I just ask that maybe you consider taking a shower?"

A soft laugh escapes my throat, thankful she is not going to push Genevieve on me anymore. "Yes, Mom," I reply sullenly as she disappears into the kitchen.

Snatching up my bag, I retreat to her spare bedroom where I put on a fresh change of clothes. I'm thankful that she grabbed my favorite pair of yoga pants—I have every intention of moving into them until the hygiene Gods evict me.

"What the hell happened in here?" Rachel shouts.

She must have found the small heap of technology I left crumbled on the floor of her kitchen.

I pop my head out of the bedroom and shrug, feigning nonchalance. "Phoenix wouldn't stop texting me."

"So you broke your phone?"

"I didn't mean to break it," I lie. From the instant I threw it, I knew I was going to have to result to more extreme measures when I found it unscathed. Apparently shatterproof phone cases aren't exempt from cases of extreme heartache. I have every intention of fixing the dent in her kitchen wall once I have my first paycheck. I may even buy myself a new phone, though I don't see the point. I can't imagine having happy conversations with anyone anymore.

But once I got the screen to crack I went a little overboard. A meat pounder and a box of tissues may or may not have been involved. On second thought, that sounds like a subplot of a really bad porno.

"You know, you could have just turned your phone off if you didn't want to hear from him," Rachel informs me, trying to hide the condescension in her voice.

I roll my eyes. Really? She's going to scold me? I am at the lowest point of my life and the last thing I need is to be reprimanded.

"Okay, okay. I felt like breaking shit. I figured breaking my phone was better than chucking your television out of the window. Sue me." I turn back into the bedroom, hoping she gets the hint to just leave me the hell alone.

She doesn't, of course. She stands in my doorway, holding the piece of metal formerly known as my cell phone.

"My life is a train wreck, Rachel." I release a heavy sigh.

"No, *my* life is the train wreck. You, my dear, are the conductor on the Hot Mess Express," she responds, trying to make me smile. She tosses what's left of my phone on the side table by the door and releases a heavy sigh that lingers in the air between. "I'll leave you be for a little bit."

I watch as she shuts the door behind her, and then hide under the covers for the umpteenth time today, hugging a pillow to my chest tightly. How I wish this were the comforting arms of a warm body.

In spite of everything that has happened, I still miss him.

I want nothing more than to open my eyes and be somewhere else. To be lying next to Phoenix. To be completely oblivious to his lies. To disappear into a state of being where the lines of numbness and happiness are blurred. I want to rewind life and start things over. I don't care if I'm blissfully ignorant. At least I wouldn't be in pain.

But each time I close my eyes, I'm taken back to the night on Lake Mendota, trying to find the exact moment things went wrong. I think about all of that blood and Phoenix's outburst. Sully's silence echoes through my ears. I hear the doctor say the words "spontaneous abortion" again and again and again, breaking my heart all over.

I refuse to think about what Sully supposedly did to me. Each time that I do, the scab on my soul rips wide again and the sting consumes me to the point of hysterics. And I refuse to think about the secrets that Phoenix kept because the memory of him is the salt in the wound and I just want to bleed out.

So instead of thinking at all, I open my eyes and stare at the beige popcorn ceiling and will myself to sleep. I count backwards from one hundred and start again when I reach zero. It's all I can do to keep my mind from drifting to him.

THE MOVEMENT ON THE MATTRESS stirs me. At some point during the course of the early afternoon I must have fallen asleep. Rachel is perched on the edge of the bed holding a moving box marked "Kitchen" in bold letters along the side.

"Get up," she commands. "We're going outside."

Groaning, I put the pillow over my head. Damn it, why won't she just leave me the hell alone? Misery doesn't love company. Misery wants to hole up in peace and quiet. I am perfectly content living as a recluse in this moment. I can't deal with Rachel's saccharine sentiments. I just want to be by myself. There is no way in hell I'm going anywhere today. The pain is all too fresh and raw and I'm too busy burying myself in a landslide of remorse and self-pity.

"I'm fucking serious, Ivy. I know your life sucks right now, but that's just how it goes. Life sucks. It gets better temporarily. And then it will inevitably suck again. But I'm not going to allow you to sleep away the pain. You want to feel numb? We have some pills for that. Now get up."

Rachel yanks my arm as I sit up. Resistance is pointless. Numbly, I stand and follow her out of the apartment. But rather than taking the elevator down to the ground floor, we head up the emergency stairwell. She pushes the door open and I'm blinded by white light. For a brief moment, I envision moving on from this world. The warm breeze wraps around us like a blanket, comforting me.

I look down … *when did I put shoes on?*

The roof.

We're on the roof.

And for one fleeting moment, I welcome the thought

of being pushed off the side of her complex. I bet it would feel like I'm flying. Not falling. Because I've been falling for days and there's no ground in sight. I just want to fly. Be gone from here. Be done with all this drama.

My eyes focus on Rachel. I see her lips moving, but I hear nothing. She's talking. Nothing registers.

Maybe that's because nothing matters?

Or because I am nothing?

Perhaps both?

Why doesn't anything matter?

Rachel hands me a plate and I vacantly examine the cool porcelain in my hands. "Go ahead," she says, gesturing to the plate in my hands. "Throw it."

What? Is she mad?

"This will be much more therapeutic than putting a hole in my kitchen wall with your cell phone. Go on, Ivy. Throw it."

Yep. Rachel has definitely gone mad. I'm not breaking her dishes. This whole notion is utterly ridiculous.

I feel the heaviness of the plate in my hands. It's the same heaviness I feel in my chest and my shoulders and my soul. I reluctantly trace my fingers over the scalloped edges.

Rachel grows impatient and a pissed-off hardness punctuates her eyes. "BREAK THE DAMN PLATE, IVY!" she screams in my face.

Without thought, I obey and gently sling the plate toward the wall, watching it snap into large chunks against the rooftop.

"No, don't toss it. You feel like breaking shit? Then fucking break shit. Don't you dare pussyfoot around."

Jesus. Why is she so angry with me? I want to tell her

to chill out. She has no right to be pissed. This bullshit happened to me. Not her.

Rachel grabs a mug from the box, stretches her hands high above her head and smashes it against the ground forcefully with a primitive grunt. The mug fractures into thousands of tiny little pieces and dust at our feet.

Rachel reaches back into the moving box and grabs a small white dessert plate and places it in my hands.

"Go. It's your turn." Her eyes burn deep and her jaw is tight. I know she means business. "It is *not* okay to not feel anything right now. You are blindingly angry and are too numb to realize it. Has any of this shit actually registered with you?" Rachel squints into the sunlight and I finally notice that she is on the verge of crying.

I want to shout that yes, it has registered. And each time I recognize the devastation, I die a little more inside.

I hate myself that much more.

I hate the secrets and the speculation.

I hate Phoenix and how confused he makes me feel.

I hate this world and all of the fucked up cards I've been dealt in my lifetime.

"Break it, Ivy…" her voice trails off in a whisper as she wipes the trails of moisture streaming down her cheeks.

I clench the saucer and sling it like a Frisbee against the neighboring building's wall. Chips of white ceramic ricochet into a million tiny pieces and the shards rain down into piles on the black rooftop.

Slowly, I begin to hear the beating of my own heart deep inside my ears. Adrenaline picks up and the pulsing vein in my neck throbs as if an angry demon has been awakened inside of me. Waves of anger pulse through my body and I want to fist my hair and rip it from my skull, absorbing the pain to make sure I can still actually feel something other than anger; that I'm still capable of feeling physical pain and not just emotional pain. Instead, I fist a teacup, then wind my arm back and pitch it against the wall with so much force I fall to my knees.

I watch it burst with satisfaction.

I crave release. I'm driven by the insatiable need to damage. To break. To shred. To crush every last little thing in my path.

I push myself back to my feet and my chest heaves as I snatch another plate from the box. I will not stay down— I refuse to be defeated. I *will* come back from this shit. I bite the inside of my cheek so hard that warm metallic liquid starts to fill my mouth. As Sully invades my mind, I fight back the tears. That piece of disgusting filth makes me ill. That asshole deserves to die.

I look at the plate. *That motherfucker. This should be his face right now.* "Fuuuuuuuuuuuuuck!" Anger rips through my frame as I hurl dinnerware in rapid success.

Smash.

For the contempt I feel for my sister.

Smash.

For Phoenix.

Smash.

And every last thing I ever felt for him.

Smash.

Thought I could feel for him.

Smash.

For thinking I could love him.

Smash.

For Matt.

Smash.

Fucking, Matt that I cannot seem to get out of my life.

Smash.

For my goddamned parents and their need for appearances.

Smash.

Approval.

Smash.

For my need of their approval.

Smash. Smash. Smash.

"I hate you!" I scream as I wind my arm back and hurl the last plate in the box at the barrier wall, watching it shatter into tiny smithereens.

I crash back down on my knees. I don't know whether to laugh or collapse into a fit of sobs. I can hardly contain my panting. Adrenaline pushes and pulls through my veins.

But this feeling …

This feels …

Damn. This feels incredible.

I grab the empty box and punch the ever-living shit out of it as it caves-in upon itself. When it's finally flat, I grab it and begin tearing it apart until I'm surrounded by a messy confetti of the corrugated box.

A guttural sob rips through my soul. How has my life gotten to this point?

I throw my head back as an inhuman roar escapes my body. All of the hatred I carry for Sully is unleashed. My soul, my security, even my sense of self … it has all been violated and left in shreds.

I hate him. With every fiber of my being, I hate him. And I hate Phoenix, too.

I hate him for knowing.

I hate him for telling me the truth.

I hate him for loving me.

And I hate myself for ever loving him. I am so pathetic. And foolish.

I look at the remnants of Rachel's dinnerware scattered across the roof as the tears continue to flow. I am fully aware of my lunacy in this moment. Anyone watching would surely have me committed.

But my God ... breaking shit, breaking myself, *breaking my world* is exactly what I need. I imagine this it the kind of despair Edvard Munch tried to paint in *The Scream.*

Exhaustion sets in and my head falls to my chest, aching with each heave. Rachel lays a delicate hand on my shoulder and gives it a reassuring squeeze.

"I'm gonna go inside, sweetie. Stay up here and take all the time you need. I'll come back and clean up later." Her voice rings soft, like tinkling wind chimes. I can't summon myself to look at her in the eye, but I give her a tight appreciative nod before I hear the door close.

Grabbing a jagged fragment of broken plate, I lie flat on my back and gaze up at the sky. Clouds in shapes of my childhood imagination roll by with graceful ease. In the distance, a car horn blares, the Blue Line train rumbles, a dog barks. The white noise of the city calms my restless soul as I mindlessly twirl the porcelain in my fingers, careful not to cut myself. Heat radiates off of the rooftop as the thick summer air sticks to my skin like honey.

I learned at a very young age that the world only cares about what you can do for it. It craves discernible output. The intangible things, like kindness and love and justice, are simply nice haves. I used to believe that I wanted the tangible things in life, but not anymore. Those things aren't important.

So what is it I want for myself?

It's a challenging question to ask. But arguably more challenging to answer truthfully.

Even in light of everything that has happened I still want Phoenix. My body aches for his touch, yet I hate him with a ferocity that scares me. Everything I feel for him is an extreme of passionate emotion. Hate. Love. There is no in between. He will forever be entwined with Sully and the aftermath of that party. Of being raped. The baby that never was. It all bleeds together and feeds off of him. As much as it would kill me to let him go, holding on would be a slow, painful suicide. I need to be free of Phoenix.

I want to be independently happy from my parents, from my friends, from any potential love interest—be it Phoenix or Matt or the next dark, tall, and screwable guy who catches my eye. I know that I can't carry them with me. Whatever comes next is something I have to do on my own accord. After all, if you want something you've never had, you have to make yourself do something you've never done before. And that means leaving them all behind.

I come with too much baggage, especially now, for anyone to truly love me. I'm damaged. Used. And as much as it hurts, I'm okay with my new reality. I played that part for so long it has become second nature, but I'm not okay with what happened—I doubt I'll ever be. But I am trying to be at peace with my emotions through it all. There is a little voice in the back of my head that taunts me. It tries to convince me that I am deserving of everything I'm going through right now ... that my current reality is a penance for my past transgressions. But I know better than to feed that demon. I know that there is only one person to blame for this, and that person is *not* me.

It's amazing how in two days the world can shift and drastically change the course of your life. Everything can be taken from you without you ever even knowing it. Nothing is in control. Life is just a series of coincidences in expeditious succession. My coincidences just happened to wreck my self-being, self-worth and shattered any sense of normalcy I ever had. All it takes is one crack, and how quickly your world will shatter.

The colliding of two souls along a lake under a starry sky.

The slip of a pill.

The shout of an accusation.

The smash of a plate.

The collapsing of a soul.

My life is Newton's Third Law of Physics. For every action, there is an equal and opposite reaction. Cautiously give your heart away? It'll be torn to smithereens. For every moment you feel alive, there is a point of emotional death. But in order to pick up the pieces and become whole again, you need to allow yourself the opportunity to crumble, and be less than perfect. Vulnerable.

Pieces of porcelain litter the rooftop. My fingers still. And the world moves in slow-mo.

My eyes catch a black cloud of sparrows circling the sky above. They float, dive and shoot back up into the sky in unison, over and over, like an amoeba dancing in the air. I can't help but wonder, with wings and freedom and the ability to fly anywhere in this world, why do they stay here, in this neighborhood, flying in the same circle over and over again.

I'm just like those damn birds.

Except for I have the sense to break free from the rut.

I have the capacity to chart a different course for myself. Nobody but me gets to write the ending to my story. And I refuse to let the hand I ache to hold be the hand that holds me back.

I will start over. Pretend none of this ever happened. Pretend Sully doesn't have this horrible, humiliating claim on my life. Pretend Phoenix was just another meaningless name on my laundry list of guys. Leave all the bullshit, deceit, and unnecessary drama in Chicago.

This is it.

I'm moving to New York.

22

THREE QUICK RAPS BEAT THROUGH the door and echo down the hallway to the kitchen where Rachel and I stand hugging each other. I've just told her about my decision and she is unbelievably supportive of me moving, even though I know it's killing her inside. She is, hands down, my rock through all of life's dramas.

"Ivy! Rachel? Open up. I know you're in there!" My heart crumbles at the panic in Phoenix's voice. He beats on the door again with such force that we can hear the chain on the back of the door rattle. "Come on, Ivy. We need to talk."

Yes, we need to talk, but I can't talk right now. If I see him, I will slap him so hard that we'll both go back in time so he can have the opportunity to make all of this right. I want to hurt him like he hurt me. I want to open him up and tear apart his insides so he knows how it feels to be violated. But more importantly, if I see him now I know I'll cry. And Phoenix is not worthy of seeing me in tears.

Rachel releases me. "Do you want me to get rid of him?"

I choke back the tears as I nod. The weight in my chest is heavier than a loaded gun. I sit down on the wooden chair at our kitchen table and fold myself in half. I need to be small. Invisible. I want to disappear completely and forget about him. This is all just too much to take in right now.

In the background, I hear Rachel crack the door open and say something to Phoenix—what, I'm not sure.

"I'm not leaving until she talks to me!" he shouts as he tries to assert himself through the doorway.

"Hey! Back off, jackass. She needs some space right now!" Rachel throws her shoulder into the door with a grunt, slamming it shut. That is sure to leave a mark. "I mean it. Leave her the hell alone."

I have never heard such an acidic tone from her before. She massages her shoulder gingerly as she returns back to the table.

A string of obscenities floats through the air from the hallway. A low thud makes me question if he's starting to kick the floorboards. Perhaps Rachel should offer him a plate to break and send him on his way.

Returning to the kitchen, my best friend's eyes look haunted. She doesn't say anything but shakes her head and slides into the seat across from me.

"You know what we need right now?"

More plates? A restraining order? A time machine so I can go back and be fourteen years old eternally before all of the drama began? Any of these would be welcomed right now.

"Pancakes," she says with a small, sympathetic smile.

Yes, I do believe that breakfast food would help. While it won't solve my problems, it will at the very least help make my stomach stop growling.

"Go in the other room and relax. I'll grab you in a bit when it's ready."

I do as I'm told and retreat back to my temporary bedroom. The mouthwatering scent of the batter sizzling on the griddle fills the apartment as Phoenix's assault on our door continues. This incessant ruckus has got to stop. I grab my iPod and crank the volume up to eleven, but even the melodic wails of Trent Reznor aren't enough to drown him out.

WHILE RACHEL BUSIES HERSELF IN the kitchen, curiosity gets the best of me and I stupidly decide I need to see Phoenix one final time. I creep quietly into the living room and glance through the peephole, convincing myself that all I need is one quick peek. I can hear him, but he's hidden from my view so I crack the door, keeping the chain latched to the lock so he can't force his way through. Upon seeing me, his jaw softens and he appears lighter. His beautiful face is anguished, like he hasn't slept in weeks.

"Are you okay?" he asks softly.

I divert my eyes quickly to the floor. Am I okay? No, I am most definitely not okay. Frankly I don't know if I ever will be okay again.

"I'm fine," I say, the lie becoming easier each time I say it. I'm not fine. I'm anything but fine. But I've learned that other people need to hear those reassuring words more than I do.

A bewildered laugh escapes his throat.

"Fine. Fine. Fine. You're always just *fine*, Ivy!" I

can't tell if he's angry or annoyed, but the sound crescendos from his soul as his voice raises. "But you know what? Sometimes it's okay to not be fine. Sometimes it's okay to bleed, and be shattered. Show the world you're vulnerable and be really fucking pissed off. And it's okay tell people how you really feel. Anyone who has suffered through what you have this past week, hell, through the past twenty-two years of existence with that family of yours, is certainly not what I'd call fine."

I flinch as his fist meets the doorjamb in a jolting thud.

"I'm sorry, I didn't mean to yell..." He trails off in thought. My eyes catch his and his chest heaves as he tries to catch his breath. His jaw is square as he grinds his teeth, calculating his next move.

Minutes pass and Phoenix's voice turns softer as he begins again. "From what I've gathered, you get involved in relationships—if you can even call them that—for all the wrong reasons. They're empty. Meaningless. A distraction from how shitty you *think* your life really is."

How very true this is.

"But this..." His voice cracks as he waves his finger in the space between us. "*This* wasn't meaningless. Not to me, anyway. You completely turned my world upside. And I don't know what to do. I know I've only just met you and it's so damn hard not being around you. This distance is killing me."

Slowly, gently, he starts pounding his forehead against the doorframe.

I didn't think it was possible, but my heart just shattered a little more. I want to push the door shut and unlocked the chain so I can throw myself into his arms. Tell

him that it will be all right. That I forgive him. That this—
that *us*—can work.

But I can't.

I don't.

He looks at me expectantly. Yet all I can do is stare at
him as words fail me.

My body fails me.

I'm paralyzed.

Phoenix's soft tone escalates and he's practically
shouting at me now. "Open your eyes, Ivy! Your life isn't
terrible. Sure, your family is messed up, but whose isn't?
You have been dealt some shitty cards, especially as of
late, but you've got a lot of really great things going for
you, including me, which you're rejecting because all of
your past relationships didn't work."

His fingers wrap around the side of the door and he
presses his forehead against the trim, like he's capable of
liquefying and slipping inside. I notice the dust dancing in
the hall amid the glow of the sunshine the pours in from
the window. It's mesmerizing and I try to numb myself so
his words wash right over me. I want to tell him that he's
right—that I'm not fine. That I'm devastatingly hurt. That
ever since he told me what Sully did to me I've been having nightmares so bad that I'm terrified to close my eyes,
which is infuriating because all I want to do is sleep away
the pain. I want to strip him down and expose him and
make him defenseless like he's made me. I want to rattle
every ounce of his confidence and rip away his security.

But I know I need him gone.

If I don't let him go now, I never will. The time has
come to cut him loose.

It has become painfully obvious that no matter how

much you may be drawn to a person, sometimes two individuals were simply not meant to be together. Harold once told me that everyone we meet serves a purpose in our life for that particular place and time. And I realize that Phoenix walked into mine that fateful night to push me to the edge of living my own life.

But there is no longer a place for him.

"I … I think you should go. This … us … we were a mistake."

"Ivy! Wait…"

I freeze momentarily and my eyes meet his through the crack in the door. I know exactly what I need to say to drive the dagger into his heart and him free, so I focus on the painful truth. The truth he deserves to know.

"I slept with Matt last week," I say, my voice void of emotion.

I say it to come clean with myself and own my shit because the old Ivy would never confess her sins.

I say it to push him as far away from me as possible because the old Ivy would have just strung him along.

I say it to fulfill my preceding reputation because even on their deepest level some things will never change.

My confession visibly guts him and I watch the man before me crumble and cave in on himself. When I can no longer bear to see the agony in his eyes, I quietly push the door shut and lock the deadbolt. I stand there for a moment, forehead pressed against the door, fingertips touching the knob, silently saying my goodbyes inside my head while he continues to knock and beg from the other side.

"I don't care about your mistakes, Ivy. I don't care how you've fucked up. We all have fucked up—believe me, but it's how you come back from the fall that counts.

Just don't self-destruct on me."

I try to stay strong, but my tears betray me.

"This is what you do, Ivy—you run!" he shouts through the door as anger takes over. "You ran away to Italy when things with Matt and your family got too shitty to deal with. And you're running away from me right now. You have this need to keep everyone, even Rachel, at a distance. Is that why you liked me so much, or rather the idea of me? Because you could finally have a relationship that you could keep at a safe distance? I know deep down you don't want to hurt me. But you are so consumed with your own pain that you are blind to the fact that your actions are hurting others."

I close my eyes absorbing his painful words. It hurts so much because it's true. Minutes of silence drift between us. I press my hand against the door and imagine his hand mirroring mine on the other side. So close, but so very far apart from physically touching.

"You have a choice here," he starts talking again. "You can run away or *we* can try harder."

The way he emphasizes we gives me a flicker of hope, but my mind does everything to extinguish the thought.

"I'll tell you what, Ivy. You can try to push me away. You can try to run and build up walls around you. But each and every wall you put up, I'm going to tear it down brick by fucking brick. I'll give you some space, just know that this isn't the last of me."

I pull back and look through the peephole in time to see him run his hands through his hair and take off down the hall.

I can't do this.

He needs to just walk away and be done with me. I need to learn to stand on my own two feet. I will always love the man I made him out to be in my mind, but I don't need him in my life.

I turn around to find Rachel's pitying eyes sizing me up, debating whether or not I'm going to cry again. She makes her way to me in three steps and wraps me up in the biggest bear hug she can muster.

"I'm okay," I whisper hoarsely to her, everything in my eyesight a smeared, wet blur. "I'm fine."

But this time the lie is for me. I need the lie because lies are truths that you convince yourself are real.

THE FIRST BATCH OF PANCAKES burned. The scent of charred batter will surely linger for days.

Rachel's second batch of pancakes fed my broken heart.

The third batch feeds my soul and offers a glimmer of hope that one day I will be whole again.

We eat the pancakes off of paper towels because, as my best friend so candidly put it, "I'd offer you a plate, but you broke all of mine." Leave it to Rachel to find humor on a day like this.

We spend the rest of the afternoon wrapped in an oversized fleece blanket, shades pulled down, curtains drawn, shutting out the rest of the world. She is the glue holding me together. I fear the minute we come out from under this blanket I will unravel into an inconsolable heap.

This is our farewell party.

In my best friend's solace, I know that one day I will be all right. Definitely not today. And probably not tomorrow. But one day I will recover from this and truly be fine.

With the help of lots of therapy.

And lots of pancakes and waffles.

And probably lots of alcohol.

Whoever said love hurts had it entirely wrong. The act of loving someone is never what hurts. That part of love is beautiful and amazing and liberating. It makes life electric and vibrant. It makes you the best possible version of yourself. It's when the person you love falls short of your expectations that drive the stake relentlessly through your heart.

That is the part that hurts the most.

AIRPORTS ARE A MOSAIC OF emotions. There are people constantly coming and going. Saying goodbyes. Being reunited. Stoic businessmen crunching numbers to meet that bottom line. Vacationers in anticipation, or disappointment, of being home. And, of course, the dreaded assholes who are convinced that their oversized carry-on is the exception to the rule.

And somewhere in between, there's me.

I'm completely and totally lost. But at least I'm lost heading in the right direction, which is anywhere but here. For me, there are no sayonaras, there will be no greetings on the other end, and there certainly are no expressions of affection.

Airports: they are equal parts overwhelming loneliness and overflowing love.

But do you know the best part about airports? They have bars that open with the first flight and have bartenders who don't judge.

It's only ten thirty-six, but I already need a drink. My eyes flash to the clock behind the bar and I remind myself that it's five o'clock somewhere.

Saddling up at the empty bar, I flick my driver's license onto the wooden counter, requesting a draft I can barely pronounce. The bartender examines my ID then studies my face.

"I know. I look like I could be in high school." I shrug, acknowledging his unspoken concern. He sighs as he pours my beer, not being mindful of the abundance of foam toppling over the rim.

The first draw I take is bitter but the ale warms my insides. The second long sip helps me forget all of the good that came into my life the past few weeks. And with the third I force myself to let go of the things I cannot control.

The dark mahogany décor reminds me of the interior of the Washburn Observatory during my only date with *him*. I refuse to even think his name; it hurts too much, so I quickly focus my attention on a toddler running wild in the terminal with his mom in hot pursuit, pushing his memory out of my mind.

The bartender wipes down the counter with a dingy, tattered rag and turns the volume up on the television. The station is showing highlights from last night's Cubs game. Another mark in the loss column. My chest tightens at the mere mention of the Chicago Cubs. Before I would just roll my eyes and push thoughts of hot summer days at the ballpark with my dad from my mind. But now, the memory of being *his* Cubby Bear plagues me.

Everything I do and everything I see reminds me of him. It's infuriating.

Among the crowds of people throughout the airport, I realize just how alone I am in this world. Don't get me wrong, I'm used to being alone in every sense of the word, but this is the first time being alone has actually felt lonely. His presence, even at a distance, filled a void that I never knew existed.

I miss knowing he is just one quick phone call away.

I miss waking up to a text he sent during the night.

I miss his laugh.

His jokes.

His stories.

Hell, if I'm being entirely honest with myself, I just miss *him* even in spite of everything.

My God, how we've both fucked things up beyond recognition. It's hard to not be angry with the pair of us.

Downing the rest of my beer, I slap a few singles on the bar and sling my bag over my shoulder. The bartender gives an appreciative grunt and I make my way back into the crowds of travelers.

I've waited my whole life to truly break free and venture out on my own. And now it's finally here. It feels strange to find myself standing on the edge, ready to jump. Much like reading that final page of the never-ending novel—I'm excited for the resolution with the characters but so incredibly sad to see their journey end. I wish my story would have the resolution I thought I was once destined for, but sometimes it's up to ourselves to write our own happy ending. I'm ready for the end of this novel; to turn to a blank page of a different book and simply write my own story.

An automated voice pulls me from my thoughts. "Ivy Cotter, please pick up the red courtesy phone for a message. Ivy Cotter, please pick up the red courtesy phone for a message."

Rachel is the only one who has my flight information, so I can't help but wonder what I've forgotten at her apartment, or what she forgot to tell me before leaving. Maybe I really do need to buy a replacement phone when I get to New York?

I make my way over to a gate agent and ask where the closest courtesy phone is. The young woman points down the main way and I find myself tucked in a quiet corner, overlooking the sea of travelers.

Lifting the receiver in confusion, I speak.

"This is Ivy Cotter."

"Ms. Cotter, you have a call. One moment, please." The line clicks over and I hear the familiar sound of my father's heavy sigh.

"Dad?"

"Hey sweetie," he says with a sadness in his voice. "You were asleep when I stopped by last night. Did Rachel give you everything?"

"Yeah, she did. I really appreciate you bringing me some of my dress clothes. And thank you so much for the picture." I smile thinking about the photograph of us at Wrigley Field. He hid the frame in the middle of a stack of pants. It reminded me of how he would leave hand-written notes in the middle of my workbook when I was in second grade.

"Listen, kiddo. I'm headed to New York on business in a few weeks. If it's okay, I would really like to come see you."

"Yeah ... that'd be nice," I reply, actually meaning the words.

"Well ... I wanted to track you down to say good-bye ... and good luck. You'll be great out there."

"Thanks, Dad. I love you."

In the background, I hear the incessant babbling of

my mother and she grabs the phone before he has a chance to reply. "Ivy, where the hell do you think you are going?" My mother's voice barks each syllable sharply on the other end. "You up and disappeared before your sister's wedding, ruining everything for her as always. You haven't returned any of my messages. And now you are just leaving without saying a word? This is unacceptable."

Of course Genevieve married that asshole in spite of drugging and raping me. That girl will go to the ends of the Earth to keep up appearances. But I find delight in the fact that my dad didn't share my plans with Mom. Her attitude is the exact reason I couldn't bear to go back to my parents' house to gather my things on my own. Rachel secretly called my dad late last night and had him bring me the clothes I would need in New York. She even coordinated temporary housing with her cousin who is attending NYU during the summer session until I can find a place of my own. I'm really going to miss her.

Mr. Horesji was quite understanding when I called him and asked if his offer was still on the table since I had missed the deadline to follow up with my decision on the position with him in New York. I explained that I was hospitalized without the ability to reach him and otherwise disposed. While he had started the process of interviewing more candidates, he felt confident enough in my abilities and ceased his search. There are no words to describe my utmost appreciation at his compassion. I'm sure the fact that I am Professor Whitman's prized pupil played a large part in his flexibility. I was certain that I had fucked that opportunity, but good old Whit must have really done a number with his recommendation. He will receive my eternal gratitude.

"Ivy? Ivy, are you there?" my mother snaps.

Deep breaths.

I do not need my mother's approval.

I do not need my mother's approval.

I do not need my mother's approval.

I exhale and steady my voice as best I can. I can do this. "Mom…" I begin and tuck a loose strand of hair behind my ear.

"Well, what do you have to say for yourself, Ivy Elaine?"

"Mom, I'm on my way to New York. I accepted the Associate Curator position at the gallery. My flight leaves in fifty minutes." The words come out faster than the speed of sound.

"Excuse me? Stop rambling and speak clearly, Ivy."

Of course she didn't hear me. For twenty-two years, she has never listened to a word I said. Why would she start now?

I swallow any traces of fear, lift my chin, and summon confidence into my voice. "I said, I'm moving to New York," I repeat slowly.

"No, you're not, young lady." Her voice is calm but stern. It's the same one she used when I was a child being punished for crimes of curiosity, like painting the walls with bright red nail polish or shaving the dog's legs. It's downright frightening. "You're coming home right now."

I can't help but guffaw at her audacity. How disconnected could she really be? A lot has happened since I left for Italy last year. I discovered myself and fell in love with art on a deeper level. When I came home a few weeks ago, I fell in love all over again, only this time with a man, and then had my heart clawed from my chest. In spite of it all,

I know I will be stronger for it. There is no way this woman is going to try and keep her hold on me anymore.

"I am less than pleased with you right now."

There's a surprise. I exhale quickly through my nose, suppressing a laugh. I'm fairly certain the last time she was pleased with me was when I was voted homecoming queen my senior year. Anything to keep up appearances for the family name.

"I took the liberty of confirming that job at the Museum of Contemporary Art with Mr. Ramirez on your behalf. They are expecting you this Wednesday at nine."

I hardly register what she says as my eyes are drawn across to a tall figure across the busy terminal. The man is tall, with dark, shaggy hair much like *him*. His shoulders are hunched over sadly as he looks around lost in a sea of people. The phone in my hand trembles and my heart seemingly stops all together as air escapes my lungs. My emotions betray logic as every fiber of my being wants it to be Phoenix.

Needs it to be Phoenix.

Demands it to be Phoenix.

And for a brief moment … I am certain it *is* him.

I can only imagine that this is just the beginning of moments like this—I will, no doubt, see his face in crowded rooms for a long while. I'm not sure I will ever be truly free from his ghost.

"Yeah…" I say slowly, shaking my head to bring myself back to earth and the crowd before me. "No. I, uh … I gotta go, Mom."

I put the phone back on the receiver before I hear her say anything else, then I sling my bag over my shoulder and begin to follow the figure. My pulse finally returns to me and races as I weave through the throngs of travelers until I lose him in the crowds.

It's not him.

Surrendering to my imagination, I embrace the heartache once more and head back toward gate B11.

As our plane pulls up to the jet bridge, I take a seat by the window, looking out over the tarmac. The day mirrors my mood: gloomy, air so thick it slows the world's momentum down to the speed of molasses. The sky above is cloudy with a chance of a shit storm. How convenient. Like my life, a turbulent flight is inevitable.

As the passengers start to de-board the plane, I pull out Rachel's well-loved copy of *Pride and Prejudice*. The cover is desperately clinging to its spine from all of the times she has read it countless page corners are creased from late nights of reading to flag the last page read.

It's been ages since I read the classic, high school probably, but I vividly remember falling in love with Mr. Darcy. They don't make guys like him in real life, but I'll be damned if I don't try to find my own modern day Darcy in New York. Flipping to the first page is like being reunited with old friends.

Just as Mr. Bingley and crew are about to attend the ball a foreign hand delicately touches my shoulder I spin around defensively, shutting the book firmly. My breath is taken away from me at the sight of him.

Phoenix.

He looks horrible. Still breathtakingly boy next door beautiful, but horrible. Like he hasn't showered in days, eaten in weeks, slept in years. His hair is completely disheveled, and the dark circles swallowing his beat red eyes heighten the sadness of his face.

I want to jump out of my skin. Wrap my arms around him so tightly that my body pushes through his to the other side. Show him in actions what I am incapable of putting into words. I want, no, I *need* to kiss him with all the fervor and passion and fire that has built up within over the past few weeks since his lips melted into mine on the terrace in Madison. That no matter how royally he fucked up … how royally *I* fucked up … he is the reason I've changed.

Slowly, he comes in front of me. As I stand to match him my body quakes. In excitement? In nervousness? Probably both. But I instantly know that this is one of those defining moments that will stay with me until my dying day.

I open my mouth to speak. To tell him thank you.

That I believe him.

That I hate him.

That I love him.

That no matter how angry I may be, I can't shake him from my soul.

That I don't think I can stand to live one more day without him physically next to me, capable of reaching out to take my hand.

That I want to fight for us. To try and see if we can try to overcome everything that has happened and work to build that trust back.

But before I can say anything, he presses his index finger to my lips, quieting my mind. His touch is delicate. His skin is rough. A perfect juxtaposition of man.

"Shh … before you say anything, before you push me away for good, I needed to see you again."

Stunned at his words, all I can do is blink.

273

"First of all, I'm sorry ... so incredibly sorry. Those pathetic little words do nothing in comparison to how I feel for what happened with Sully. I will never let myself live that night down. The minute I suspected something in that moment, I should have told you. I should have kept a closer eye on you, camped out against the door of the bedroom that night and kept closer tabs on his whereabouts. I should have done *something* more.

"I won't ask for your forgiveness because I know I don't deserve it. But know that if I could turn back time, I would have done things differently and done every last thing in my power to protect you."

I open my mouth to speak again, to remind him that he wasn't the one to take advantage of me that night. That he was not the one who drugged me. That he took a damaged soul who didn't even realize how badly she was broken and helped make her whole again.

"Second of all, you were right." His eyes search my face for answers. "Last night I called my dad. I needed to clear the air with him. I've spent the last decade with so much pent up anger and hurt, I never considered that he lost the love of his life and his son at the same time. I feel like such an asshole."

My heart warms at his admission. Phoenix actually called his dad. My stunned look must take him by surprise. He extends his hand as if to take mine, but hesitates and draws it back into a fist and hooks his thumb into his front pocket sheepishly.

"He told me his biggest regret beyond cheating on my mom was not going after her the day we left. He realizes he should have gotten up and followed us right out the door, refused to let us walk out of his life." He takes a moment to reflect introspectively.

"I will not do what he did. I'm not going to spend a life of regret and I don't want to lose you for good. I will not sit back idly and go down without a fight." The intensity in his eyes blazes right through me, leaving a burning trail of ash and smoke in its wake. "If you're leaving, Ivy, I'm following. If you go, I go with you. I'm trusting my instinct for once. I refuse to live a life without you. My heart, my instinct ... it has to be enough. It just has to."

My eyes grow wide as I slowly begin to process what he's insinuating.

An ember deep inside reignites and words fail me.

Slowly, he guides me into the chair and crouches down in front of me, looking up at me with sad, hopeful eyes. He's practically on his knees before me, begging.

"Phoenix, I..." Tears begin to pool in my eyes and my heart is on the verge of exploding.

"Ivy, the hardest thing to do in life is figure out what it is that you want and then having the courage to say it aloud." My pulse quickens. I look down to see my hands shaking. He hesitates for a moment then reaches out, taking them in his palms. His thumbs tenderly trace the inside of my hands.

"It's you that I want, Ivy. Only you. You're perfect."

After all the drama and hurt, it's me that he wants? After seeing me hit rock bottom. Seeing me completely lose it. After I've pushed him away again and again. After knowing that I am not just damaged goods—I am completely and eternally ruined. After all this, it's still me?

"That is, of course, if you'll have me..." he trails off softly.

I want to ask him why but my mind says something

completely different.

"I'm hardly perfect." I need him to see the real me. I want him to hate me as much as I hate myself. "I've done all sorts of horrible things. And I have a long history of hurting people. I even slept with Matt … I mean, I didn't *really* sleep with him … well, I did … but I stopped him and—"

"Stop it, Ivy!"

I look down at my fingers. I have gnawed my nails down to my cuticle beds the past few days. He repositions himself below me so he catches my gaze once more.

"All of that, it doesn't matter. You're perfect to me. You're perfect *for* me. And I love you enough to let you be imperfect."

Phoenix's words seep into my soul and I slide off the chair and into his lap before the floodgates open. I bury my face into his neck and I don't care that I'm making a spectacle of myself. I need this man more than Rembrandt needed his paintbrush. His breath hitches subtly and he wraps his arms around my so tight I can hardly breathe. His chest shakes against mine and the tears start to fall.

"You love me?" I croak between sobs.

He pulls back and takes me by my shoulders, looking directly into my eyes with a silent smile. If I listen closely, I know there is a voice that doesn't use words; a love that silently screams to be explored and nurtured.

"I know we've only just met, and have barely spent any time in each other's presence, but I *know* you. I know the you that nobody else does. I know how you would eat breakfast food for every meal if you could. I know that no matter how much you think you hate your parents, you secretly enjoy being your dad's baby girl and you would never admit that out loud. And I know that you murmur to yourself in your sleep, and it sounds as if you're singing a lullaby. It feels like I've known you a lifetime. And knowing you like I know you is to love you completely.

"I've never been so sure of anything before. My heart has been threaded to yours since that night in Madison. You breathed fresh life into me and awakened me in every sense of the word. And when I thought I'd lost you last week, when you refused to talk to me … God, Ivy. I was wrecked. I never want to feel that way again. Ever."

His words spear right through my heart and my pulse starts flying fast. I take a deep breath in an attempt to slow it down. For the first time ever, I am part of a relationship that isn't measured by what I have, but rather by why I give. And I want nothing more than to give Phoenix the peace that his heart deserves. In order to heal, I need to let him in deeper. I'm ready to surrender.

Phoenix's expression is a cross between pleading for mercy and somber confidence. I press my forehead to his and close my eyes, committing this moment to memory.

"You are going to be the death of me," I whisper.

He sucks in a sharp breath and I open my eyes to meet his.

"Good. Because once you find what you love, you need to let it consume you and then completely kill you. I dare you to find someone who needs you more than I do. Who wants you more than I do. Who loves you more than I do. I dare you, Ivy."

I pull back and look right through him. I can feel his honesty, his pleading in my bones. He's right. I know I won't find anyone else like him. Phoenix has already proven that when things get tough, he isn't going anywhere. We may fight, and I may cry and try to kick him out of my life, but he will hold me and dry my tears. Even when we are angry with each other, he still cares. Of this, I am now certain.

"What about your father? The project you're supposed to lead? You're just giving everything up?" I ask, my voice barely a whisper.

"We'll be okay. He wants me to follow my heart. He knows the importance of finding love, the real thing, and never letting go no matter how many times I may manage to fuck things up. As for my job? Eh, there will be others. My mom always told me that life is too short. I know she'd be proud that I'm following my heart. I just hope I can do her proud and not fuck things up even more."

Wryly, I smile to myself and shake my head. "Just shut up, Phoenix. You can't possibly fuck things up between us."

I see a hint of confusion mar his beautiful, stubborn face milliseconds before my lips crash into his. I pull him tight, fisting his hair, choking back tears and devouring him like he's my final meal. I kiss him for all of the kisses lost to distance, to stupidity, to jealousy, and rage. I kiss him to drain myself of all the hurt and self-deprecation I've been harboring and fill myself with the one thing that will keep me going day in and day out—hope.

Pulling back, a shy smile plays his lips. I smile back, finally coming to terms with what I've been feeling.

"I love you too."

And for the first time in my life I mean those three little words with every fiber of my being.

The gate agent announces the boarding call for our flight to LaGuardia. Phoenix stands, fishing his ticket from his pocket, and I'm struck with the realization that he's coming with me today. In a few moments, he is going to take my hand and walk down the jetway with me.

We are starting over.

Together.

I stand to meet his gaze and reach up, connecting my lips to his once more. Each kiss we share is better than the one before. We are lost in each other, only breaking apart when the gate agent is calling us both by name. In what felt like mere seconds, all of the passengers have boarded.

I don't know where we're headed once we land in New York. But I know that I'm strong enough to overcome all of its bullshit as long as Phoenix is next to me.

As he reaches for my hand, I note that the heat I hold in my palm still burns brightly, slowly, and passionately. And like our undeniable, unwavering connection it shows no sign of extinguishing.

PHOENIX

WE HAVEN'T EVEN BEEN FLYING for twenty minutes before Ivy falls asleep on my shoulder. I'm amazed she is able to calm herself with all of the turbulence that threw down during takeoff. Usually, I'm not nervous to fly, but for a moment I seriously thought we were all going to be goners. How fittingly tragic that would have been for us.

With everything Ivy has gone through the past few weeks, it wouldn't surprise me if she slept until winter. She is clearly exhausted. I watch her chest slowly rise and fall, purring like a kitten as she softly snores. Even with that tiny crease of worry between her eyebrows, this is the first time since the moment I laid eyes on her that she actually looks at peace with her life.

And I'm the lucky bastard who gets to be a part of it.

I suppose it's a miracle I'm even sitting here next to her right now. I know that I wouldn't have forgiven me. And technically she hasn't forgiven me, but she didn't cast me to the wayside at the airport gate, so I've got that going for me. We'll get there eventually. We're just going to have to work through it all, come to peace with the bullshit and figure out how to move forward. Together.

When Ivy pushed me away at Rachel's apartment a few days ago, I didn't know what to do. I couldn't talk to Sully about it, and all the guys who were up for the wedding wouldn't believe what happened even if they lived it, so I shoved my pride aside, picked up the phone, and heard my dad's voice for the first time in years. I probably stared at his number for a good hour before growing a pair and hitting call. I told myself that if my mother could find it in herself to forgive the man who completely annihilated her heart, I owed it to her to at least try.

And try I will. It's just going to take some time. Maybe one day I'll get to that point. Just not today.

When I showed up to Rachel's apartment this morning, she was more tight-lipped on Ivy's whereabouts than the Gestapo. I had to convince her to tell me where she ran off to, which meant I had to confess how pathetically head over heels in love I am with her best friend. My admission left her in a puddle of emotion in her doorway as I sprinted to O'Hare with nothing but the clothes on my back and bought a ticket for the first flight to New York City. Before she left, she had to know how I felt—even if it wasn't reciprocated. I raced around the terminal aimlessly looking for her before retreating to my departing gate in defeat. And by sheer, dumb luck I ended up on the same flight as her. I just knew I couldn't let her slip through my grasp, especially after hearing Dad talk about his regrets.

I never thought I'd say this, but the old man is right. He said, "Even though your mother is gone, I have never stopped loving her. I love her more today than yesterday. And I love her less today than how much I will love her tomorrow. You see, son, as you get older you learn that time will make a fool out of everyone. But in the end, only love will make a fool out of time."

I immediately understood what he meant and I knew I couldn't waste another damn second of my life.

When I told him more about Ivy, and what is arguably the biggest laundry list of fuck-ups in the history of fuck-ups, *he* was the one to push me to go after her. The man I've grown to loathe helped me realize that I had to throw caution to the wind and chase after her. In a split second, I have managed to flip my life around on its head. Was it hard to walk away from the freelancing project? Abso-fucking-lutely, but I didn't second-guess myself. Sure, it would have been some damn good money. But there will be other jobs down the line; however, there will never be another Ivy. I have to prove to her that she is the one for me and I will not back down easily. After all, relationships are a game of high stakes poker—you have to be willing to risk everything and go all in; otherwise there is no way you can ever win big.

I have no clue if Sully ended up marrying that bitch; although those horrible assholes deserve each other. I haven't seen him since I left the hospital, but looking back I should have killed the motherfucker when I had the chance.

As I flex my hand, I wince at the stiffness in my knuckles and the burning sensation when I clench it back into a fist. My skin is a blend of watercolors—faded shades of green and purple and blue pulled taut over sinew and bone. I think back to Sully's face and the satisfaction that raged through my body as I delivered each blow and I know it was totally worth it. I just wish I could have done more damage.

No. I wish I could have protected her from him.

What really needs to happen is for Ivy to press charges. Fuck his future up real good and make that sick son of a bitch pay. We'll have to talk about that sometime soon.

It's funny how all this shit works, like the universe wants you to believe it's nothing but a series of random coincidences. But really, I think fate is the one orchestrating the push and pull of our lives. Even if I hadn't met her in Madison at Sully's bachelor weekend, we would have eventually crossed paths. I was destined to meet her. Some things are just meant to be.

The powers that be made no mistakes in our relationship; the only mistakes that rose were from simple human error—or rather, my own fucking stupidity.

How do you tell the love of your life that she saved you from yourself without scaring her away? The past year has been one of the darkest of my life, full of bad decisions, amazing stories, and epic mistakes that I am too ashamed to even remember. But I finally feel like I am headed back in the right direction when I am pointed toward her.

That night in Madison, Ivy appeared as the brightest star in my sky, placed there just for me, bringing me out of darkness and into light.

I was immediately attracted to her. Not in the physical sense—I mean, don't get me wrong. Ivy is hot as fuck. She has legs for miles, smokin' tits, and an ass tighter than a drum just begging to be banged. Plus, she has to be the most gorgeous girl who has ever given me the time of day.

But from the moment I first laid eyes upon her, and heard the lightness of her laughter, my heart caved in on itself and I didn't just see her hot body. I saw *her*. It was like my soul had found its missing piece the moment she walked into the party and I immediately knew I was home.

She became my home.

Ivy makes it easy to forget and lets my past stay in the past. And believe me, there is plenty to forget, especially over the past few months. If she were to ever find out what really happened with Hailey, she would probably string me up by my dick and leave me to die. I mean, I never lied to her. We weren't *technically* together. I just gave her a bunch of half-truths. I've spent my adult life being so afraid of turning into my dad that it happened organically without my knowledge.

I suppose the apple really doesn't fall far from the tree.

But I know it's only a matter of time before the demons I'm leaving behind catch up to me, even though Ivy doesn't deserve to be burdened with my bullshit. Only I deserve to live with every ounce of regret and guilt and internally wrestle with my past indiscretions. She has enough on her plate and doesn't need anything else to worry about. I just hope to God that if it ever comes out she doesn't see me as the piece of shit I really am.

I don't know what is going to happen with us, but I do know that in order for us to work we need this fresh start in New York.

A clean slate.

A new canvas.

I'm just hoping that together we can paint over our history and make a new masterpiece.

Want more Ivy and Phoenix? Stay tuned in 2015

Acknowledgments

FIRST AND FOREMOST, I WANT to thank my husband Mike. Without you, these words would never have been penned. I know this entire process has taken us on quite the ride, but thank you for being here for me through it all (even when I disappeared behind a computer screen and you wanted to throw me off a cliff). You took on more than your fair share so I could go after what is arguably the most terrifying thing I have ever done. I wish I had the words to explain just how much I appreciate having you in my life. You make everything richer and I am so, so lucky to be your other half. I love you more than you could ever begin to comprehend.

Thank you to my children, Thing 1 and Thing 2 … for being a constant source of inspiration. I realize you are too young to understand everything that happened over the past year while writing this book, but I want you to know that you are never too old to chase down your dreams. I love you both fiercely and you're not allowed to read this until you're at least forty-five.

To my family who cheered me on once I finally confessed that I was writing a book … thank you. But I meant what I said, if you start reading into these characters and situations, you will never be allowed to read anything else

I write. You are all crazy and there's not a damn thing I can do about it. But I wouldn't have it any other way.

Jennifer Roberts-Hall ... where do I even begin? From the moment I first messaged you to ask about your approach to editing, I knew I had made a dear friend. Thank you for holding my hand throughout the editing process. Thank you for giving me confidence. Thank you for being so fantastic from start to finish. Your kindness, patience and guidance are unparalleled. You are a BAMF.

Sharon Goodman and Melissa Saneholtz... you loved my baby as if it were your own and I could never thank you enough. You two worked tirelessly to help get me noticed and I want you to know just how much I appreciate your hard work. Thank you for rocking my socks off through this whole process. If you're looking for a power team, hunt down Sassy Savvy Fabulous PR!

To all of my beta readers who helped shape this story into the best possible version of itself ... we did it!!

Angie Albertson, you are undoubtedly the world's greatest secret keeper and one of my favorite cheerleaders. You saw this story when it was in its ugliest, rawest form and looked beyond the hot mess to help push this in the right direction. Your feedback and your friendship are invaluable. I love you, dearly.

Erycka Thesing ... I want to get on a plane and just give you the biggest hug imaginable. Thank you for religiously holding our Sunday night sprints sacred. Thank you for letting me vent when I couldn't find the right words. And thank you for celebrating each and every last letter that made it onto the page right along with me. You are amazing and wonderful and kind and I am so lucky to have you as my critique partner and friend.

Amy Preston Rogers, thank you for your countless support along the way—from helping build my fan base, to creating teasers, to sharing my passion for storytelling. Your enthusiasm for these characters is unprecedented. I hereby give, devise and bequeath Phoenix T. Wolfe to you, my dear. He's all yours, baby!

To Melanie Peterson, for not only scouring Target stores for a pair of ridiculous cats in outer space leggings for me, but for also loving Phoenix and Ivy's story so much. Deana Wolstenholme for being the first stranger to read this and think, "There's something here." And to Sara Johns, for finding the holes and helping answer medical questions that nobody ever wants to have to ask. Thank you! To Terrie Johnson for answering all of my miscellaneous syntax questions with a smile. And, of course, my trio of "fresh eyes"—Marisol Herrera, Janelle Stevenson and Alexis Durbin who helped find those last minute glitches before hitting publish.

To all of the ladies in the Berry Brigade … I am so lucky to have your friendship and support through this entire process. It truly takes a village and I could never have done this without your support.

Thank you to all of the bloggers who have supported me, especially Sassy Savvy Fabulous, Chicks Controlled By Books, Three Girls and a Book Obsession, Judging Books by Their Covers, Schmexy Girl Book Blog, Devoured Words, 101 Ways to Make Love to a Spoon, A Book Junky's Obsession, A Book Whores Obsession and Livin' Simple. Thank you for your support – not just of me, but for the entire indie author community! No author out there could do this without you.

To Najla Qamber … you took a small idea and completely surpassed all of my expectations with the cover design. Thank you for understanding my vision and for creating a stunning piece of art. Your talent is unmatched. And to Julie of JT formatting for helping bring my baby to life and answering my endless stream of technical questions over the past few months.

I want the world to know that the one and only Heather Markey is responsible for giving me the perfect "hot guy" name. Also, I need to confess that I stole one of her jokes. Thank you for being a constant source of hilarity, you slut monkey.

All of my ladies from "the sandbox" … :grouphug:

To the one and only Charles Bukowski, who may or may not have said the *Falsely Yours* quote on the opening pages of this book.

To all of the authors who have imparted wisdom, encouragement, feedback and love to me throughout this whole crazy process, I am forever indebted to you. I'm especially looking at Mia Asher, Angie McKeon, L.U Ann, Deena Bright and L.B. Simmons. You push me to be a better writer and "thank you" simply does not do my gratitude justice.

And finally, it would be amiss to not thank *you*, the reader. Thank you from the bottom of my heart for taking a chance on a no-name indie author and reading my debut. I have spent many a sleepless night worrying that nobody other than my mom would read *Love Nouveau*. I sincerely hope you enjoyed reading this little piece of my heart as much as I enjoyed writing it. If you are so inclined, I would love to hear from you!

About the Author

B.L. BERRY IS MANY THINGS. A New Adult author. A self-proclaimed music whore. A long-course triathlete. A marketing savant. And a full-time working mom. While there are never enough hours in the day, she does the best she can to get things done and hopes for technological advances in human cloning.

When she's not hiding behind her computer writing, you can find her spending time with her family or catching up on her favorite TV shows. Rumor has it she'll sleep when she's dead.

She is Canadian by birth. Mexican by marriage. Chicagoan by heart. Kansan by choice. Jayhawk purely by common sense.

Residing outside of Kansas City, she lives with her husband, two children and black pug. Each day her family thanks the makers of e-Readers, because without which they would be living amongst stacks and stacks of romance novels. Conversely, each day B.L. Berry thanks the makers of e-Readers for hiding her book-hoarding tendencies.

* * * * *

I'd love to hear from my readers … let's connect!

blberrywrites@gmail.com
FACEBOOK – http://www.facebook.com/blberryauthor
BLOG - https://blberrywrites.wordpress.com